THE BOOK OF ROGER

"His Discovery and Adventure of Cruiser 5.0"

By

Kyle R. Smith

KRS DataCom LLC.
kyle.r.smith@thebookofroger.com

First Printing, 2014

ISBN-13: 978-1500410049

ISBN-10: 1500410047

The Book of Roger
www.thebookofRoger.com

This book is dedicated to the childhood memories that inspire us and put smiles on our faces no matter where we are. These precious memories keep us thoughtful of who we are and what we have done that only we, as individuals can recall for our very own, whether they be good or bad.

Also thanks to all who have helped inspire, push and wait for this work to be complete. Those youth in my class that helped to awaken the story of Roger and the idea of putting him in a book. To my dear family I live for and love. Finally to my good faithful friends, I would never have made it without ALL of the rewarding memories you have given me.

CHAPTERS

Chapter 1

The Beginning

"RUN, get out of here! Now Roger!" shouted a voice in the room now half filled with smoke. Roger found himself standing in a large room surrounded with the sounds of explosions and computer equipment overloading. He could barely see the silhouette of the young man who was shouting at him because of the thick smoke and bright lights from the explosions. The voice sounded familiar, but his heart was racing and sounding in his ears as he tried desperately to find the young man as he stumbled toward his screams. The smoke was causing him to cough and his eyes were watering as he stumbled forward a few more steps. The tears, from being scared were now starting to burn from the smoke. The chaos caused him to try to yell out to the young man but he couldn't say a word through the coughing that was overtaking him as he struggled for breath. He stumbled down to one knee after tripping over debris from some equipment that was blown across the floor, but was quickly back on both feet. As he rose up he saw a second silhouette of a much larger man running toward him from a different direction where the screaming young man had been. As this other man was coming toward him at full speed he reached out and-

"Roger, Roger, wake up." He was being shaken softly on the shoulder by his father. He had fallen asleep at the desk in his room. His head was laying on his English book, a little drool trickling down his cheek, dripping on the pages.

His head jerked up quickly, a little startled with a page of the book briefly stuck to his face from the wet drool. He sat up fully, looked at his father and wiped his cheek dry with his sleeve.

"Hi dad, I guess I dozed off a bit there. English has always been a little boring for me," he chuckled as he wiped his face again.

His dad laughed and said, "I thought you said you had to come up and finish your English homework, not go to bed early," as he smiled at his son.

Roger returned the smile, reached out and hugged his dad sideways, "I guess I should finish reading this chapter."

"Yes, good idea," chuckled his father as he turned and left the room.

Roger Dexter was a young, dark haired boy, just a few weeks away from turning fifteen. He was an excellent student, bordering on genius. He stood up to stretch and take in a breath of the cool night air as he stood at his open window. It had just finished raining that May evening in the mountain town of Belford. He loved the smell of the rain mixed with the cold river air that ran next to his house.

Next to Roger's desk were piles of small boxes and old broken electronic devices that people had given him. His family, friends and neighbors had become accustomed to giving him their old and broken devices like television sets, remote controlled cars, radios, toasters, and anything else that ran on batteries or electricity. He loved receiving old broken devices so he could take them apart to learn and explore. He would use the parts for his experiments and inventions he enjoyed creating. He had become a master at repairing broken devices. The stash of broken devices and pieces he kept always cluttered his room and drove his mother crazy with the mess.

Numerous times Roger had to repair his mother's vacuum cleaner after it was damaged from sucking up pieces of debris from projects that were left behind. In fact, it currently sat broken next to one of the numerous knee high repair piles. The side of the vacuum was stained with black smoke from an earlier incident involving a small fire. This time it was damaged after sucking up a few small pieces from an old blender he had left on the floor. His mother had missed the small parts while doing her normal visual scan of his room prior to vacuuming.

Roger couldn't help but laugh inside as he looked at the vacuum. He remembered the sound of his mother's scream while he was downstairs watching TV.

"Aahhh," came her scream, over the loud noise of grinding plastic and metal as the pieces of debris got sucked up and killed the vacuum cleaner. As he climbed the stairs to the second floor to see what had happened, he smelled the all too familiar odor of melted plastic, fried electronics and smoke. He chuckled at the memory and was glad for the distraction it gave him from reading the boring school book.

"I need to finish reading this book for my report," he mumbled as he sat back down, "Focus, focus."

A few moments passed as he read the dreaded book, then he turned in his chair and began to stare outside again. He was a sucker for being easily distracted, so he placed a paper clip in the book on his current page and laid it down next to a picture of him with his older brother Randy. The photo was taken a couple of years ago during a family picnic at a park next to an old steam train engine. He looked at the photo with sadness. Randy had died in a car crash that he and Roger had been in just over a year ago and he missed his brother a lot. He leaned back in his chair locking his fingers behind his head with a big stretch. He took a deep slow breath, smelling the cold outside air again and closed his eyes thinking back to that day with his family at the park.

BANG! The door to his bedroom was kicked open by his eleven year old little sister Jenny.

He jumped and quickly turned to see the dark haired girl with cute glasses coming into his room, a toy helicopter buzzing just above her head as she entered. She was holding the remote control and was steering the small army helicopter toward the left side of his head.

He was sitting up now and was looking over at her with frustration from being startled, but then grinning at the attack that was heading his way.

"FIRE MISSILE ONE!" she shouted.

A small "click" was heard from the side of the helicopter. Immediately a small red plastic missile the size of a crayon was speeding straight toward his forehead.

He had no time to react. It appeared to be happening in slow motion as he was saying "Noooo-"

Then a hollow "THUNK"....a direct hit to his forehead. Roger flung his head back and his body following, toppling over his chair, landing with a "Thud."

Roger lay on the floor, hanging his tongue out like they do in cartoons as he pretended to be dead. While on the floor, he did a few little jerks for a dramatic dying effect.

After a few seconds he peeked from one eye to see Jenny laughing as she knelt down next to him. She pounced up to him and started to do pretend CPR on his chest pushing down crying out,

"DON'T YOU DIE ON ME!" with a small giggle.

Roger then burst into laughter, sitting up and grabbing his little sister and taking her under his arm in a football tackle move. He began to tickle her under the chin and arm making her squirm and laugh trying to escape his grasp.

In the distance, the small uncontrolled helicopter bounced off the wall and crash landed on his bed. They both sat up and with grinning smiles gave each other a high five.

"Great shooting Jenny," said Roger.

"Thanks, I've been practicing on the cat all day." And she smiled proudly.

They both laughed and got up. Roger picked up the helicopter from his bed and held it out to Jenny.

She grabbed it. "Thanks bro," running out of the room heading down the hall.

"You are dead meat and better watch your back!" he called out as she ran toward the stairs.

Roger walked over to the window, "What have I created, practicing missile techniques on the cat!" as he laughed under his breath.

He sat back down at his desk and picked up his book, opened to his paperclip book mark and began to read with a half grin on his face. Jenny's distracting attack was just what he needed to relax. He read on for an hour until he was tired and decided to go to bed.

The next morning Roger awoke to the sound of his alarm. "Man, that is the worst sound I have ever heard" he said as he rolled over punching the top of the alarm clock to stop the hideous noise. He fell back over onto his back and looked up at the ceiling. "Friday is finally here," he said, letting out a deep breath. Then he kicked off the covers as he got out of his warm bed.

After a quick shower and getting dressed, he threw the covers sloppily over his bed to make it look made, just to please his mother and show he had made an effort.

He walked over to his closet and pulled out his favorite jacket. It was the color of his favorite baseball team and had the team logo "CUBS", on the front and back.

This jacket was no ordinary jacket. The jacket was the crown jewel of all of his inventions and hard work, and he was aching to wear it to school today. He picked up the heavy jacket and slid it on very carefully. He stood staring at the jacket in the mirror that hung above his dresser.

Behind him, in the reflection of the mirror, he saw that Jenny was watching him from the hall.

"You're going to actually wear your precious CUBBIES jacket" she said in a sarcastic girly voice.

"Quit spying on me!" he hollered as he did a backward kick with his right leg to slam the bedroom door in her face.

He heard her laughing faintly through the door as she walked towards her own room. Roger looked at himself again in the mirror, this time with a huge grin stretching across his face. He opened the jacket and reached inside the left side.

There was a small "click," and he quickly pulled his hand out as a deep hum started to rumble from the jacket. The hum was a deep base, and began to sound like a small jet airplane powering up with a slight winding noise. A women's soft voice came from the collar of his jacket, "*System power at 100%.*"

Roger was grinning wide, showing all of his teeth as he looked in the mirror. He raised his left hand and with his pinky finger, touched a small button on the lower side of the cuff.

With lightning fast speed, a small metal rod about a foot long came shooting out of his left sleeve staying attached to the inside wrist of the jacket. It was glowing blue, looking similar to a magic wand. A few small bluish sparks erupted from the tip as it glowed with electricity. When the rod came out of his sleeve, a small touch pad screen with controls opened up where the small button he had first pressed used to be. The jacket control panel was displaying the power levels and system status. This panel allowed him to adjust how much power would be used to electrify and charge the glowing rod sticking out of his jacket sleeve.

"No more bullies today," he mumbled as he did a small karate move with the rod and his arm. "Take that," he said doing another small chop, at the same time pressing a green button on his control panel causing the rod to spit out blue and red sparks.

"This little bugger is going to shock the pants off those bullies," as he did another chop, emitting more sparks.

"Roger!" shouted his mother from the kitchen, "you're going to miss your bus!"

"Crap," he replied softly.

He quickly pressed the jacket shutdown button with his pinky. A small "click" sounded as the rod retracted into his sleeve followed by the control panel into the jacket. He reached inside the jacket and clicked the button to power off the jacket. As the jacket powered down the small jet engine noises slowed to a silence.

Roger grabbed his books while running out of his room heading for the stairs. He rounded the corner of the kitchen at a slow run, grabbed his brown paper lunch bag from the counter and kissed his mom on her out stuck cheek as he passed. "Bye mom, thanks for the lunch," he waved as he raced out the door and down the driveway and onto the bus.

The old school bus door squeaked to a close. Darrin the bus driver announced over the intercom in his cool voice. "Ok little dudes, sit back and hold on, we'll be there soon."

The bus bumpily drove down the road, heading into town with the sound of The Beach Boys music playing from Darrin's IPod over the speaker system.

Roger walked down the bus aisle looking for an empty seat, mumbling under his breath, "please, not today, not today," as he approached "bully" row. This was the row where the school bullies sat and created his fellow classmates worst nightmares.

A very large boy by the name of Gary Crawford jumped up in front of Roger, right before he got to the dreaded row, halfway down the bus aisle. Loudly Gary spoke "What's with the dorky jacket, dead meat?" facing Roger, lightly punching his open palm with his fist, looking mean and intimidating.

"I hate being called dead meat," Roger thought, "That's when the pain starts."

Roger quickly reached for the jackets power button but had no time to press it before a leg shot out from one of the boys behind him. Gary shoved Roger in the chest pushing him backward. The outward stretched leg caught Roger behind the knee, and he went tumbling over backward onto the floor of the bus.

"WHAM" the hollow sound of his back hitting the hard metal floor, followed by a moan after the air from his lungs went gushing out.

Roger was gazing up at the ceiling as he heard the distant laughter of the bullies. Turning his head he caught a glimpse of the high fives they were giving each other. With his right hand he slowly reached into his jacket and pressed the power button. A small deep hum now winding up could be heard. *"Power at 100%,"* sounded the voice as Roger pressed a little button on his jacket sleeve with his pinky.

Instantly a small noise sounded as the metal rod and blue sparks shot out from his CUBS jacket cuff ready for action. Gary was turned around facing away from Roger and was taking high fives from all of his buddies.

Darrin heard the commotion and looked in his rear view mirror to see Roger laying on the floor and Gary getting congratulations. He hit the brakes and the bus quickly began coming to a stop. As the bus momentum slowed, this made Gary stumble backwards toward Roger as he was sitting up on the floor who was holding his arm outstretched with the highly charged electric rod projecting outward in front of him.

Before anyone knew what was happening, a shower of sparks came from the glowing rod as it made contact with Gary's right butt cheek.

This sudden powerful jolt of electricity sent Gary airborne and heading for the back of the bus, squealing like a baby pig. Gary hit the emergency exit hard with his forehead, falling hard on the floor dazed and confused.

"What the heck was that!" screamed David, one of Gary's crew and the one who had tripped him.

He leapt out of his seat to confront Roger who was getting to his feet.

"That is what I call the '*toasted butt cheek sandwich*' and if you don't want one, you better step aside and get away from me, *NOW!*" Roger said in a heated voice.

David's face had a mean grin, and he lashed out to grab Roger's coat with one hand.

Instantly up went Roger's arm with the rod to meet the boy's hand, but instead the wand caught him right in the junk. A shower of sparks flew as David shot straight up hitting his head on the ceiling of the bus, crashing back down on the floor where he lay, moaning in pain.

Roger held the electric rod up, ready for another attack from Gary's bully friends, but they all stayed back, nervous and in their seats not wanting to be electrocuted, ending up in pain like their two unfortunate buddies both crumpled on the floor of the bus.

Roger did a fake Karate chop-, like he did that morning in the mirror before he left for the bus. The boys jerked backward, flinching. Roger now smiled ear to ear as he finally had rid himself of these bullies once and for all.

Wham! Before he knew what happened, a large fist knocked him in the back of head, slamming him forward and falling. Gary had returned and was fuming. His punch to the back of Rogers head propelled him quickly forward, causing him to lose his balance. Roger started to put his hands out to stop himself from slamming into the front windows of the bus, but his hands were too late.

As he slammed into the windows, his power rod snapped in half spraying sparks into the air and pieces of metal to the floor. He fell hard to the ground, his head aching from Gary's punch and he gasped for breath.

"That's enough from you boys!" shouted Darrin, as he put the bus in park and quickly stepped out in front of the oncoming Gary to stop him just as he was reaching out for Roger to grab him and give him a heavy pounding.

"Calm down," Darrin said and he directed Gary back to his seat by angrily pointing at him.

Darrin reached down and picked the moaning David off of the floor and placed him into a seat. He told Roger to take a seat next to the driver and told the kids that were sitting there to move to new seats in the back, then turned to Gary. "This is the last warning you're getting Mr. Gary Crawford", said Darrin, "Then your butt is off this bus for good!"

They all sat down as Darrin slid back into the driver's seat, pulled the bus back into traffic and continued the drive to their school. Shortly after they were underway Darrin leaned over to Roger, "That was the coolest thing I have ever seen!" softly laughing. *"You gotta do that again!"* pausing-*"but not on my bus!"*, and they both laughed.

Darrin had taken a liking to Roger the past two years driving his school bus. Every day he would chat and visit with Roger. Darrin tried to have Rogers back on the bus because he was always teased and harassed by the bullies that were members of the Gary crew.

The bus squeaked to a stop in front of the school and the doors flung open. Roger had quickly gotten up and was the first one off the bus. *"See you later little dude"* he heard Darrin say as he hurried down the steps towards the school building.

Roger held his hand up while walking away in a single wave, "See ya," and he hurried up the walk and into Belford High School.

Chapter 2

School

Roger was in the hallway at his locker after his home room class. He had just slammed his locker shut. Behind the locker door was a boy with crooked glasses staring at him with a goofy grin. The boy was his best friend, Aaron Cate. He stood there, his face beaming with a huge smile.

"Nice work," Aaron said with a grin, "I'm so mad that I missed the *Shocking show* on the bus. *You did a live test of the jacket without me!"*

"I didn't mean to," explained Roger, "I had no choice, I'm sorry."

Aaron stood, listening in amazement as Roger relayed the entire story in great detail about what happened on the bus on the way to school.

"I really wanted to just wear the electro jacket to show Mr. Moody today." Roger said, "But it got broken when I did the face plant on the windshield of the bus.

Mr. Moody was the awesome advanced electronics teacher they had for their last class of the day. He had given the class an assignment at the beginning of the term that was due next week. It was an experiment he left entirely up to each group to create. They each had a partner assigned to them for the project. Mr. Moody knew that Roger and Aaron were best friends so he made them partners for the project.

"He would have loved to see it," said Roger.

"I know, we would have gotten an A for sure," replied Aaron disappointedly.

Roger lifted the broken electro jacket out of his locker and showed Aaron the broken rod part that was destroyed during the conflict on the bus.

"Let's work on it tonight and over the weekend," said Aaron, "then we can show it to him next week. It's not due until Friday."

Roger sighed, "Oh man I can't, I am going to my grandmas house with my family tonight for her birthday party. But we can start the repairs tomorrow sometime."

"OK, I'll come by later tonight to hang out when I see you get home," said Aaron.

Aaron lived half a block away and on the same side of the street as Roger. They had grown up together and were the best of friends. Aaron was a shorter blond haired boy and fourteen years old. He had a great sense of humor and his nerdy characteristics and personality could make anyone smile.

"Sounds like a plan," said Roger as the bell sounded for their next class.

In English class the teacher Mr. Wilkins was up front discussing the new vocabulary words for the upcoming test. He was often mean to Roger and other kids. He loves birds, especially pigeons. His class room looked like an aviary with photos of the award winning pigeons he raised plastered around the classroom walls. He even had a stuffed pigeon mounted and perched on a rock that he used as a paperweight on his desk. As Roger sat bored out of his mind, he stared out the window. While he was staring, his mind wandered again to the scene he had in his mind last night. His thoughts drifted back to the large computer room full of electronic devices and equipment. This time he saw himself standing in the corner of the chaotic room full of explosions when he heard the young man's screaming again, but it appeared that he was yelling at someone he thought looked like his father. He was surrounded by flashes of light as this man came running into the large electronic computer room,

"MR. DEXTER!" sounded a loud voice causing Roger to jump and drop his pencil. It was his teacher Mr. Wilkins calling out to him.

"Distracted again are we Mr. Dexter? I asked you a question." snarled his teacher nastily.

Roger started stuttering and looked a little confused, "Sorry, what was the question sir?"

"I asked you, what the word *defenestrate* means?" he replied with the same nasty tone.

Roger regained his thoughts, and then looked up at him saying, "I have no idea sir."

Looking frustrated and angry, Mr. Wilkins loudly replied, "To throw something out of a window!" And he began to approach Roger in an angry manner.

"That is what it means young man!" he snidely replied as he leaned over him. "That is what I am going to do to you, if you don't study and pay more attention in my class!" hissed Mr. Wilkins softly in his ear.

A few girls nearby who overheard the teachers comment to Roger laughed at him as soon as the teacher had turned away heading back up to the front of the class. The bell rang and the students quickly rose being free from the class. They all gathered their belongings and then headed for the door. The snotty girls who had laughed at him getting scolded stayed behind to talk with the teacher and wish him luck on the upcoming bird show for his pigeons that weekend.

"Remember, the test is on Monday!" Mr. Wilkins spoke loudly over the noise as the students were departing and heading into the hallway.

It was now lunchtime and Roger headed toward the cafeteria to meet Aaron and Maxine. Maxine or "Max" for short was Rogers's other neighbor. She was one tough girl. She was a little taller than him and definitely stronger. She was stunningly pretty with beautifully kept hair and minimal makeup. She was an avid Gymnast, very athletic and toned. She had black hair and big brown eyes. She was not really into boys yet and just loved gymnastics and being a very intimidating girl. Her strength and toughness made her distant from other girls. Not only was she prettier than most, but could beat up any one in the school if she wanted to. She knew it as did the whole school.

As Roger rounded the corner to the entrance of the cafeteria he heard Max's familiar voice, this time it was loud and very mad.

"You messing with my friend again?" he heard her ask as he looked up to see Max stabbing her finger into Gary's chest.

"No!" he said in a quaky voice, "No harm done."

As Roger walked up to Max and Gary, he spotted Gary's friends standing behind him.

"How's the butt cheek?" Roger asked with a smirk and a grin, looking at Gary.

With an angry look on his face Gary turned to Roger, "If it weren't for your *girlfriend* protecting you right now I would-"

"YOU would what!" yelled Max at Gary. "I am not his girlfriend you *butt fried loser,*" she continued yelling, "I'm going to knock your-

"Break it up Max, what is going on?" questioned Ben, the school guard who just appeared on the scene. "MAX, leave the kid alone," he said, as he was breaking up the gathering crowd. "All right, everyone get back to lunch, break it up, nothing to see here".

Max stepped away from Gary with her finger still pointing at him, a nasty glare still on her face as she stepped backwards.

"Let's go eat, guys," she said to Roger and the newly arrived Aaron who had just walked onto the scene.

"Man, what did I miss this time?" asked Aaron, with a very disappointing whine in his voice.

"Nothing big" said Roger, as the three of them turned to go find a place to sit for lunch. As they walked Roger filled Aaron in on what he had just seen Max doing to Gary.

"Thanks for watching out for me," Roger told Max.

"No problem little buddy," said Max, "I like charity cases and besides, I like the limp you gave to Gary and the waddle his friend now has from you electrifying his-

"That's enough!" said Roger, cutting off Max raising his hand signaling stop, with a laugh in his voice before she could mention any more about the boys misfortune to his lower region.

They walked out to the courtyard and sat down at an empty table. As they sat eating their lunch, Roger spoke, "I am having those day dreams again guys."

Both Max and Aaron looked up, their mouths filled with sandwich, eyes wide and silent.

"When did they start again?" asked Max. "They had stopped a couple of months ago."

"Last week," answered Roger. "I stayed up late one night working on my jacket, and fell asleep with my brothers IPod on again."

Both Max and Aaron continued to stare at Roger with full attention. "I had a small nightmare that night and a really vivid one last night when I dozed off reading my English book," explained Roger.

They continued to stare at him. "I have no idea why I am having these more frequently lately," he said with frustration in his voice. "At first I just remembered the screaming and the flashes of light. Now, as they keep happening, the exploding room full of smoke and fire seems to get more detailed all the time. I think I'll talk to my Dad about it. He might have some answers or ideas why I am having these weird dreams."

Max looked over at Roger and asked, "Why do you think your dad might have some ideas?"

Roger looked over at Max and Aaron, their eyes still glued to him.

"I have no idea, but I am going to find out, *I have to find out!*"

The bell rang and they all got up to head back to class for the rest of the school day.

"See you in sixth period," Aaron waved to Roger, as he turned the opposite direction to his math class.

"Let me know what you find out when you ask him, OK," said Max.

"Of course I will," replied Roger as they headed down the hall to class.

Chapter 3

Silver Box

"Let's go" shouted Rogers's mom from the kitchen, "We're going to be late to Grandmas for her birthday party!"

It was almost 6:00PM and the family was getting ready to go to Grandma Dexter's for her 74th birthday party. She lived in the small town of Cove Creek, a short 25 minute drive away. Rogers's mom always hated to be late and she always liked to arrive 15 minutes early to any appointment she had.

"*Where is your Father?*" said his mom Alicia, in a stressed voice.

"Outside in the shop," answered Jenny.

"CALVIN!" yelled Alicia out the kitchen window, "get in here *NOW*, we are going to be late to your mother's house!"

"I'm coming, I'm coming, be there in a second," came his voice from the back steps.

The back door opened and Rogers's dad entered the kitchen. "Sorry guys, I was in the middle of a project."

He grabbed the car keys from the holder and they all headed out the door.

"WAIT!" said Alicia. The door quickly opened again as she hurried back into the kitchen, walked over to the counter and picked up a delicious cheesecake she had made for Grandma Dexter's birthday. She turned and hurried back out the door to the car.

They had begun the drive to Grandmas house and just entered the freeway to head across town, "Dad, what were you working on tonight in the shop?" asked Roger.

"Just tinkering on my old motorcycle" said his Dad. "It helps me unwind after a long day of work."

Rogers's father worked for the local power company called Eagle Pass. He had been a supervisor the past fifteen years. Roger had many fond memories with his brother Randy when they were younger and they would be allowed to work with their father for the day. They were able to drive around town with him in his cool big work truck. He remembered watching his dad work on high voltage power lines and the poles that held the wires high in the skies throughout their hometown.

Roger turned his head and looked out the wet car window from the small drizzle of rain just beginning to come down. He remembered a time with his brother Randy a few years before he had died. Randy had just gotten his driver's license and wanted to take Roger out for a drive in the old classic Chevy he had fixed up. He wanted Roger to be his first passenger after he got his new license. Roger clearly remembered driving down State Street with his brother at the wheel. The sound Randy's old Chevy car made was so cool and tough. It made a deep, low rumble as they drove along in the old muscle car. Randy handed Roger his license as they drove so that he could check out the new privilege he had just earned. Roger looked at the cool photo of his brother on the license, flipped it over checking it out and then handed it back to him.

"Let's go get ice cream and fries at the diner," said Randy.

Roger smiled and was happy to be hanging out with his big brother. Not many young boys had a cool older brother who actually wanted to spend time with them. Roger was very lucky to have such a good older brother. The two of them were very close and never did have disagreements or fights. They got along so well and really enjoyed each other.

"We are here!" said Calvin, as they pulled into the driveway of his grandmas house. Roger snapped back from the deep memory he had drifted into. His breath had made the window foggy while he was staring out of it as he looked up see his grandmas house. He loved coming to visit his grandma Enid. She was widowed and lived in a huge old house on top of a hill with a beautiful view of the city.

The rain had just ended as they all entered the house. They were greeted by the cutest grandma you could imagine, followed by her little dog Chester. She had big, puffy, curly grandma hair, large glasses and a huge smile for them.

"Hello come in, come in," said Grandma with big grin.

As she kissed Roger and Jenny on the cheeks, they stepped away and looked at each other laughing. They were laughing at the big red marks on each other's cheeks left from Grandma Enid's bright red lipstick. As they were wiping the traces of Grandma from their faces, the family went into the kitchen followed by the small guard-dog Chester. Roger's mom placed the cheesecake she had brought into the refrigerator while they all visited.

I'm so glad you came," said Grandma Enid.

"We are glad to come," replied Alicia.

"My girlfriends took me to lunch today at the Sizzler downtown and we had a lovely visit," she told them.

"That sounds like you had fun," replied Calvin.

As Alicia and Calvin sat down in the living room with Grandma, Roger and Jenny snuck away and headed down to the basement. Old people talk was boring to them and they liked to explore the huge house. Her house had lots of neat things and places to explore and check out. Grandpa had died five years earlier and Grandma Enid had left his things scattered around the house in the rooms that he had spent a lot of time in. The basement was kind of creepy to them, but was fun to explore. It was old and partially unfinished. It had piles of things all over and plenty of space to move around. Most of the time Jenny and Roger would play hide and seek. Because of the size of this old house they could play this game for hours.

The house was so too big for two old people to share so Grandma and Grandpa had converted part of the basement into an apartment. They rented it out and had different tenants living there the past few years. Some of the renters Roger got to meet and know had been college kids. After they moved on, a newlywed couple lived there briefly. Roger's favorite tenant had been Bart the bachelor. He was so funny and a good friend. He would help Grandma around the yard with upkeep, mowing the lawn and helping her plant a small garden in the back behind her garage. Plus he played soccer with Roger and Jenny sometimes when they were over. When he left unexpectedly a few months ago she rented it to the current tenant, a man named Carl Massey. He was a very nice, clean cut younger man, just a couple of years out of college. They would see him some days when they were exploring the house and would chat with him to get to know more about him.

"Jenny and Roger!" they heard their mother call, "come up stairs so we can sing to Grandma."

They both came trotting up the stairs to see both of their parents wearing ridiculous cone shaped birthday hats. They had one on Grandma Enid over her big puffy hairdo. The rubber band under her chin made her cheeks squishy and she looked like a giant squirrel with fat cheeks. Calvin had even managed to get a party hat on Chester who was not happy about it. He was growling at Calvin as he held him making him keep it on. Roger and Jenny had just put on their hats when they saw Carl walking toward his entrance to the basement apartment. They waved at him getting his attention and motioned for him to come in.

"Hey Carl," said both Jenny and Roger.

"Here you go," said Jenny as she handed Carl a blue cone hat to put on.

"What do we have going on here?" asked Carl.

"*It's my birthday!*" Grandma replied.

"Well congratulations," said Carl, 'what are you now, 30 or 31?" he asked with a grin.

"Oh stop it" said Grandma as she flirtatiously slapped him on the shoulder, "I am 35," she said with a giggle.

After everyone stopped laughing at her young Grandma comment, they started to sing the famous happy birthday song. They all sang along, except for Chester who was looking like he wanted to bite Calvin. After Grandma blew out her candles, they all enjoyed the cheesecake Roger's mom had made.

Calvin asked Carl how he was doing. "Fine," answered Carl. "I got a promotion today." He explained what he was doing at the computer company he was working for. Roger and Jenny finished their cheesecake and ran off to explore some more of the house; this time upstairs. They heard Carl say 'goodnight' and were watching him leave as they looked through the window in Grandpa's office on the second floor. He walked out of the side of the house and around to the back. Jenny went to another room to explore but Roger was still watching Carl as he reached into his pocket and pulled out a small 2 way radio.

"That is odd," he thought to himself. "I wonder what he uses a 2 way radio for?"

He continued to stare at Carl as he walked to the entrance of his basement apartment having a conversation with someone on the radio. Something about Carl's behavior and the way he kept looking around as he continued to talk on the radio kept Rogers attention. Carl finished his radio conversation and put the radio back into his black leather coat and walked down into his basement apartment, disappearing from Roger's sight. He continued to stare out the window when he heard his name.

"Roger!" sounded Jenny's voice behind him, making him jump.

"CRAP," he said as he turned around to face her. "What do you want Jenny?'

"Mom sent me to get you," chuckled Jenny, laughing from just scaring him and making him jump, "We are leaving for home," and she ran out of the room and down the stairs.

As Roger turned to leave his grandfather's office he knocked over a lamp on the desk accidentally with his elbow. The lamp tipped over but didn't break. As Roger leaned over reaching for the lamp, something on the bottom of the lamp caught his attention. It was a small silver box, about the size and shape of a cell phone and it was stuck to the bottom between the extended legs on the base. He looked closer at the small box then he pulled it from the base of the lamp and placed the lamp back on the table standing up correctly. He stared down at the box in his hands, turning it over several times, studying the detail. The tiny silver box had small combination lock wheels on it like a bike lock with the numbers zero through nine on each of them.

"What is this thing?" Roger said in a small voice to himself as he flipped the box over and over again in his hands, concentrating on the small thing.

"Roger!" called his father.

"I'm coming Dad," hollered Roger, as he slipped the small box into his pocket and ran out of the office and down the stairs. As he jumped the last few steps he came bouncing into the living room, saw his grandma Enid looking at him.

"Happy birthday old lady," he said as he gave her a big hug with a goodbye kiss on her cheek, then walked out the door to the car.

As they were driving home Roger kept reaching into his pocket to touch the small silver case wondering what in the world was in it. He wondered what the combination could possibly be to open the box and how could he figure it out. They pulled into their driveway to see Maxine sitting on their porch swing enjoying the cool night air. She was obviously hanging out, waiting for them to get home.

"Hey girl" said Roger as he came up the walk. "What are you doing here this late?"

"Just taking a walk to clear my mind."

"Well, come on in and have some leftover cheesecake from my grandmas wild 35th birthday party," said Roger.

She had a confused look on her face. "Uh-all right, sounds good to me," as she followed the family inside.

After Roger explained the joke to her, he handed her a plate of cheesecake and they both sat down at the counter. Just then Aaron came walking into the kitchen, "I heard cheesecake was in the house, I'm starving for some."

He took a double helping and grabbed a fork from a drawer. It was just the three of them in the kitchen.

"Guys, check this out," as he tossed the small silver box from his pocket over to Max. It sailed high over Aaron's head as he shoved an entirely too large bite of cheesecake into his mouth. Max reached up and caught it with one hand, her other hand shoveling cheesecake into her open mouth.

"Uutt is thus?" she tried to speak with her mouth full.

Aaron popped his head up to see what she was holding.

Roger was pulling his finger from his mouth after small taste of cheesecake, "I have no idea" he said. "I found it on my grandpa's desk stuck under an old heavy lamp."

He held his hand up facing Max, signaling her to toss the box back over to him. As the box was flying toward him Aaron's hand shot up and caught it before it reached Roger.

"How long do you think it has been there?" asked Aaron as he stared at it.

"I have no idea. But my grandpa has been dead for five years."

Just then Jenny came into the kitchen and Aaron quickly chucked the small box to Roger who caught it speedily and shoved it in his pocket in one quick motion.

"Hey little buddy," said Aaron to Jenny.

"What's up?" Jenny replied to Aaron. "Save me some of that cheesecake for tomorrow! It's Saturday and after I sleep in, that's going to be my lunch."

"No problem mini Dexter," replied Aaron.

Jenny took a slice of apple from the fridge, closed the door and left the kitchen.

They quickly finished their cheesecake snack and the three of them headed to the shop out back to talk in private.

Chapter 4

Meeting Place

The teen trio walked into his father's workshop from the backyard, shut the door and gathered in the back corner. His father's shop was very large and had two spacious work areas. One area had an old Ford Mustang that was in the process of being restored by him and his father. It was a great looking old classic car and was in need of a paint job. The other area where they were gathered was a nice work area with a couple of work tables that had some tools and projects laying on them. On the edge of the area was a rustic looking mini kitchen with a sink. There was a small area for seating with some stools, a small table and an old leather sofa. It was the best hangout ever and they enjoyed spending time together in it.

"Does anyone know you took that tonight?" asked Max.

"No, I found it on accident after I knocked over the lamp," replied Roger as he stepped up to the work table and placed the small silver box on it. They were all staring at it as Aaron made a movement to pick it up. The door slid opened startling them all, causing them to jump and turn around to see who it was.

"Whatcha doing?" asked Jenny, as she walked into the shop and over to the small refrigerator under the counter.

"Just hanging out and isn't it past your bedtime little girl?" quipped Roger.

She gave him an angry glare as she pulled a bottle of cold root beer from the fridge.

"Knock off the big boy talk, you loser," she said as she opened the soda and took a long gulp from the cold bottle. Then she chucked the bottle cap at Roger, missing him completely when he ducked and it sailed off somewhere clinking to the floor. She looked over at the three of them gathered around the table and noticed Aaron trying to cover the small box on the table with his hand, standing there trying to look very casual.

"You're a terrible giveaway Aaron," she said, "You couldn't be more obvious dude. I see you trying to hide something in your hand."

Aaron had tried to move the box with grace to his pocket but she had spotted it.

"Just show me what you've got and I will leave you alone."

"FINE," Aaron said with a sigh, but as he started to pull it from his pocket Max stepped in.

"Don't show her, it's a surprise!"

"What do you mean?" asked Jenny.

"Duh, it's a small treat we got for your grandma for her 74th birthday," said Max, as she turned her head so only Roger and Aaron could see her cheesy grin and a small wink with her left eye.

"We'll show you later, now take a hike little punk, get in the house to bed!" said Max, in a joking manner. She reached over turning Jenny towards the door and gave her a little push.

Max slid the shop door shut and she turned and came back to face Roger and Aaron in the room.

"Nosy little turd," mumbled Max, "but, she's a cute kid."

They all grabbed a bottle of root beer following Jenny's lead, Aaron and Roger sprawled out on the sofa. Max took a seat in a chair facing the sofa.

As Aaron sat comfortably in the soft sofa, he tossed the box straight up in the air, catching it with one hand a couple of times, pausing in between tosses to stare at the box. Max had just taken a sip of root beer and held out her hand toward Aaron, signaling him to toss the box over to her. As she caught it, she heard something inside the box make a small jingling noise. She paused, looking at the box, then held it up to her ear giving it a little shake. She could hear something softly rattling inside and shook it a few more times.

"What do you think?" she asked Roger as she tossed it over to him. He was mid sip with his root beer and quickly reacted with his other hand to catch the box as it sailed toward his forehead. He too heard a small jingling inside the box as he caught it. He shook it, examined it closely and lifted it up to his ear giving it another little shake.

"I wonder what my grandpa used this for?" he said. "Should I ask my grandma if she has seen it before?" he asked.

"I guess it couldn't hurt" said Aaron. "Do you think she'll be mad you took it?"

"I hope not. Maybe we could ride our bikes over to her house tomorrow. It's Saturday and we don't have much planned," said Roger.

"I can't, I have to go shopping with my mom in the morning," said Max. "I have a gymnastics meet next week and she promised to buy me new clothes for it and besides, she is only in town for the weekend and then she goes back on the road for her *busy* work life," she said in a frustrated voice.

Both Roger and Aaron could see the pain in her face as she said those words and caught the tone of disappointment and hurt in her voice.

"Sorry your mom had to go back to work," said Roger. "It must suck to see your parents get a divorce," he said.

"Yeah it really does," said Max. "I sure miss both of them. But that is why I have you two *losers* to keep me company."

"Anytime," replied Roger and Aaron. They had smiles as they held out their half empty root beer bottles for a toast among friends. All three of them clanged their bottles together- "To Friends," taking a gulp from their bottles.

"I'm hitting the sack," said Roger, "I'm kind of beat from the busy day."

And he stood up to and tossed his now empty bottle in the recycle garbage bin next to the counter.

"See you tomorrow" said Aaron and Max and they all three headed out the door of the shop and turned off the light.

That night, Roger lay in his bed with his ear buds in, listening to a new top 20 song he had downloaded earlier. As he stared up at the ceiling he held the small box in his hand and flipped it over and over and then noticed some very small writing on the side. He looked at it closer and saw the letters, "FOR RRD" inscribed in small letters. He hadn't noticed them before but stared at them now.

"What is FOR RRD?" he asked himself. "Did someone misspell the word FORD?" He wondered. "No, it must be some ones initials or something," he thought as he turned it over and flipped through the small combination of numbers to see if they moved.

He continued to thumb through the dials and randomly picked some numbers to see what would happen. There was no button or switches to try, even if he thought the numbers were correct, so how was this thing supposed to open, even if he picked the correct numbers?

"Oh well" he said, reaching over to place the box on his night stand and turned off his lamp. Rolling over to his back he took a deep breath and closed his eyes listening to the music and quickly drifted off to sleep.

Chapter 5

Flashback

Roger again found himself in a large room, the sounds of bursting light bulbs and flashes of bright light were surrounding him. He looked up and couldn't see very well because of the smoke filling the room and the sounds of chaos. He heard a young man's voice screaming, "Run, Run!"

Roger looked to see where the familiar voice was coming from. He looked around the room and was shielding his eyes with his hand from the brightness and flashes of light and small explosions. He was squinting and walking quickly forward. He had just started to pick up his pace when he was hit hard from the side by someone large and running full speed into him.

The person, who had slammed hard into him, had his arm wrapped around Roger's body as his body smashed into him in a football tackle, grabbing him firmly. They both hit the ground hard and the air was knocked from his lungs as he hit the white floor and rolled onto his side. The grip around his waist from the man was now softer as they lay together on the floor. There was smoke in the room and bright flashing lights. The loud sounds were increasing with small explosions from power and computer systems going into overload, bursting into small puffs of smoke and sparks.

"What is going on!" he tried to scream as he knelt next to the man. But his voice was not as loud as he wanted it to be, because of the wind being just knocked out of him. It was hard for him to take in a full breath of air.

As Roger knelt trying to get his breath he looked up in front of him,

"No Way' he whispered," R-RANDY!" He was starting to scream. He saw his brother across the room with one arm up over his head as he was moving quickly down the panel of instruments, switches, and monitors. He was frantically pushing buttons, turning knobs and switches, screaming as loud as he could

"Get out, get out fast! DAD."

"What!" Roger said as he looked over and saw that it was his father next to him getting on his feet.

"Dad, what is going on?" Roger yelled. His father was pulling him up, turning them toward the back door of the room.

His father was just starting to take a second step toward the door, when a giant gust of wind hit both of them hard from behind, immediately with it was a tremendous 'BOOM' from a huge explosion going off right behind them. He felt his body tumbling in the air, being carried in the path of the explosion, pushing him and his father in the air toward the door they were once trying to get to.

He saw a giant fireball engulf the room as he flew through the air. He felt like he was seeing everything in slow motion from the explosion. The fireball was headed rapidly toward his dear brother and starting to engulf the equipment around Randy, destroying the computer systems. It just started to knock his brother off his feet when all of sudden Roger hit the floor.

He was violently awakened from his nightmare and was lying face down on the floor next to his bed. He had fallen out of bed from the thrashing he was doing in his sleep.

"Randy!" he cried out loud, "Dad!" he yelled.

His bedroom door burst open as his father and mother rushed into his bedroom.

"What happened!" exclaimed his breathless father.

"I fell out of bed Dad," he said as he gasped for breath. "I - I had a nightmare."

"You were screaming out to Randy," said his mother as she helped him off the floor and onto his bed, taking a seat beside him.

His mind was clearing and his breathing was returning to normal as he became calmer.

"I don't know what happened" he said and tears stared to roll down his face. "I saw Randy getting blown up."

He turned to face his father, "What is going on Dad?" he asked as he looked up into his father's handsome rugged face. "That dream felt so real, like- I had been there in real life," said Roger.

His father glanced up at his mother with a look that Roger had come to know. It was a serious look, one that always came with some bad news. His father looked back over to Roger with a concerned stare.

"Son" he said, "we thought you had lost that part of your memory."

Roger looked upset now and glanced up at his mother, then back to his father's face.

"My memory?" His heavy breathing starting to pick up again and a little panic in his voice. "What are you talking about?"

His father knelt down next to him as he sat on the edge of his bed with his mother.

"We didn't know how much you would ever remember son, about the accident." explained his father. "There was an accident in the lab that Randy was working in," his father paused, looked into his eyes, "and Randy died in the explosion, son."

"NO! That's not true," barked Roger. "You said, I was told-" he stuttered in unbelief from what he was hearing. "You told me Randy died in his car from a crash while taking me to get ice cream!" gasped Roger. "I was in a coma for weeks recovering and missed his funeral!" he yelled.

"SON!" said his father in a loud, deep fatherly voice, getting Rogers attention and causing him to look at him. "We couldn't tell you what happened," he explained, "there is so much to tell you, but we have been prohibited from talking about it." Roger focused on his dad.

"Listen son, the work Randy was doing at his lab was very secretive and the government was involved somehow. We don't know how they were involved, but after the explosion we were instructed by them, about what had happened and we were restricted not to speak about it to anyone."

His father leaned and whispered in his ear, "We had to follow their cover story son, we have so much we need to talk about, but we can't right now, we are being watched." His father whispered, "I promise, I will tell you what is going on soon, just please be patient with me and your mother. We will tell you when we can," assured his father looking at him sternly and directly into his eyes. He reached over to Rogers face and wiped away some tears now starting to roll down his cheeks. His hands cupped Rogers face, using big thumbs to clear more tears. He held Rogers face in his hands, "Please, be patient, I need some time before I can tell you," whispered his father again then looked up at his mother, his face showing some emotion and a half scared smile.

His father's look was powerful and Roger could see the love in his eyes as he looked at his mom as she stood up. His father stood up, leaned over and gently pulled Roger's bed covers over him, kissed his forehead and walked out of the room.

His mother leaned over and picked up his music player that he had fallen asleep with. It had fallen on the floor after he fell asleep and had the nightmare. She reached over and placed it on his night stand along with the tangled headphone cord. As she placed it on the night stand, she saw the silver box sitting there.

She saw that Roger had seen her face after she noticed the silver box. Roger could tell that his mother was familiar with that box. He thought to himself "she has seen it before" as she picked it up, looked at it with concentration, like it was a lost item she had been looking for. She continued to stare at it and appeared to be very deep in thought.

Roger lay there in bed silently watching her for some sort of reaction.

"Nice little box" she said, as she sat it back down on the night stand.

Roger took notice that she turned the box so that the small combination wheels were facing him and she reached up to turn off his lamp.

"That little box used to belong to your brother." she said with a smile.

Roger looked at her with a confused face, his mind now racing with more questions.

"What do you mean, do you know what it is, or how to open it?"

Then she reached over, clicked off his lamp and kissed him goodnight. "No I don't Roger. I had seen him with it before. Where did you find it?"

Roger didn't want to get in trouble by saying that he had swiped it from grandpa's office, but decided to be truthful and replied, "I found it while exploring grandpa's office."

"Really, well don't lose it, it might be important," she told him.

"OK mom," he said.

Then she turned and left his room shutting the door behind her.

Roger lay in bed now with his mind at full speed as if he had polished off a large Mtn Dew soda and was loaded up on caffeine. He was thinking about the silver box and after a few minutes switched thoughts to the terrible dream he just had. He was studying it over in his mind trying hard to remember. He closed his eyes and with deep concentration, playing out the scene again in his head and tried to focus on what was in the room that he might have missed. After about an hour or so of deep thought he grew tired and drifted off to sleep.

Chapter 6

Weekend

The sun was breaking through the morning sky, reaching into Roger's bedroom stretching over his face. The light hitting his closed eyes was causing him to stir. He slowly opened his eyes, looked up at the ceiling, then turned over on his side pulling up his covers to shield his face from the bright room. He lay facing the wall, trying to stay sleepy so he could fall back to sleep again. It was hopeless to try anymore, he thought to himself. He then remembered his nightmare as his mind started warming up.

He sat up quickly kicking off his covers and looked over to his nightstand to see the small silver box he had swiped from his grandmas house. On the night stand he could only see his iPod music player, but no silver box. His heart jumped and he shot out of bed searching around the nightstand. He was frantically looking around, moving the alarm clock and the iPod searching for the silver box, but he could not find it.

"No, no, no, where is it? It was right here!" he gasped as he pointed with both of his hands at the nightstand with his palms up. His heart was racing at full pace. He crawled around the nightstand again and the area surrounding it on his hands and knees looking frantically, searching to see if it had fallen off and landed somewhere. When it was nowhere to be found, he let out a sound of frustration.

"No," he moaned as he slowly let his body lay completely flat on the floor. He cupped his face after rolling over on his back motionless on his bedroom floor.

"Where did it go?" he said, as he dropped his hands to his sides.

As he looked up toward the ceiling, he caught a glimpse of a face looking down at him. The face was upside down and looking at him with a cheesy grin spreading across the little girls face. "Jenny, what are doing?"

"*Did I scare you?*" She asked Roger, as he started to sit up.

"NO, you didn't, but you look like a freaking Vulture hanging over me getting ready to pounce."

"Mom sent me to wake you for breakfast. She has some biscuits and gravy ready so you better come down to eat."

Roger stood up to go eat his favorite breakfast, waiting for him downstairs. He was still upset about losing the silver box and was very frustrated. A hunger pain groaned in his teenage stomach, he could smell the biscuits that were in the oven cooking, filling the house with the tasty aroma. He glanced around his messy room. It was full of broken electronics and inventions he had made, but he was hoping to spot the silver box in a pile somewhere. He wanted to look one more time, just in case he missed the place where the stupid little silver box was hiding from him.

Jenny was standing in the doorway and preparing to walk down to breakfast with him when a little sound could be heard from inside his nightstand. "BEEP," then a pause and another "BEEP, BEEP." He looked down at the night stand and then at Jenny.

She was looking at him, "That thing is annoying Roger."

He looked at her, "What do you mean?"

Jenny took a step back into the room and said, "That dumb alarm box you have."

"Wait, what alarm box?"

"The one I put in your drawer a half hour ago."

She took a step over to the nightstand and slid open the top drawer. They both were looking down into the open drawer. Rogers's heart skipped as he reached down into the drawer and took out the silver box. "BEEP", small pause, then "BEEP, BEEP" sounded from the silver box.

"Yeah, it keeps changing tones like that," explained Jenny. "When I first came in to wake you for breakfast, I heard the little box making one small 'Beep' every few seconds. So I tried to change the numbers on the front to get it to stop." She told him. "Every time I changed the small numbered wheels it would beep in a different sequence. It was getting very annoying, so-I tossed it in your drawer to keep it from waking you up. I decided to let you sleep a little longer since mom hadn't quite finished making the gravy." Then she closed the drawer and stepped back.

"What is that little thing anyway?"

"I have no idea," he replied. "I found it in grandpa's office yesterday."

"Does grandma know you took it?"

"No, she doesn't, but I'm going to take it back Sunday when we go over for dinner."

"Whatever, *you liar*," accused Jenny. "Hey, that's the thingy that Aaron was hiding from me last night in the shop, isn't it?"

Roger looked down at the silver box, then back up at Jenny, "Yeah, so."

"You and your friends are ALL liars," she scolded him, "A present for Grandma, LIAR!"

"Sorry Jenny, it was a secret," he explained, "and I'm going to take it back, I am, really. And mom knows I have it," he blurted out before he could stop himself. He remembered his mom handling the box last night after his nightmare. He thought if he told Jenny that mom knew he had it, he could stop her from interrogating him any further.

"I'm starving," trying to change the subject quickly. "Let's go eat." He proceeded to walk out the bedroom door, slipping the box into the front pocket of his pajama shorts.

Jenny shouted, "COMING THROUGH!" As she ran past him, she gave him a soft elbow to the side as she went speeding by taking the stairs 2 at a time.

Roger quickly took off after her; he couldn't let her take him in a race to breakfast. He sped down the stairs behind Jenny. They spilled off the stairs into the hallway, Jenny out front with her arms high, making a noise like a crowd at an Olympic race cheering the winner as they came into the kitchen together giggling about the race. They slowed down and walked over and sat at the table.

"Not going to be so easy on you next time Jenny."

She was smirking at him, still holding her champions arms up in the air, taking in the win, rubbing it in that she had beaten him.

"Smells good mom," they both said as they inhaled the delicious aroma.

Their mother was busy making white country gravy at the stove. "Should be done in about a minute," she said. "Will one of you go out back and get your father?"

"I'll get him mom," said Roger as he jumped up and walked out the back door and mumbled, "I want to ask him more questions about what he told me last night."

As he walked toward the shop out back, he heard country music playing on the radio they had in the shop. Roger had been hoping for a chance to get his father alone so that he could question him about what he told him late last night about "being watched" and how he couldn't tell him right then about his dreams.

Roger slid the door open and quietly started to walk into the garage to tell his father about breakfast. At first glance around the shop he looked over by the old Ford Mustang that they owned to see if his father was working under the hood, but he did not see him anywhere in the shop. "Dad," he called out, to see if his father would answer him. But no reply came from his father. Roger then said "Calvin!" a little louder.

He and Jenny had a funny ritual; to get their parents attention they would call them by their first name instead of saying "Mom, or Dad." This usually would get their attention and a nasty look with it, but it would get their attention. This time he got what he was looking for.

"What!" came the sound of his father's deep voice from underneath the old car.

Roger looked down and saw two legs sticking out from under the car. His father was laying on his back on a mechanics dolly working.

"Breakfast is ready," said Roger. "Mom sent me to get you."

Roger heard small wheels start to move and saw his father starting to emerge.

"Let's eat." As he sat up and reached out to Roger with his hand to help pull him up to his feet. "Oomph," came a groan from his father.

"What was that noise you made there?" Roger said with laughter in his voice.

"That was an old man groan" replied his dad as he came to his feet and gave Roger a soft punch on the arm.

He then reached for a shop towel on the tool chest to wipe his hands and started to turn around to head to the door of the shop.

"Wait, dad," said Roger. "I wanted to ask you something."

His dad stopped walking, paused wiping his hands clean and tossed the towel onto the counter. He turned to face Roger and spoke.

"You don't waste any time, do you?"

"What were you talking about last night in my room, when you said you couldn't tell me right now?" asked Roger. "I want to know what-

His father cut in, "Roger, I think we need to get in the house like your mother wanted," and he made a gesture with his face, as if to say with body language, not right now, this is not the time.

Then he winked at Roger and pointed his chin up at an old license plate nailed to the wall. Roger caught what his father was saying with body language and looked at the license plate.

Still a little confused Roger motioned with his chin at the license plate and mouthed the words "bugged?" and pointed to his ear.

His father looked at him, winked again, shook his head up and down and at the same time said, "Let's go eat, I'm starving,"

While walking from the shop toward the house his father leaned over and whispered, "I found some sort of listening device behind that license plate on the wall. I don't know who put it there."

Roger looked back at him, *"Seriously Dad?"*

"Seriously Roger! I can disable it when I'm in the garage working. I have a scrambler that Randy and I made. I use it to block the transmission signal and rebroadcast a recording of the sounds I want whoever is listening with that thing to hear. So, whoever put it there hears only shop sounds and useless banging around so it appears that I am alone and just working." He explained, "But I didn't have it on when you came in so I had to cut you off like I did, sorry about that."

Roger continued to stare at his dad in amazement and his mind was now racing with questions he wanted to ask his dad, but they had arrived at the house on their short walk returning from the shop.

"Listen son, I will get you up to speed soon. This afternoon we are driving over to grandmas and we'll talk during our drive, OK?"

"Ok," replied Roger as they walked through the back door into the kitchen.

"About time," said Rogers's mother, "your food is getting cold."

They both sat down at the table with Jenny. Alicia brought over a basket of biscuits and a small container of delicious white country gravy and she took a seat with all of them at the table.

As Roger reached for the biscuits his mother snapped his hand with a lightning fast move with a wooden spoon, "We pray for thanks first," she reminded him.

Roger was holding one hand with the other, rubbing the back of it with a startled look. He was caught off guard from being 'Mom Slapped.'

"I will say the blessing," said Jenny. "I'm starving after waiting forever for you guys."

She prayed quickly and they all started to eat and enjoy the time together as a family for a late breakfast.

"What time are we going to grandmas today?' asked Roger.

His dad replied "We'll go this afternoon. I'm going to fix a bathroom faucet for her after I get some parts from the hardware store."

"That sounds good" said Roger as they chatted about their upcoming plans and ate the delicious food.

Chapter 7

Lazy Days

After the family finished eating breakfast and cleaned up the dishes, they all went their separate ways in the house to spend some personal down time relaxing and taking a break from the busy week they had just had.

Roger went into his bedroom and got dressed for the day, then took out the CUBS electro jacket that had been broken on the bus. He was looking at it while it lay on the workbench he had in his bedroom and then he spotted his mother's broken vacuum cleaner sitting in the corner. He remembered that he promised he would fix it soon for her. The vacuums motor was destroyed when she ran over some debris Roger had left on his floor from one of his inventions. So he pushed aside the jacket and went over to get the vacuum. For the next hour he worked repairing it with spare parts from pieces of a broken DVD player and an old blender. His mother came into his bedroom when she heard the noise of the resurrected vacuum cleaner and saw him pushing it for a test run across his bedroom floor.

"Hey there," she said with a smile, watching him push the vacuum around his room cleaning the carpet. "I don't know what makes me happier, the repaired vacuum, or *to see you actually using the vacuum to clean your room*," she laughed.

Roger smiled and then turned it off and rolled up the electrical cord, attaching it to the cleaner. "Sorry I didn't get it fixed sooner mom," he said as he pushed it over and stood it next to her.

"Don't be sorry Roger. I'm just glad I didn't have to take it to the repair shop. Thank you for doing this for me," she said and pushed it out into the hall and carried it down stairs to try it out in the living room. Roger stood at the top of the stairs and hollered down to his mom, "Remember, you have a free one year warranty on the service," then smiled as he returned to his room.

The broken jacket lay on the workbench next to a few inventions he had made. There was a broken IPod with other electronic devices that he had been tinkering with. He had used the screen from the broken IPod to be the master system screen on his electro jacket. Roger was definitely talented with electronics, mainly because he was mentored by the best technician in the world, his brother Randy.

He took the jacket and laid it flat on the work bench and went to work repairing it. He had just removed the broken piece of pole from the sleeve of the jacket when Aaron came walking into his room.

"Hey man," said Aaron.

"Hi bud," replied Roger, as Aaron walked over to see what he was working on.

"I still can't believe I missed the first voyage with this jacket," said Aaron. "I had that dang dentist appointment. If it wasn't for that I would have had a front row seat to the show on the bus, up by Darin."

"I'm sorry you missed it too bud, we'll just have to fix it and put on an encore show for you."

"It's a deal." He pointed the broken piece of pole to the side of his head, made a small noise, Ka Chang. "I just made a mental calendar note," and smiled.

"You're such a dork," said Roger, laughing along with Aaron.

They worked on the jacket for a while and appeared to have it working again. Roger looked at it and commented, "I think we are finished, we just need to do a test to see if it is working," and he turned to Aaron.

"I know how to test it," said Aaron. "JENNY!" he hollered out of Rogers's bedroom door.

"No way! We are not testing it on my sister. My mom would kill me."

Aaron had the electro jacket on in a flash and was ready for the test. "Power at 100%" came the small voice from the jacket. Aaron had already powered it up and was waiting for Jenny to come running into the room.

"Not going to happen," said Roger, then reached over and hit the power down button on the cuff of the jacket. "We can test it later," and the small sound of the motor winding down could be heard coming from the jacket. Aaron slipped it off and handed it to Roger. He took it over and put it on a hanger and hung it in his closet.

"Where did you get the power source for that thing?" asked Aaron.

"Randy made it from some old TV parts and other gadgets before he died."

It was a very powerful system that his brother had started to make while he was in college at the local State University. Randy had been a senior in some very advanced classes in Physics, Electronics and Engineering. He was a genius and loved teaching Roger about what he was working on at school. Right before Randy died he had showed Roger his latest invention. He was worried about it and the grade he would receive from it. Roger really couldn't remember much about it, only that it had something to do with electricity and he was working on harnessing its power into a mini power source.

This little experimental power source that Randy made with Roger was pretty small and compact. Roger had installed the power source into his jacket and it could generate just enough power to run all of the electronics in it and provide power for the shocking end of the power rod. It worked really well and almost survived the first field test too.

"Now that we have our assignment fixed, what do you want to do?" asked Aaron as he flopped down on Roger's bed.

"My dad and I are heading to my grandmas house to fix a sink later today," replied Roger.

Aaron reached over to a small shelf next to Rogers's bed and grabbed a small garage door opener. He pointed it at the bedroom windows and pressed it. The windows automatically began to open to let in the afternoon breeze and the fresh air began to fill the room.

This amazing automatic window opener was an invention Roger made for his science fair project earlier that year for school. The invention contained parts from a dishwasher, garage door opener and other parts from broken VCR recorders. It was the best thing ever for lazy people because it not only would open and close his bedroom windows while he lay in bed, but would also open and close his bedroom door with a different button on the remote. It could even turn his lights on and off with a pulley systems that he made with the motors and wheels from a broken tape recorder. This device made you feel like the 'King of Being Lazy'. The main reason that Roger invented it was because he wanted to be able to use it when he would watch a scary movie or TV show before bedtime in the dark. He could jump into his bed with the lights on and get all covered up and feel safe, snuggled in his blankets. Then with a "Click," he could turn off his lights or shut his door and windows.

"This thing is so awesome" said Aaron, as he pressed the other button to open, then close, then open, then close the bedroom door.

"OK, OK" said Roger, as he plucked the control from Aaron's hand, "you are going to wear it out, *it's not a toy,*" he laughed.

"Any more thoughts on the little silver box you ripped off from your granny?" asked Aaron.

"I didn't rip her off," replied Roger, "I only borrowed it and NO, I don't have any thoughts on how to open it or what the heck it is," he said as he took the small box out of his pocket. He had put it there while he got dressed that morning after breakfast. He then tossed it to Aaron who caught it and continued to examine it for a moment. Aaron then tossed it back to him and he put it back into his pocket.

"Do you think you should ask your Mom or Dad?" asked Aaron.

"I was going to ask my Mom again," and he told Aaron about his recent nightmare and how his mom had spotted the box on his nightstand and checked it out.

"She told me that she had seen it with Randy before and to be careful with it. She said she didn't know how to open it after I asked her more about it."

"Did she get mad that you took it without asking?" asked Aaron,

"No, she didn't say a word about that and I didn't get in trouble, "replied Roger.

"So, what are we waiting for, let's go ask her some more questions dude," said Aaron as he picked up the opener and pointed it at the bedroom door, pressing the button. The door made a click sound and slowly opened up.

As they looked out the door into the hall, they saw the top of a head with black hair and then a pretty face with a smile, bobbing up the stairs toward them.

"Hey Max" they both said as they walked up to her and then back down the stairs she had just came up. She made a U turn and followed.

"Did you get your new gymnastics stuff?" asked Roger.

"Yea, but I had an argument with my mom at the store. She was flirting with the salesman and trying to get him to ask her out. I got sick of it and told her I wanted to go. I told her that I had what I needed and messed up her chance of getting a date. But he was way too young for her. And then I called her a cougar," said Max. "I kind of feel guilty."

"OH dear" uttered Roger. "And how did she take that?"

"Well, let's just say that I might be grounded right now," she said with disgust in her voice. "And besides, she got called into work, so I am now home alone with Mrs. Jenkins watching me."

Mrs. Jenkins was a lady who lived up the street across from Max's house. She lived there most of her life and was the best neighbor. She helped to raise Max after her parents' divorce, while her mother was traveling for work. It was very hard on Max being without a dad and left alone a lot but she was too prideful to admit it. If you dared to bring it up you were in for a pounding. So it was better left unsaid and ignored. Roger and Aaron knew they were always going to be there for her as her best friends.

"Well at least you'll get some great home cooked meals," said Aaron.

Mrs. Jenkins had always cooked and loved to bake. She was a pudgy woman and very tender hearted. She loved to have the three of them over to visit and eat her delicious goodies. She was actually the best baby sitter you could ask for. But a word of caution right here, do not tell Max she is being watched by a babysitter. A verbal thrashing or physical attack will shortly follow if you do.

"I know, she sure makes a good stuffed chicken breast," said Max. "And the cheese that melts from the middle as you cut into it, is to die for."

"STOP" said Aaron while holding up his hand to stop her describing more of the delicious meal. "We get it and we are jealous that you get to eat so well when your mother leaves town."

"So where are you guys headed?" asked Max.

Roger quickly filled her in on what he told Aaron earlier about his nightmare and the box. Now they were headed to question his mother further and fish for information.

"I am joining you" said Max "I want in on this mystery."

They all headed into the kitchen to look for Roger's mom, but she was not in there.

"Mom!" hollered Roger out into the hall, hoping to hear a reply from her.

No reply came, only silence. "Alicia!" yelled Roger down the hall, trying the trick he had used earlier on his dad to get his attention.

"What do you want?" sounded his mother's voice from down the hall. The three followed her voice toward his parents' bedroom.

His mother was laying down on a small sofa on the edge of her bedroom, with a small tablet computer in her hands relaxing and watching a movie. Her corner bedroom had large picture frame windows and a beautiful view. An antique king sized bed was in the center of the room covered in pillows looking very soft and comfortable.

All three of them came into her room and stood next her. "Hey mom, we have a question for you," said Roger.

She sat up on her sofa, paused the movie she was watching and faced the three teenagers standing before her.

"Yes son, what is it?" and she noticed him slowly pulling the small silver box from his pocket. "I knew it wouldn't take you very long to come ask me about that."

"I want to know what this is?" he said as he stared into his mother's eyes.

She paused a long moment, "Roger, you seem to have stumbled onto something very big. How long have you really had that box?"

"I really found it yesterday at Grandmas house on accident. I tipped over a lamp in grandpa's office and saw that it was stuck to the bottom of it as it lay there on the desk."

She put down the tablet she had been watching a movie on. "Roger, can we have a private moment between just us?" She motioned for Max and Aaron to leave the room.

"*Mom-*, whatever you tell me, you know I'm going to tell my best friends. So it's really easier if they just stay, don't you think?"

His mother smiled and rose to her feet, took a deep breath, exhaled, then turned to look out the window of her bedroom.

"I guess I can tell your friends. They are here enough to be considered part of our family anyway. I didn't want you to get involved in this. I don't want to lose another son." She was sounding as if she had a lump in her throat on the verge of crying. She had moist eyes as she looked at the teen trio. "I don't want to tell you son, I am scared," and she turned and sat back down on the sofa looking down at the floor.

Roger had a confused look on his face, "What are you scared of mom?" he said with concern in his voice as he reached and took her hand. "What is going on?" he asked as he knelt down next to her, "I want to know."

Now deep in thought, Roger looked past his mother. He thought back to his nightmares and the visions he had in his mind about being in a large room with numerous explosions going on around him. It was the lab his father had told him about last night he thought to himself. That was Randy's lab I was in. "I remember being in a lab with Randy," he said as he looked back at his mother. "Dad told me Randy died in an explosion last night, I remember it more now," he said. "I remember him screaming something at me and Dad. I remember seeing him throw-, wait a minute," paused Roger as he turned to face his Mother. "I saw Randy throw *this silver box* to Dad in the lab when it was starting to blow up, just before Dad tackled me as we were running out of the lab." He looked up at his mother who was staring at him intently.

"You're catching on real fast son," and she reached down and took the silver box from his hand. She held it, her eyes scanning the box and turned it over and over in her hands.

"What I am about to tell you is, well, it could get us into a lot of trouble with the government," she whispered.

"What are you talking about?" said Roger, in a concerned voice, with Max and Aaron staring wide eyed and open mouthed at him and his Mother from across the room.

She sat up and used her tablet computer to start an app, not saying a word. She typed some codes and the tablet made a few beeps and she looked up.

"I just turned on the jamming devices Calvin installed in the house a few months ago. The jammers are like the one in the shop and block the transmissions of any possible hidden microphones in the house. We don't know if there are any more hidden in the house. Calvin found two of them a while ago and disabled them. We still search constantly through the house and have not discovered any new ones. But we still need to be very cautious," explained Alicia.

"Bugs, jammers, hidden microphones? "What are you talking about," questioned Max and Aaron.

She told them about the hidden bug they found in the shop and filled them in on the jamming devices that Randy and Calvin built to block the device and any other hidden devices from anyone listening in on them. Roger was aware of the shop device, but did not think about the possibility of any hidden inside of his house. After she finished filling them in on security, she put down the tablet and looked at the three eager faces in front of her. Their curious faces made her smile as she had their full attention and began to tell her story.

Chapter 8

Boy Genius

His mother spoke, "Randy was a genius, a real genius. When he was in high school his teachers quickly discovered just how smart he was. He was rapidly excelling at everything he worked on. His math teachers were amazed how quickly he picked up and solved their toughest problems and formulas. He enjoyed it, it was fun and just very natural to him. He never seemed to struggle and enjoyed learning new things. His brain was like a giant magnet and seemed to pull knowledge into it."

"The government somehow caught wind of how smart he was. This particular division, we later found out, monitored schools through science fairs and competitions in search of extra talented, young, smart people. They would follow up on reports from ex-military officers and would pay a bonus pension to the officers who found potential recruits. So they actually tracked students' progress and monitored them so that when they were older and ready for recruitment, they could persuade the student to come work for them. I'm not sure how they monitor and keep watch on young talented minds, but they have their means. I think Randy was first brought to their attention by a substitute teacher named Mr. Stewart. He took notice of Randy's abilities while filling in at his school. Mr. Stewart was a retired Army Major from the intelligence division. He was volunteering as a teacher with his free time and was a great mentor and friend to Randy in the electronics class that he was teaching. Randy knew about Mr. Stewart being retired from the Army and did not want to be involved in the military at all. Randy told us Mr. Stewart approached him a few times to get him to join the Army Intelligence Division and he could put in a recommendation for him. But Randy was not interested. In fact, Mr. Stewart arranged a recruiting type field trip to the military base down in Bell Grove for a group of interested seniors from school."

Roger looked at her. "Did Mr. Stewart know dad from when he was in the Army?"

"No, he was much older than your father when he was in the service and did not know him before he came to teach at Belford High. Besides, your father was in a different division."

She continued to explain, "You see, some high schools used to arrange for types of field trips with the military for their senior students. They did it to give the students some interaction with the military and to see if it was a possible new career path they might want to follow if they chose not to attend college. The recruitment trip was pretty luring for Randy. He told us about it when he got back, but it did not change his mind, he still did not want to work for the military. Besides, he was too young. He was a senior for this trip because he had moved up a couple of grades in school. Randy graduated from high school two years early so he was young when he entered college. He had bigger dreams of creating new inventions for the world and for using his inventions to help people and make life better for them and not pursuing a military career."

She stood up and now was starting to pace the floor as she continued her story with them. It seemed like she was having a burden lifted from her as she confessed this past with them.

"I swore to myself years ago, that I would never divulge this to you Roger. But when you found that silver box and started to question things from your dreams, I changed my mind about the promise and decided to tell you."

Then she went on to talk more about Randy.

"He just loved making inventions and had a natural ability at it. During his senior year of college, a government agency recruiter contacted him. They had been closely monitoring him since high school. They were getting very curious as to what he was up to. He had secured numerous patents for electrical devices he had made at school under the direction of his teachers."

"So they were monitoring him from the patent office?' asked Roger.

"It's very possible they were. They were starting to get very nosy and were trying even harder to recruit him. It was getting to the point of being ridiculous. He would come home and tell us that the Government stopped by his lab and that they made excuses to be there. They would then start in with the questions, "What are you working on, or did someone ask you to make this?" She continued.

"It entertained Randy to see them so curious about what he was making and would infuriate them because he did not want to work for them. Your father told him not to taunt or mock them because they were very powerful and he didn't want Randy getting into any trouble with them. But before his accident at the lab, I remember him coming home upset the night before. Randy told us that someone had broken into his lab at the college. Someone had taken the project he had been building all semester and smashed and busted up the lab to make it look like some kind of vandalism or a robbery. But he knew that someone had done it just to get his senior project."

Roger asked, "What kind of project was he working on?"

She replied, "It was some kind of computer thingy, a device or gadget of some kind. I really can't recall what it did," as she continued to pace, deep in thought about the question. "He said it was for a computer system or some kind of network I think."

"Mom, what do you-?"

She held up her hand in a stop motion at the trio, "I don't know what it did or what it was for," she quickly spat, cutting them off before any more words came out of their open mouths.

"Randy was very frustrated about losing it and the college term was near an end. He had to try to re-build it again to be graded in a few days. This project was also going to be his entry into the '*Collegiate Inventors Competition.*' The Collegiate Inventors Competition is a national competition searching for the invention that will make the biggest impact on the world. It is a great honor to win, along with big prize money for your school. And it makes your resume *very impressive*. Students who have won this competition in the past have always received excellent job offers to work at huge, powerful companies and went on to lead very successful careers." She continued the story. "The next day he was working in the lab very late at school to get caught up. Since we live pretty close to the college, you and your father were taking him dinner and were going to eat in the lab with him."

"When you guys arrived, your father saw smoke coming from the windows of the lab. Then there were flashes of light, the smell of fire and loud explosions. You both ran into the lab and saw Randy running around trying to turn off the electrical equipment and then- the lab blew. You were knocked unconscious and into a coma from the blast. The doctors were worried at first, but later after you woke up, they said you would recover just fine and that you were going to be ok."

Roger's eyes now wide, "So I wasn't in a car crash" he said.

"No, No, you were not. But when you finally woke up from your coma, you had lost your memory of the whole incident, even the explosion. You couldn't remember anything about the explosion. The explosion destroyed Randy's classic Chevy that was parked in back of the lab. That is how we introduced you being in a car wreck, since the car was destroyed. And then there comes the crazy stuff. The whole accident at the lab was covered up strangely by the FBI and CIA. We had the FBI and CIA tell us that we were not to talk about the incident to anyone, that it was matter of national security and if we did tell anyone, even you, then we would be prosecuted as terrorists and locked away in prison. We were scared into keeping silent by this one woman who was so pushy and intimidating."

Roger spoke, "That's crazy Mom and what about Randy and the explosion, what about his funeral? I missed it!"

"The fire from the explosion was so hot and intense that it melted the building. Everything inside was obliterated and destroyed. The metal computer racks and the lab contents were literally melted and incinerated into ashes. The firemen and rescuers only found part of a leg from Randy that apparently had been blown into the parking lot from the explosion when he was killed," she said sadly.

They all looked at her horrified and she continued. "We had the funeral and buried his remains with some of his belongings while you were still in a coma in the hospital. As far as everyone knew, his whole body was buried at the funeral. Roger, we didn't know when you might wake up, *or IF* you would ever wake up." She looked down with tears in her eyes, "I sure miss my son" she said. "And that is why I am so scared to lose you," she said as she looked over at Roger.

"Lose me?" he said, "How will you lose me?"

She turned to Roger and held up the little silver box she had taken from him, "From this." She said.

"How can that little thing get me killed?" Roger questioned.

"It's what's inside this little box that will lead you to something special, something Randy built and hid. Something he might have been working on before he was killed."

They were all now seated apart in the room, Aaron and Max on the sofa, Roger and his mom sitting on the edge of the bed. His mom handed the box back to Roger.

"I don't know what's on the inside, or the combination to open the box, but I know you three will figure it out."

Roger took the box, turned it over and spun the wheels of the combination a few times and then tossed it over to Aaron and Max for them to have another look at it. Roger hugged his mom and said, "I can't believe you told me I was in a car crash with Randy."

"*I am so sorry son*, but we had to at that time, we were so scared. *You* were in a coma, *Randy* was dead and gone, the CIA and FBI were telling us to keep quiet. We were devastated and scared; we did what they told us to do."

"Dad showed me the listening device in the shop this morning," said Roger to his mother. "I understand how we might still be under surveillance and being watched by someone. Who do you think is doing it?" asked Roger.

"I don't know. I wish we did, maybe then we could fight back," she replied.

Max and Aaron had both turned their heads and looked at Roger, "What listening device?" they asked.

His mother said "Randy spent a lot of time in the shop with Calvin. I think whoever put it there is trying to find clues to something Randy may have hid in there. Part of his invention, or something from his school lab, or something he and your father might have talked about. Your father was always working with Randy and knew about some of the things he was working on at school. They would talk while they worked on the cars together in the shop. I think they are still listening to see whether your father talked about it or might know something about it."

She continued, "After Randy's death the agencies came by and searched the shop and house. They had some Federal search warrant or something and said that Randy might have had some illegal chemicals stored in there, but they didn't find anything in shop or in the house after they searched them both thoroughly."

She emphasized to all three of them, "We need to be very cautious about what we discuss from now on. We have to be on our guard now that I have told you this information, we need to be extra careful."

She looked at them all, "If we are going to try to figure this out, you need to get started on that combo to the silver box. Be careful with it, don't lose it."

"This is kind of cool," said Max, "we have a secret mission and a bit of homework to do to figure this out."

As the three of them stood up and started to leave the room, Alicia spoke.

"Please be careful. Keep me updated on anything you find out," she ordered them.

"OK, OK, mom" said Roger as they all headed to his room to discuss what they were going to do on this mystery they had been assigned to solve.

Chapter 9

What's in a Name?

Max and Aaron followed Roger into his room. Aaron picked up the small remote control from the top of the dresser and pointed it at the door. With a "click" the bedroom door automatically closed behind them.

"I love this invention," he said to Roger.

Their minds were buzzing with questions and the lingering images they had from the story Roger's mom just revealed to them. Roger was holding the silver box and thumbing through the combo wheels, small faint beeps being emitted every time he turned a wheel on the combo.

"This thing is going to drive me nuts," said Roger.

"WHAT THING?" came a loud voice from behind Aaron.

"WAHHH!-" screamed Aaron as he jumped up holding his chest and turned around to see Jenny kneeling on the floor behind the side of the bed laughing loudly, pointing at Aaron.

"You should have seen your face" she laughed and then she made a small scream like Aaron did "Aahhh-" and continued to laugh as Max joined in.

"What are you doing in my room?" asked Roger angrily.

"Don't get your panties in a bunch" said Jenny. "I came in here to find the missile from my remote controlled helicopter. I lost it here the other night when I *shot you in the face with it*. I thought it might have landed behind the bed. I was down here looking for it when you came in. I saw that you didn't see me and I just couldn't let the chance to scare someone go. I just had to do it," Giggled Jenny.

"Fine, now get out of here," ordered Roger.

"I'm leaving, I'm leaving, Mr. grumpy," said Jenny as she stood up and started to lazily cross the room.

"Hey scared chicken boy" she said to Aaron, "do you mind opening the door?" gesturing at the closed door with her hand.

"Oh," said Aaron. Then he used the remote he still had in his hand to click open the door.

"Nice one Jenny," said Max and smiled at Jenny and gave her a high five as she passed by.

"Thanks" smiled Jenny as she left the room, the door closing behind her.

The three of them tried to refocus on why they came to Roger's room and to discuss the recent meeting they just had with his mom and all of the information they were flooded with.

Roger and Max turned to look at Aaron because they heard him mumbling something,

"Little punk, I should have-

"Let it go Aaron" Max cut in, "she was just messing with you. And besides, you really are fun to scare, you make an easy target. We need to work on you and build you some nerves of steel."

"Whatever, I will get her back, someday Jenny will pay." Aaron vowed.

"OK, another time" said Roger, "lets worry about something else right now, like this weird silver box and what it does."

"Do you have any clue what Randy might have hidden in that thing?" asked Max gesturing at the box.

"No-, I don't," said Roger, "but I need a soda and I want to try something on this box in the shop. Let's go down there." He pointed to Aaron to open the door as he walked toward it. After a point and click it automatically swung open.

They headed down the stairs cutting through the kitchen toward the back door leading outside. Jenny was sitting at the counter eating a sandwich and chips watching the small TV on the counter. They all walked passed her out the door with Aaron in the rear. Jenny was just starting to take a drink of milk from a tall glass as Aaron was passing by her. He slowly reached his hand out, quickly tipping the bottom of the glass of milk higher in the air, causing milk to spill up into her face.

"Aahhh, the sweet taste of revenge," chuckled Aaron softly as he walked away, the sound of Jenny behind him coughing and hacking from the flood of milk that went flowing up her nose.

"You will pay for that you loser!" she yelled at the door behind Aaron as he continued toward the shop. *"YOU HEAR ME AARON CATE!"* Then she wiped her face with a paper towel she pulled from the roll on the counter.

"What is Jenny yelling at you about?" Max asked as they walked.

"No idea," Aaron shrugged and shook his head. After Max turned back to face the shop entrance, he smiled to himself in triumph.

They all entered the shop and went over to the small refrigerator below the counter. Max grabbed a bottle of nice cold root beer, while Aaron and Roger chose cream soda. Roger took a long swig from the cold bottle and went over to the tool box and took some pliers from one of the drawers. He shut the drawer and turned toward the work bench. He placed the silver box on it, adjusted the pliers and tried to pry the box open. He had no luck in even making a small dent on the box. It was made of some type of strong metal, very light and extremely strong.

"This thing is tough," exclaimed Roger.

He abandoned the pliers and moved on to something stronger. He was now using a small chisel and a hammer and was trying to pry the box open. He was hitting very hard with the hammer and still the small edges of the box showed no sign of giving or being pried open.

"Give it here weakling," challenged Max reaching and taking the hammer and chisel away from him.

Max began pounding on it with the hammer and chisel. The box withstood the blows and showed no signs of cracking or breaking. "I don't get it" said Max, "this thing is incredibly tough and there's not even a scratch."

"OK guys, let the muscle take over from here," Aaron told them as he stepped up taking the tools from Max. "You see, you have to be smarter than the box."

He turned and flipped the switch of an electric grinding wheel that was mounted on the edge of the workbench. The grinding wheel and motor spooled up to full speed with a loud hum. As Aaron put on a pair of safety glasses, he turned to Max and Roger,

"Now, pay attention to how the master does it." He proceeded to place the edge of the silver box up to the grinding wheel.

Sparks were immediately flying from the edge of the box as he pressed it to the spinning wheel. All of a sudden, the box slipped out of Aaron's grasp and it shot out of his hands like a bullet upward. It ricochet off the top of the grinding wheel plastic face cover so fast

Aaron had no time to react. After it bounced off the cover it ricocheted off the back of the mount and then bounced off Aaron's forehead zinging across the shop. As Aaron's head was blown backward from the force of the blow, his safety glasses also flew off when his head whipped backward. The scene happened so fast, Roger and Max just stood soaking it in. It took a few seconds before they began to scream in laughter. They were laughing so hard they couldn't speak from what they had just witnessed.

"Did you see the look on his face," Max tried to utter in between laughing and trying to breathe.

"I did, I did," said Roger, trying to catch his breath from laughing.

Aaron was holding his forehead where a big red spot was and a nice bump was starting to take form. Luckily no blood, just a large growing red bump.

"Oh man, that hurt," said Aaron, "you can stop laughing now, the side show is over, OK," as he continued to rub his forehead. He reached over, turned off the grinding wheel and picked up the safety glasses that had flown off his face. He took a seat on the couch and held his cold soda bottle to his forehead with his head tilted back, "That's going to leave a mark," he uttered and then let out a small giggle of embarrassment as he looked over at Max and Roger.

All three were laughing at the show that Aaron had just put on for them. Max and Roger walked over to Aaron and patted him gingerly on the shoulder,

"Thanks for the belly laugh," they both said and looked around to see where the box had finally come to rest.

"Where did it land?" asked Roger as he searched around the area that he thought the box had landed in.

"I thought I saw something flying over to the corner by the car," said Max, as she walked over to that side of the shop, scanning the area for the box.

"I see it, there, under the front tires," pointed Roger.

Max got down on her knees in front of the Mustang, reached under the car, grabbed the box and pulled it out. As she rested on her knees she glared at the box and noticed there wasn't one scratch on it from the grinding wheel or from the short flight it took across the shop off of Aaron's forehead to its resting place under the car.

She read aloud the inscription on the box, "FOR RRD"

She looked at the front of the car she had just put her hand on. She was beginning to push herself up from off the shop floor and noticed right next to her hand was a Mustang horse. Instantly her mind went to the make of the car she was kneeling at.

"This thing is a FORD!" she said loudly and quickly stood up. She said it again, this time pointing to the car, *"This thing is a Ford!"*

She was sounding a little hysterical.

"Get over here now guys!" and she motioned to them to come over to the old Ford Mustang.

The car had been in the family as long as Roger could remember, he thought as he walked over to where Max was now standing. Aaron was getting up off the couch still holding the soda bottle on his forehead as he slowly walked over to where Max and Roger now stood.

"Of course it's a Ford. It's a classic Mustang," said Roger.

Max looked at him and then Aaron, "FOR RRD, that is what this little indestructible box has written on it," she pointed out. "Look!" as she held up the box pointing to the letters FOR RRD. "This has got to mean something," she said and looked to see how Roger and Aaron were responding to her discovery.

They both stood there with confused faces gazing at her.

"Here look," she said and she pointed at the side of the car fender at the word *'F-O-R-D.'*

"Don't you see, they are almost spelled the same way," and she handed the silver box to Roger. "Look at it," she ordered both boys. And they peered down at the box.

"I don't know," said Roger, "Ford is spelled with the letter "R" wrong, it has three of them in it. It could be some kind of initials or something."

Instantly Aaron's face lit up with a burst of new knowledge. He grabbed the box from Roger and spun it around so the words "FOR RRD" now were facing him. He mouthed the words in silence "FOR RRD" and then his head popped up looking at Max and Roger with their eyes glued on him.

"You just said the clue Roger!"

"What do you mean?" Roger responded back.

"You said initials or something like that, right?" and he looked at them both. They still looked confused about what he was trying to describe to them.

"Come on, you guys, don't you see it?" then he paused for a moment to see if they got what he was hinting at.

"OH MAN," Roger let out grabbing his head with both hands, "You don't think it is, do you?" he asked Aaron.

"What am I missing?" exclaimed Max, "what is it?"

Roger and Aaron both turned to Max, "Do you know my middle name? Have you ever heard my mom call me by my full name?" Max shook her head no.

"My full name is *Roger Roy Dexter*." He announced then looked at her to see her reaction.

A funny grin started across her face and she said "Seriously, *'Roy'* is your middle name?" and let out a small giggle. Then she took the box and turned it over in her hands looking at the inscription, "FOR RRD."

"Do you think it means "For- Roger Roy Dexter?" and she looked over at Roger and Aaron staring back at her.

"It does. I think it does!" replied Roger. "I think Randy left it for me to figure out. He was always doing things like that and leaving little clues about things. He liked to make you think hard about something. He didn't like to give you the answer right away. He told me that when he would help me with my homework. I knew he would have the answers, but he wouldn't give them to me. He made me study again and try harder to figure it out. I hated it when he did that, but he told me that it would make you smarter to try to get answers to questions by studying hard and always thinking for yourself."

Roger looked up from the box and started pacing the floor of the shop. He took a sip on his cream soda and spun around with a scared look on his face. He frantically motioned at both of them to be quiet and put his hand over his mouth signaling them to be quiet. He pointed at the old license plate mounted on the wall of the shop and gestured to them to go outside and then he spoke in an overly calm voice, "Let's go into the house and get a snack," he called very loud to Max and Aaron.

"OK," they replied, with faces that wondered what he was up to. They left the shop heading toward the house, but Roger passed the house walking down the driveway. Max and Aaron were quickly on his heels as they headed toward downtown.

"I totally forgot about that stupid listening bug in the shop! My mom told us to be careful and we might have already blown it!" he said in a frustrated voice as they continued to walk down the street toward the center of town.

Max had a worried look on her face, "I don't think any of us really gave away any secrets, do you?" Max asked them both as they continued to talk and walk.

"We only talked a little bit about the Ford and your initials, we never said they were on the silver box," replied Aaron,

"If anyone was listening they wouldn't know what we were talking about. And if someone was listening, they were probably wondering what we were all laughing so hard about after that box went bouncing off my face," laughed Aaron.

This comment made Roger smile, putting him more at ease.

"I guess you are right," said Roger. "I am just really worried now and especially knowing someone put a listening bug in our shop."

Max and Aaron both agreed with Roger and felt that they didn't say anything that would have given them away as they were talking in the shop.

They continued their walk another mile downtown to the local diner where they would get ice-cream and fries. It was right next to their other hangout at the local park. The diner was named, *The HiSpot* and was a great place to hangout and eat. They loved the food there because it was delicious and best of all it was cheap.

Chapter 10

The Car

They entered the diner and stood waiting to be seated. This diner was a great place to get tasty food and had been in business for over 50 years. It was just off the city square and was on the old Route 66 trail. It was a classic looking place, decorated like it had been in the 50's.

The owner of the place was a guy named Marlow. He still worked behind the grill as the proud owner of the family-owned restaurant. Marlow had been working there since he was a young boy. He loved to have teenagers in the diner and enjoyed the youthful feeling they brought.

"Hello you three," came a deep voice from behind the order window, "find an empty seat and Laura will be with you," Marlow said, in the middle of flipping a hamburger on the grill.

They walked over to their favorite corner of the diner and slid into their favorite booth still discussing the silver box. Aaron looked around the diner with a look of concentration and excitement showing on his face.

"Where is she?" wondered Aaron as he quickly scanned the diner in search of *Laura*. His eyes found her across the dinner. He slowly leaned back into his soft vintage red seat with a huge smile stretching across his face. A beautiful looking waitress approached their table. Aaron's heart was pounding in his chest as the blond haired, dark brown eyed woman approached them. She had three menus under one arm, holding a pot of hot coffee in the other. When Laura McKell reached the table she greeted the group with the nicest smile, sat the menus down and leaned over to give Roger a sweet hug. He returned her hug and sat back down across from Aaron and Max.

"It is so good to see you kids," said Laura with a beautiful smile, her lips gleaming with bright red lipstick. "How are the folks?" she asked Roger.

"They're doing pretty good," replied Roger, "they've been wondering when you might be coming by for dinner again?"

Laura looked at him with a little frown, "I know, it has been quite a while since I've been by the house. I planned to come by tomorrow for a visit and to say goodbye before I leave next week."

"LEAVING!" blurted out Aaron, "What do you mean leaving?"

"I've decided to continue school at Illinois State this fall. But don't tell your parents, I want to let them know myself."

"I won't say a word, but they are going to miss you Laura. You were a daughter to them," said Roger.

Laura had been engaged to marry Randy. She was a few years older than Randy when he first met her at college. They met each other in college and she invited him to come take a Karate class that she was teaching at the local dojo. She was a tough black belt. During his first class, she accidentally punched him in the nose, giving him a nosebleed while they were partners for one of the drills. Randy was in love from that moment on. They were going to get married after they both graduated from college. She had a real hard time with his death. She dropped out of college and was very depressed. She got a job at *The HiSpot* and became good friends with Marlow when he learned of her heartbreak.

Aaron had fallen in love with Laura when she got the job at the HiSpot. He was hypnotized by her beauty and she would flirt with him just to mess with his head. It would crack up Roger and Max the way she could manipulate Aaron and control him just flittering her eyes at him, or touching him ever so gently on the shoulder while she would laugh at his stupid jokes.

"I can't believe you would leave us," Aaron moaned at Laura with sad puppy dog eyes.

She took his hand and then placed her other hand on Aaron's shoulder. She looked him in the eyes and had his full undivided attention. Then she moved her hand and held the side of his face in a motherly fashion and said, "I will miss this handsome man," she sighed, then turned away as Aaron took a deep long sad breath. Laura looked at Max and Roger and winked knowing she just twitterpated Aaron. Max and Roger returned a smile holding back the laughs. "I'll be back with your usual root beer sodas," as she walked to the kitchen.

"Please put a scoop of vanilla ice cream in mine," said Aaron to Laura. She waved her hand to signal she heard him. "I need the ice cream now for my breaking heart." Aaron let out a deep sigh, "I can't believe she is leaving me." And then suddenly his head snapped forward from a blow that Max gave him to the back of his head, *"Come back to reality Lover Boy."* He looked over at her with anger spreading on his face from the soft blow, "And don't be a baby, that didn't hurt, you're just mad I interrupted your Laura fantasy."

"OK, OK I'm back with you now, I just can't help it, she is so-, *Bee-u-tee-ful,*" he said with that glazed look starting to overtake him again, "and her accent is adorable."

Max raised her fist this time ready to punch him but when he saw her fist ready he quickly snapped out of his oncoming trance.

"We should eat and then get back to the Mustang in the shop," said Roger. "I was planning to see if there were any clues to the box, but I totally forgot about the stupid bug behind the license plate on the wall. Man, I feel so stupid, I can't believe I forgot someone could have been listening to us discuss the silver box."

"Don't beat yourself up," said Max, "We didn't talk that much about it and I don't think we gave away any information. But let's ask your dad how to turn on the device he built to block the signal so this doesn't happen again. We need to do it before we check out the Mustang again."

Roger wondered to himself again if there were more hidden bugs spying on them in the house or somewhere that his dad might have not found.

"I hope you're right," said Roger. "Let's eat, then go back to my place and talk with my Dad."

Laura came out and gave them their root beer sodas and took their order. They continued to discuss their latest adventure and what they planned to do that day.

After they had finished eating, they paid the check and Laura came out to give them their change. "What time do you think you will be coming by my house tomorrow?" Roger asked Laura.

"I'll be coming over around six tomorrow night, so I will see then," said Laura as they were all getting up to leave.

"OK, see you then," said Roger leaning in for a goodbye hug from Laura. She gave him the standard quick hug and turned to walk away, but a whiny *'what about my hug?'* from Aaron caught her attention.

She turned her head sideways over her shoulder to speak as she walked away, "I'll have a nice hug for you tomorrow, *lover boy,"* she replied with a slow bit of sarcasm, but Aaron took it as pure love for him.

Roger and Max laughed "Let's go *lover boy-*" as they both pushed Aaron from behind aiming him toward the doorway so they could leave the diner.

"Thanks for coming kids," they heard Marlow say from the back of the kitchen.

"Anytime Marlow," replied Max and Roger as they were pushing Aaron all the way out of *The HiSpot* diner.

They all walked sluggishly toward Roger's house, their stomachs full from the delicious food.

"We need to pick up the pace guys," said Roger, "I told my dad I would help him this afternoon at my grandmas house. We have to fix her bathroom faucet." And they started to walk a little faster toward his house.

When they arrived at his house they saw Roger's dad loading some tools into the back of his old pickup truck parked in front of the shop, the doors to the shop open wide. With doors open they all could see the Ford Mustang sitting in the corner. They were anxious to go check it out and look for clues when they heard Roger's dad,

"There you are Roger! Are you ready to head over to Grandmas?"

"Sure Dad," said Roger and he walked over to where his dad was standing. "Do you need me to get any more tools from the shop?"

"I think I've got them all," replied his Dad. Then his dad turned to Aaron and Max, "I would love for you both to come along with us, but I need to discuss some family stuff with Roger on the drive, OK guys?" he told them. "No problem Mr. Dexter," replied Max and Aaron at the same time. "I need to practice for my gymnastics meet anyway." said Max. "Plus I have to mow my lawn today," replied Aaron and the two of them left to walk the short distance home.

"OK, let's get going Roger," and they climbed into the truck.

The drive was pretty quiet the first few miles as they headed toward Cove Creek and then his father spoke. "I hear you had a very interesting talk with your mother, *I guess she spilled the story to you and your pals.*"

"Yeah, she told us the whole story about how Randy really died and that *you both lied* to me the last year Dad!" replied Roger in a frustrated voice

"I am so sorry for keeping the truth from you son, but we both felt it was for your own good," explained his dad.

Roger cut in "It still hurts to be lied to Dad! It's very frustrating and I wonder what else you might be lying to me about."

There was moment of silence from his father, then he spoke. "Roger, you have to know how hard that was to keep from you. I'm truly sorry we kept it from you, but we had one son die and I was determined to protect you after the explosion at the lab. We knew how much you loved and looked up to Randy. You always tried to follow in his footsteps and be more like him. We were worried that if you were to find out what Randy was working on when he died, that you would want to actively pursue his research when you were older."

"So Randy's projects are in need of being completed?" asked Roger.

"Yes son. I know a lot about the projects that he was working on. Your mother told me that you apparently have found a piece of one."

"You mean this box?" And he pulled the small silver box from his pocket.

"Ahhh," said his Dad as he took the box and glanced at it. "You seem to have found his pet."

"His pet?" questioned Roger. "It's just a tough little box."

His dad laughed. "There is so much more to this little box than you know. I hid it in my dad's office after Randy died, because he told me it was a key to something. He didn't tell me what, only that I needed to keep it hidden and safe should something happen to him," and he handed the box back to Roger.

"What are you talking about Dad, I'm confused."

"First, let's get Grandmas bathroom faucet fixed," he said as they pulled into her driveway.

Grandma was sitting on her front porch in a rocking chair and waved with a big smile as they pulled in. Next to her was a small table and on it, a plate of cookies. Her little dog Chester sat nearby looking at the plate, possibly planning a way to steal some cookies. They both got out of the truck, took the tools and parts from the back. They went up to her, kissing her on the cheek as she stuck it out for them. They took a seat next to grandma on the porch and had a few cookies. They talked a minute and then went in to work on the sink.

Roger was relentless trying to pull information from his father as they worked together on the bathroom faucet. Shortly after they arrived, they were alone together and working on the faucet when Roger spoke,

"OK Dad. Spill it, what is this thing and how is it Randy's pet?" as he held the silver box out.

"Alright, settle down," said his Dad. "I'll try to explain."

"Randy had a science project in high school working with robotics. You remember, he had a couple of really cool spider robots and a small ninja one. The ninja would jump and hop around yelling funny Kung foo slang. He used to torment you with the ninja when you were sleeping and send it to attack you and kick you in the head. Randy thought that it was pretty funny sending it after family members. He won the state championship for it and was granted a great college scholarship.

"Oh yeah, I remember that stupid ninja robot. I hated that thing. He called it Servo because of the little servo motors that were built inside of it, controlling all of the moving parts. I started to know when an attack was coming because I could hear the little servo motors quietly moving as it slowly snuck up on me and got close," said Roger.

"Yeah," laughed his dad, "he loved to make it scare the dickens out of your mother. He would hide it in the dishwasher, the fridge or cupboard and when she would open the doors, the screaming Servo would attack and then quickly retreat to where he had programmed it to hide. In fact, your mother ordered me to shoot it with the shotgun one day. It came out of the fridge and made her drop a dozen eggs after it kicked the container she was holding right out of her hand, showering her and the kitchen with eggs. Boy, she was not a happy mother," laughed his dad as he remembered the scene.

"Your mother destroyed the ninja. She finally caught it one day and inflicted a severe beating with a rolling pin after it came jumping out of a kitchen drawer at her. That was one sad day for Servo and Randy."

"I would have loved to see that!" laughed Roger.

"I know, me too," said his dad as he continued working on the faucet repair. "So after the destruction, Randy took the salvageable parts from it and some parts from his other spider robots. He rebuilt and updated the Ninja robot his college freshmen year. It was now small and sleek, about 6 inches tall, very agile and sneaky. He kept it at school in his dorm and sometimes in his lab. He kept it very secret. When I would visit him he would show it to me and would let me goof around with it. I was amazed at how lifelike that little thing was and how much it could do. The next year he showed me part of his newer design for his robot and what it now looked like. It had newer features and some new metal armor he had built for it. He had created some amazingly strong armor. I'm not sure what kind of metal he made it out of but it was very strong. So you seem to have found the robot I hid in grandpa's office. What I think you have there in your hand is Servo."

Roger looked down at the silver case in his hand.

"Dad, how do you open this box?" He asked.

His dad started to answer him but quickly stopped talking when Grandma entered the bathroom to see how they were doing on the faucet.

"How is it coming in here?" she asked. "All done mom," replied Calvin as he snapped his toolbox closed.

"Thank you boys for coming to fix that dripping thing. It was driving me crazy," said Grandma.

"No problem mom," replied Calvin, "I love to help you out, but we do need to be going now though," and he kissed his mom on the cheek. Roger gathered the old parts and the toolbox and put them back in the truck. They said goodbye, each took another cookie and headed back home to Belford.

Immediately Roger began to explain to his Dad what they had discovered about the inscription on the box and that he thought it was his initials on the box that Randy had intended for him to find.

"So you think there is a clue on the old Ford in the shop?" He asked.

"Yes, I do Dad," replied Roger.

"OK then, let's check it out when we get home," said his father.

They pulled into the driveway and it was getting dark outside. The automatic lights in the driveway clicked on from the motion of the truck entering. They got out of the truck, unloaded the tools and put them away placing them in their correct drawers and locations.

Roger's dad made eye contact with him getting his attention and making a signal to be quiet, placing a single finger over his lips.

He then reached down and opened the top of an old record player that Roger thought was just sitting on a bottom shelf taking up space. He turned a small knob, pressed a button and immediately some sound effects were now coming from the digital device concealed in the record player. The hidden jamming device was now powered up, blocking the monitoring bug that had been hidden secretly behind the license plate on the wall.

"OK son, we are clear to talk, the signal is being jammed and being fed some garage noises and banging around.

"So that is how you turn that on," said Roger and his father quickly demonstrated how to use the jamming device he and Randy had built.

"Dad, what about inside of our house, are there any of those listening bugs in there?"

"I found two of them a few months ago and disabled them. I left them in their locations but cut the wires. One is in the kitchen in the smoke detector and the other is in the upstairs smoke detector above the landing. I continually scan looking for more and verify that those two are not working. I have a few small hidden cameras I installed in the house to monitor and see if anyone comes by and fixes or replaces them. I'm hoping to get a lead on who it was that put them in our home. But so far no one has come back for them," explained Calvin.

Roger looked a little startled by this news that someone had put them in the house, but felt better knowing that his father had disabled them and that it would be an ongoing process.

"Alright let's check out the Mustang," said Calvin and they opened the front doors and sat down inside the car, Roger in the driver's seat, his dad in the passenger side. "OK," mumbled his father as they both looked around scanning up and down. The inside of the old car had been restored by Randy. The interior was immaculate and the restoration made it look brand new. The seats were a soft blue and dash board was a flat black. They searched for anything out of the ordinary on the inside of the car, opening the glove box compartment, looking in the cubby spaces, behind the visors, under the seats and floor mats. Then they went to the back seat looking for any kind of clue and sat there taking a small break. They had searched everywhere then got out and continued their search another half hour, going entirely over the outside and the engine area of the old car.

"You want a soda?" Calvin asked as he headed toward the fridge.

"Sure," answered Roger. His dad returned with two root beers and handed one to Roger as they both sat back in the front seats again, Roger at the wheel. They finished their sodas and Calvin said, "Fire up the engine Roger, let's take this out for a spin and see if anything is different." He got out of the car and tossed the empty bottles in the recycle bin and pulled the garage doors open, returned to his seat riding shotgun.

With a turn of the ignition key and a roar, the loud powerful engine came bursting to life. Calvin instructed Roger to ease out of the garage. Calvin had been teaching him to drive his mother's car for the last year. His dad believed that as long as he was supervising him and driving with him at a younger age, that it would make him a better driver for when he was 16 and ready to get his license. He would only let him drive on a few select quiet back roads, but it definitely was improving his driving skills.

Roger pulled the car out of the shop and stopped in the driveway while his father got out and closed the garage doors and returned to the car. He then drove out onto the street into the cool evening night. As they drove up the road a mile or two, Roger would look down to closely monitor his speed and noticed that the mileage odometer was not turning. He kept looking down as he drove to be sure and definitely noticed after driving another couple of miles that the mileage was stuck on 96,321 and not turning.

"Dad, look at the odometer, when did it stop working?" asked Roger.

"What do you mean?" replied his dad as he looked over at the odometer.

"Look," said Roger pointing to the numbers 96321, "they are not turning dad." His dad continued to look at the odometer as they drove back towards the house. "Yep, definitely not working." mulled his dad thoughtfully.

"When did it work last?" asked Roger,

"I really am not sure," answered his dad. "Randy was the last one to work on that part of the car," said his dad. "We had just rebuilt that dashboard when he installed all of the gauges. It was about thr—

His dad stopped speaking, then after a moment softly said, "Roger, pull over and hand me the silver box."

Roger pulled the car over to the side of the road and came to a stop, put the car in park and turned off the engine. He pulled the box from his pocket and handed it to his dad. His dad took the box and turned it around in his hands so that the five combo wheels were now facing him.

"No way, I wonder," he mumbled to himself and he turned the first wheel to match the first number of the odometer displayed on the dashboard of the Mustang.

When he turned the first number so that it displayed the number "9," and small beep was heard.

"It always beeps when you turn the small wheels," said Roger.

His dad looked at him and then back at the box. He turned the next wheel, "6" and a slightly louder beep sounded. Then the next wheel, "3" and loud double, "BEEP-BEEP" came out.

Then the next dial, "2", "BEEP-BEEP-BEEP" and a flash of blue light came out of the box and quickly went out. His dad looked over at Roger and smiled when he saw his expression and open mouth. He looked back at the box and turned the last wheel.

"1." Multiple beeping noises started loudly coming from the box. It began to glow blue, and as the brightness began to increase it suddenly zapped Calvin's hand with a small bolt of electricity causing him to drop the box on the floor of the car.

"Ouch!" shouted Calvin as he grabbed his shocked hand with his other hand and looked down at the box as it fell and bounced under the front seat.

"CRAP," uttered Calvin and he tried to reach down under the seat to grab the box, but he couldn't reach it. He and Roger could see the blue light glowing from under the seat and at the same time they heard multiple strange clicks and noises coming from under the bench seat.

Startled, they both picked up their feet from the floor quickly putting them on the seat, looking like they had just been scared by a mouse or a spider.

A small whirring noise started to come from under the seat of the Mustang, it sounded like a tiny computer fan winding up, spinning faster and faster and had a deep hum to it. They both continued to peer down at the floor where their feet once rested to see what was going on. As they both continued to stare down at the front floor of the car, an object began to rise ever so slowly in the back seat behind them while they continued to gaze down at the ground. A soft bluish light started to fill the car as the object rose behind them. They both looked up as the object started to rise. When they heard the soft whirring noise as it rose closer to the top of the roof of the car directly behind their heads, they both felt cold chills and the hairs on the back of their necks stood straight up. They both slowly sat up facing the windshield. Roger was seated in the driver's side of the car. He had a view to the back seat of the car from the rear view mirror. He glanced at it to see a light blue object, 6 inches or so in size, whirring softly right behind his head and hovering like a miniature spaceship. He couldn't keep his eyes off the object as it bobbed up and down ever so softly and just seemed to be staring at him and his father. The silver box had transformed into a small square flying spaceship with rounded corners. It had small twin tails each with a small engine spinning, keeping it aloft. Two little metal arms hung down from the sides with tiny hands and small fingers.

Roger looked over at his dad and saw that he was smiling, then started to chuckle. The small robot spaceship was now hovering between them and slowly piloted to the front of the car and turned to face them. The small craft had two tiny bluish headlights glowing on the front like tiny little eyes staring at them. The tiny lights were scanning over each of their faces. As it hovered looking at them, it made small blips and beep noises, along with the soft low hum of the small engines keeping it aloft.

"Servo, is that you?" asked Calvin. Then the tiny craft quickly turned and faced him. A small green beam of light came from the craft and scanned Calvin's face and then Roger's. A female voice sounded, "Identity Confirmed," and immediately the crafts lights began to flash wildly with the brightness increasing inside the car. The once soft whirring engines were spinning faster and were increasing like it was winding up ready to explode. The winding sounds were getting louder and louder, the whirring getting faster. A few seconds passed and then everything went silent. Immediately an intense and sudden bright flash of light blasted through the car. There was pure silence as they sat in the car in total darkness, their eyes temporarily blinded from the bright flash of light.

Chapter 11

SERVO

The instant flash of bright light from the little aircraft momentarily blinded Roger and his dad. They sat in silence rubbing their eyes.

As their sight slowly came back they could see the small aircraft 'Servo' sitting on the dash board where it had landed and sat facing them with its little eyes. A few moments passed then the two little headlight eyes began looking from Roger to his dad, back and forth, like a dog does when you are holding an outstretched bone.

"What was that all about?" asked Roger out loud. Servo then answered with the sound of a beep, did a small hop in the air about an inch, then landed back on the dash, the headlights still going from Roger to his Dad as if it was waiting for something.

"Roger, this is Servo," said Calvin with his outstretched hand introducing him to the aircraft. "Servo, this is Roger," pointing back over to his son.

The small craft made a beep and a tiny little hand extended from its side, outstretched to Roger for a handshake. Roger took the tiny hand, "Pleased to meet you" he said and a small beep from Servo returned the greeting to Roger as the tiny robot hand released Roger's grip and fell back to its side.

Calvin then asked Servo, "Do you want to take Roger for a trip?"

Roger gave his dad a curious stare, then looked back at Servo. Instantly Servo beeped and hopped up and down on the dash with his little ship body waging back and forth.

"Is it waging like a dog?" Roger whispered, glancing sideways at him and then back at Servo.

"Yes," laughed his Dad, who reached up and patted Servo, just like scratching a dog on the head causing Servo to let out a small relaxing *beeep.*

"OK, Servo," said his Dad, "let's go."

Servo beeped, lifted off the dash into the air and started zooming around and around inside the car in excitement. Then, Servo slowed to a stop in midair right up between Roger and his dad in the front seat by the car radio. One of the small robotic arms came out of Servo and pressed some buttons on the radio, apparently in order, because instantly the radio flipped on and a small door on front opened that was the size of Servo. It looked like a miniature garage door opening for the miniature flying robot.

Servo flew partway into the small opening and blips and beeps were coming from the radio speakers inside the car. Servo had docked with the car radio and appeared to be communicating through the radio.

"What is Servo doing?" asked Roger.

"Synchronizing with the system," replied his father with a grin.

"What do you mean?" asked Roger.

His dad looked up at Roger with a crooked smile, "Just be patient son, this is the cool part."

Roger continued to stare at Servo and take in the fact that what he was seeing was real and that his brother had made the coolest little flying robot in the world. He then had a second thought about what his Dad had just said.

"What do you mean, have you seen this before?" he asked.

"Randy showed Servo to me in the form you see now. But I have never seen Servo folded down into the small box form that you found it hidden in. "I'm so glad you found *her*," said his Dad looking over at Roger.

Roger was in a trance staring at the little spaceship robot.

"HER?" squeaked Roger, "That thing is a SHE?"

"Yup, Servo is a girl," replied Calvin. "Randy designed her over the years. He said girls were perfect, so he wanted to follow the trend and make his invention a girl."

Roger let out a small laugh, "He always was girl crazy Dad, you know how he was about Laura." Then his mind clicked, "Oh yea, I saw her today at the diner. She told me she might be coming by to visit tomorrow evening."

"Good, I miss her. I hope she is doing OK," said his father.

Roger remembered the news she had to tell his parents but decided not to break his promise and tell his Dad like she had asked.

"She looked good and seemed very happy," Roger reported.

Rogers mind was now spinning with questions. Why hadn't Randy shown Servo to me? How did I not know he had a cool robot called Servo? What else does dad know that he hasn't shared with me yet?

All at once the engine of the muscle car roared to life. It appeared that Servo had just started it up. The dash board transformed and changed in an instant. The odometer and gauges flipped over and were now displaying information with LED lights on high tech digital displays. They looked just like the ones that were found in high tech aircraft. There was another display with a small map transforming on the dash to the right side of the main display. This screen showed a map of their city and the roads. Roger looked closer and noticed little blue dots illuminated on some of the roads. His father noticed. "Those dots are all of the local police cars in the city and their exact locations."

Roger's head came up as he looked at his dad. "I'm freaking out right now Dad. How is this possible?" he squeaked again.

"I know, it's crazy isn't it?" and he continued, "Randy tapped into all of the police radio frequencies and monitored each police car from its unique radio signature around town. As long as they have their police radio on, Randy could pinpoint their location. I can tell you more about that invention later. The military wanted this invention but he didn't want them to have it yet," said his Dad. "Besides, Randy really liked to drive this car very fast. So knowing where the police cars were was important. He knew where he could punch the gas and take this car for a real ride."

Roger laughed and then jumped as the car started to move. He squeaked loud, "DAD, DAD, DAD, I'm not doing this," and grabbed the wheel with both hands in a panic.

"Relax son," said his father laughing at his reaction, "Servo is taking us somewhere, it is a surprise." And the car turned and headed toward their house.

Servo drove the car back to their house, Roger freaking out the whole way. The car came to a stop right at the closed doors of the shop. Calvin got out and pulled open the shop doors. Servo turned the car around and backed into the shop. When she had parked the Mustang in its space, she turned off the engine. Calvin pulled the shop doors closed as Roger climbed out of the car. The shop was just like they had left it a short time earlier. They both stood there for a moment and then his father spoke. "This is where things get real interesting."

From inside the car, Servo could be heard winding up and small lights were blinking from the radio. A few beeps and tones could be heard and then Servo detached from the car radio and began to slowly hover over to them and picked up speed as she headed right for Rogers face.

Roger quickly ducked as Servo soared close and flew right over his head toward the work bench. Servo hovered next to the laptop they had in the shop and softly landed. Two small legs, or what looked like landing gear lowered down under the small body of the ship and she landed. A small arm came out of her side and reached over to the laptop and plugged into a small port on the side. Instantly Servo's headlights started to alternate between red and green as she sat softly humming, quiet and relaxed.

"She is updating her GPS software," said Calvin, "She connects to the internet through the laptop Wi-Fi connection."

Servo beeped and her headlights stopped flashing. She appeared to be done with her download and started to rise up into the air. She speedily raced around the shop like she was taking in the place and flew over to a small cabinet on the furthest wall in the shop. She hovered there with her headlights scanning the cabinet, up and down a few times. She made some loud beeps and backed up still facing the cabinet.

All of a sudden she lurched forward at great speed and smashed into the cabinet bouncing back a little from the collision, causing the doors to open from the force of being "robot kicked" and she fluttered inside.

Roger was speechless as he watched the little robot zooming around. "What in the world is that crazy flying robot doing now?" mumbled Roger.

He and his dad moved closer to the open cabinet peering inside. Servo hovered and then her little arm came out and she reached over to the back and lifted up a small hook. The hook was identical to all of the other hooks that were holding garden tools. One held a rake, another held a shovel and others were holding different kinds of garden tools. But this particular hook was empty. As the small hook was lifted there was a click and the back of the cabinet slid open revealing a small narrow doorway that led to staircase. As they both glanced through the small opening, they saw a dim light at the top of the stairs illuminating the narrow steps that led down. Immediately Servo sped into the doorway and turned sharply and proceeded to go down the stairway.

Roger stood speechless with his mouth open in amazement. "Follow me son," and he followed his Dad and Servo into the cabinet. His dad pulled shut the cabinet doors and then closed the secret door behind them once he was inside the passage on the stairs. They walked a short distance down the dimly lit stairs and it felt like they were now directly under the shop above. It was very dark where they stood and they could only see two headlights scanning the room as Servo sped around it, briefly illuminating the walls and workbenches as she passed by. It was hard to make out objects because she was speeding around like a tiny hummingbird.

Roger's dad flipped on the light switch at the bottom of the stairs, he obviously had been there before since he knew where to find it. The room flickered to life as lights came up to brightness, illuminating the large room. There was a thin layer of dust, apparently no one had been in it for some time. Roger looked at his dad after he finished glancing around the room.

"This was Randy's secret lab," his dad said smiling.

Roger slowly looked around the lab again, this time taking in all of the room. On one wall there were nine large monitors arranged and mounted in a giant square. They were all off, but looked cool. Two walls were each lined with a work bench. They had work stools, soldering irons, oscilloscopes and other cool electronic devices. It looked like a cool computer lab with what appeared to be inventions and projects in pieces or partially assembled on the work benches. On the final wall was a nice comfortable work desk with a computer system and giant monitor assembled on top.

"This was Randy's favorite place to work and invent," said his father, as he sat down in the chair leaning back, his arms behind his head doing a full spin around in the office chair.

"How long has this place been here?" questioned Roger as he walked over to one of the workbenches, trying to figure out what the contraption was that took up the whole workbench. "Why didn't you tell me about this place? I would be down here all of the time Dad," Roger commented as he continued to stare at the object on the workbench.

"It was too hard for me to come down here after he died Roger, I just couldn't do it, until now." He replied. "I built this lab just after Randy graduated from high school. We built this place because he was creating things that we wanted to keep secret from everyone and needed a secret place to work. My best friend Jake from work helped me build this lab. Jake was great with construction and designed and built numerous buildings, towers and power vaults for our company. We had this place completed pretty fast. No one else knows about it besides Jake and your mother. We kept a very tight lid on this place."

"How long ago did Jake die?

His father took a breath and sighed, "It's been just over a year since he had that accident at work. He died right before Randy did. I really miss that guy."

Jake Jensen was a single guy with no kids who led a pretty quiet life. He and Calvin met and became best friends while they both served in the Army Corps of Engineers. They were young and just out of college about twenty years ago. Jake would come over on weekends to hang out with Calvin and work on cars and do other manly stuff. Roger's dad always felt there was more to his death but couldn't prove it or find information to support this feeling he had. Jake had died while working at the power plant that was connected to the hydroelectric dam up at a lake about 40 miles east of town. He was working on a project when some giant wire guides collapsed and power wires fell, electrocuting him. Calvin was pretty torn up about the accident. He kept arguing with his company managers to investigate more fully into the equipment failure that killed his best friend. The company lawyers claimed they did and his death was ruled an accident.

Roger was looking at a device resting on a workbench. It was in two pieces and painted white. He was trying to pick up part of the awkward thing as his father came over and stood next to him. Roger looked the device piece up and down trying to figure out what it was. Together both pieces were about the size of a bicycle, without tires. Parts of it could be extended and snapped into place like parts from a folding chair. On the top of the piece Roger was working with was a cylinder that looked similar to a long fire extinguisher, with two pulley wheels on the top of each end. The pulley wheels were about eight inches in diameter and made with strong steel and bearings. Roger spun one of the wheels and it gave off small sparks as it spun and then came to a stop, the sparks stopping as its spinning motion ended. Calvin reached out and pointed to a few release pins and levers and pushed on one, then pulled at the same time. The piece had extended and popped into place, secure and strong. Roger now saw that there were more buttons and quickly pushed some and popped out the folded parts of both pieces of the devices until it was all assembled and complete. The giant device looked like a cross between a ski lift chair and a bicycle. Roger smiled as he took in the design his brother had created.

"This is the crowned jewel," said his father. "Randy worked on this version for years and had some helpful input from a few professors at the college. Jake even helped him out when he was building it. This is what Randy called *The Cruiser*." Roger continued to stare in amazement. "This was the first one that he made," said Calvin. "When it is hoisted up to its position, he pushes these two buttons to release and unfold the pulley wheels so they can be connected to the guide wires above."

"What do mean guide wires above? "Above what?"

Roger's excitement was showing, "What are we waiting for, show me how it works."

His dad chuckled and held up a hand, "In due time son, just be patient for a day or two." He continued to stare at the cruiser as it rested on the bench. "I went with Randy a few times on this cruiser, he even let me pilot it by myself a few times."

Roger turned toward him, "Pilot?" he asked, *"Does this thing actually fly?"* and he watched for his father's reaction.

"No it doesn't, well it kind of does, I mean it-" His father looked flustered, "it is kind of hard to explain."

"So tell me!" Roger was now very anxious, "tell me what this thing is," he demanded as he looked into his father's face.

"OK, OK," said his dad and he began to pace the floor looking down, thinking of the best place to begin and how to describe this contraption to Roger.

He looked up, "OK, you know where I work?" he asked Roger.

"Duh, you work for the power company. You work on power lines and run new wire and repair old lines on high power poles and stuff."

His dad looked up, "Well, technically, I have done that. But I am actually a supervisor now over the guys who do that every day, like I used to with Jake."

"Okay, let me give you a little history. Here son, have a seat." And he rolled the chair that was at the desk over to Roger, who caught it and plopped down comfortably in it. Roger looked up at his father who was still pacing back and forth, starting into his story.

"I have worked for the power company a long time. My department works on the power lines that stretch across the entire state. There are power lines that span the entire length of our country son and not just our country, but *ALL* countries." He continued, "Every city is connected by them, every town and every building, every house and so on. They all are connected to power lines that tie them into the National Power Grid. You've seen me climb the massive towers that hold the giant heavy power cables right?" Roger nodded, Calvin continued. "The lines span across the country, they cross over the plains, mountains, gorges, canyons and ravines. You've seen them as we drive up the mountains. The giant metal pylons and towers that stand out in the distance looking like giant metal frozen robots, with arms reaching down to hold the heavy power cables. Some of these towers are located downtown leading to and from smaller sub stations that distribute power to the city."

"So, Randy had an idea to design a device that he could attach to these massive power cables. He wanted to use the cables that connect cities to each other as a road in the sky. He made this device," and he pointed at the *cruiser*. "He could attach it to a power line and climb inside. Once he was in the cruiser and it was attached to a power line, it would draw on the power line to transform and he could use it to be propelled and travel across the cables from place to place and from city to city."

"No way," replied Roger, "are you serious?"

"Oh yes." answered his father, "very serious. I've been with him on it before. It was over a year ago and it was awesome. We went so fast and could have gone much faster. Calvin walked over to Randy's desk and turned the computer on. "I have an idea. "

He pulled over one of the rolling bench chairs and took a seat behind the desk after the computer was at a logon screen. He typed in a password and clicked the mouse, searching through a few files until he found the one he was looking for.

"Check this out," said his father and he clicked the file that started a video. Roger could hear it being narrated by his brother Randy.

The video started with a brief history of US power grids, showing a map of the United States and the current power grids encompassing the country and reaching up into Canada and to Alaska. Tens of thousands of miles of electrical cables connect the country. Randy continued to talk about using these cables for travel. The video then turned to Randy's lab where he worked at a desk with a little spaceship robot that looked just like Servo, buzzing around his head and zooming in and out of the shot. The next scene showed Randy at a different location at evening time, standing next to a giant tower with high power lines that stretch high above the ground over a hundred feet. The "cruiser" is already attached to the power cable and looks similar to a ski lift chair resting on the power cable. Only it is not a chair at all, but looks a bit more like a tandem style bike with arms reaching up above it, connected to strong pulley wheels above and below the power cable. The seats look very comfortable, full style chairs leaning slightly back with seatbelts. The video continues with more narration by Randy on how difficult it was to program the computer to follow the lines and especially where there will be sharp turns, possibly at very high speeds.

The next segment begins titled, "High Speed Turn Test." Randy is sitting in the seat leaning back slightly when then the little robot comes zooming over his head and docks in a small port on the dash board of the cruiser. It appears to be Servo and Randy confirms it is as he describes how Servo is the key to powering up the cruiser. Right after she docked, lights begin going off and the fire extinguisher shaped cylinder up above Randy's head begins to glow a soft green color and then the entire cruiser is quickly encircled by what looks like a shield of clear plastic. The cruiser has now transformed into a sleek, large oval sphere. It was similar to the shape of an American football, but twenty times larger. The plastic sphere then appears to go nearly invisible with Randy sitting inside. It is completely hidden as well as its passenger. You can hear but not see Randy still talking about the upcoming test he is about to try.

"I love this part, keep watching," his dad says.

Roger continued watching the video segment that had changed to the inside of the sphere. The front windshield showed a giant display of what looked like a road map, but it is really a map of the power grid showing all of the power cables in Belford and Cove Creek. There are two handles for steering, one for each of his hands. There are foot pedals similar to a car. Randy briefly goes over the controls and describes the numerous systems and indicators on the display screen. The video again shifts to outside of the sphere and Randy says to Servo, "Please enable the cloaking systems." The sphere has a ripple effect shimmer quickly over it and Randy is fully visible, seated in the sphere as it hangs below the power lines. He presses the foot pedal to make the sphere move forward and the stationary camera catches a glimpse of the sphere as it rockets away from the starting point like a bullet from a gun through the air, traveling on the cable that it is attached to and quickly disappears from the view of the camera.

Roger watches the video continue from inside the sphere as it is moving very fast down the cable. Randy continues describing additional systems and controls and how things are operating inside the speeding sphere. Randy points out on the dashboard display the cruisers current position on the digital map and that a sharp right turn appears to be quickly approaching. On the digital map, Randy points and shows his current 150 MPH speed and his location. Up ahead there is a small lake to the left and the power cables make a sharp turn to the right and off up a small hill just to the side of the lake. Randy describes in the video this is the first sharp turn test at this high speed on the cable. And he designed and programmed measures to help the sphere lean and turn into these types of corners and absorb the massive "G" forces and gravity that will be inflicted on the human body in this type of turn, comparing it to a fighter jet. He no sooner finishes what he is saying when he arrives at the turn at the high rate of speed.

The video then changes to a view from a stationary camera that has been setup and is positioned at the turn sitting next to the lake. It has been setup to capture this attempt for Randy's research and study. The video shows the sphere hurling down the cable toward it. Instead of making the sharp turn to the right, as soon as the sphere attempts the turn, the wheels holding the capsule to the power cable shear off, from the massive speed and force. The mounts that held the sphere to the cable burst with a spray of sparks and smoke as the sphere goes flying off the cable. The cruiser with Randy inside hits the lake and goes skipping out numerous times. With each bounce and skip you hear a grown of pain from Randy, "Ouch, Ewe, Ohh, Ouch," as he skips to a stop and slowly starts to sink in the lake, still seated inside the broken capsule. The electrical sphere that once surrounded the cruiser then disappeared depleted of its power source. A popping noise sounded and instantly a flotation device burst out and inflated around the metal framed cruiser, keeping it afloat. From the video the sound of Calvin laughing can be heard. From the stationary camera angle you see him as he walks up to the edge of the lake throwing a rope to Randy sitting in the floating cruiser. Randy unbuckled and climbed out and into the water to get the rope. He then secured it to the craft and Calvin pulled him safely back to shore.

Roger looked up to see his Dad standing next to him laughing over the video scene. The video came to an end and the frame closed. His dad reached up, turned off the monitor and looked over at Roger.

"Well, what do you think?" asks his father.

"I am completely blown away by this! I-I can't believe, I want to try-," but he couldn't speak because he was getting tongue tied with so much excitement. "I can't believe he made something like this dad!" He finally said clearly.

"That was the first of many tests and yes, he did fix the program. He redesigned the sphere to handle high speed turns, as well as descents and climbing," said his father. "Some of those cables go right down over cliffs and climb mountain walls."

"I am speechless Dad. Randy was a real genius and had unbelievable ideas. I can't believe he worked on this and I never knew it. I could kill him, I mean," and he trailed off.

Calvin spoke, breaking the silence. "His most fascinating cruiser was the last one that he created just before he died. It was far more advanced than what you just saw. It could do more *and* go faster. It could even travel underground."

"Underground?" asked Roger, "How can that be?"

"Yes" said his father, "it was truly amazing." His father then describes the latest cruiser in detail, sharing with Roger how the cruiser now used an electromagnet to hold it to the power cables, replacing the old pulley wheels.

"It was far more advanced and he designed it to work with the molecules in your body," described his father.

"I still don't understand," said Roger. "How did it work?"

"I can't tell you. I will never know the exact science of it son, but when you used his new cruiser, it would transform to take up less space. You would transform into a small shape, like a torpedo attached to the cable. While in the sphere and attached to the cable, you would appear to be a small form of energy. The cruiser was sleek and you would lay forward like you were riding a Ducati motorcycle, or a bullet bike. You would drive it leaning forward slightly bent over and racing forward at high speeds.

"So where is that model dad and when do we take it out for spin?"

"Soon Roger, very soon, it is hidden at the moment."

Roger stared at him intently. "Dad, all of these secrets are freaking me out."

In his mind he pictured the look on Aaron and Max's faces when he told them everything about Randy.

"I guess I can tell you more about the latest cruiser," said his father. "We hid that cruiser from the government after Randy died. I didn't want them to get a hold of it and I had a feeling they were getting close to Randy. They had been hounding him and were trying to get information about his projects from his professors. I think one of their agents somehow got a hold of one of the videos of the cruiser that he made for his testing and research. Randy had taken it to show his most trusted professor at school, Professor Craft. After he showed Professor Craft, I think a copy might have been made somehow and given to the government.

"Why would the government care about his cruiser project?" asked Roger.

His dad looked at him, "Oh man Roger, if you knew what they had in store for the cruiser." His dad turned white and started to pace back and forth a moment in the lab.

"After Randy was killed, you remember your mother told you that the government came out and searched the house and shop from top to bottom. They didn't find anything, but we were threatened not to talk about it or we would go to jail. We were questioned pretty heavily about Randy's school lab projects. We insisted that they were all blown up and destroyed in the resulting fire the night he died. We played dumb and told them he hadn't built anything at home since he had his lab at the college. We didn't want to give any clue about the lab we had hidden here and what he was working on. But later, I was able to find out what they were looking for and that they knew about the cruiser project. In fact I found out that they had a special name for it. They called it "Lighting Strike."

Roger looked at his dad, *"Lightning Strike?"*

His father answered, "Yep, that's what it was called. They were so sure that I had it and all of the information on it and that I would be very co-operative with them. This was pretty hard for us so soon after Randy was killed to be confronted and questioned so hard. We didn't have any time to grieve our son's loss. But they pushed us harder and said it was a matter of National Security. But I didn't have a good feeling about what this woman from the CIA was telling me. She was pretty forceful and was upset I didn't have what she was looking for."

Chapter 12

Lightning Strike

Roger and his dad continued their conversation in the lab. "I received an email from Randy a few hours before he died. He sent it to me that afternoon at work and I was really concerned about what it contained. I wanted to talk to him about the video that was attached to the email. That's why we were taking dinner to him that night. I was very worried and wanted to talk with him. In the video segment there was a download of an unknown file that looked like it was made by the military, but I couldn't be sure. In the clip they showed how they intended to use the cruiser. It depicted an animated demonstration of it being used to sneak into other countries and right up to the potential targets or threats, as they called them. Once they infiltrated the enemy's country through the power grids, they could assassinate or capture anyone, at any time. It would give them access to any country in the world that had electrical power. They had given the project a secret name, it was called *Lightning Strike*."

Roger stood there, his mind whirling. "Dad that is crazy. Who would have thought it could be used like that. I know Randy wouldn't have wanted it used that way."

His father now paced faster. "OK Roger, you now have knowledge that could get us thrown into jail or maybe even worse if this ever got out. I know the government and they have been looking for this technology since Randy died. They will not give up and probably are looking harder than ever.

"Listening bugs in the shop and house!" Roger blurted, looking at his dad.

"Yes, I don't know who it was that put them there, but someone has been trying listen in on us after Randy died. I have been very cautious about jamming the devices and signals I have found."

His father's pacing slowed down and he took a seat at the desk facing Roger.

"I can't believe the government would use Randy's invention to kill people," exclaimed Roger.

"Believe it son, if they get it, they will. Roger, I know your head was flooded with this new information tonight, but there is one more piece to this giant puzzle I need to share."

Rogers head popped up attentively looking at his dad.

"This piece of information I am going to describe to you could get us all killed if anyone finds out," he said sternly to Roger.

"I will keep quiet dad, you can trust me," said Roger.

His father turned and proceeded to tell Roger the last piece of the puzzle.

"As Randy progressed in his research, he was making astonishing discoveries with his new technology. In his discovery working with electricity and manipulating molecules, he found that he could rearrange matter and particles and that certain patterns could be found. He actually could get them to do things at his control. He could make the body physically re-arrange and change when you were inside his cruiser system so you could travel underground along the underground power lines safely. It was really amazing and there was nothing like it in the world. I got to do it with him, what a RUSH! After that it got even wilder."

"He then discovered something in the cruiser. He found that there were ways in which he could now exploit or hack into devices that were actually connected to the power grid. Randy found that he could actually tap into the power feed of any device, TV, radio and even computers.

"I don't get it," questioned Roger. "What do you mean, hack or tap in?"

"Let me explain son," and continued. "What he discovered was that while he was in the new cruiser, he was able to use his computer system to see the unique signatures that were coming from all of the different devices that were drawing an electrical current from the power outlet they were connected to. A digital TV used a special electrical signature, while a computer gave off a completely different signature feed as it was drawing power. He found that he could tap into these currents of power and could access any device or system while he was in the cruiser because it too was drawing power from the same sources the devices were drawing power from. He was tapped into the power grid and could access anything that was requiring power. He was able to tap into anything that needed power to operate. He found a passage into actual computer system networks at corporations, computer main frames big and small, home computers, government systems and yes, he was even able to gain entry at banks."

His father turned, "Can you imagine that Roger? He could access any computer system in the world without anyone knowing. The device he made to do this was called the *'NIM.'* It was his Network Insertion Module. I don't know much about it, he just had recently invented it and it was the main device he used to get into the computer systems that were drawing power."

"You see, every company is out there protecting their expensive computer networks and main frame systems from people trying to access them from the internet, or dial into them with old school modems. Some systems could only be accessed from a terminal directly connected to them. They think that you can only access a computer system from a keyboard and mouse while connected with a network cable, or terminal to their mainframes. No one out there even thinks about the power used to run a computer as a way to get in. Well that actual power connection is another gateway or a way that their systems could be accessed by Randy's NIM invention. However secure or isolated they think they might be, they could be infiltrated by Randy in his cruiser. Everyone out there is under the assumption that power only supplies a current and the ability to make any electrical device run and that it only needs power or electrical current to turn it on and function. But Randy now had the ability to tap into this back door and have access into any system he wanted in the world by coming in through the power lines that were keeping the computers running. He didn't need a network connection. In fact he could get into systems that were designed to be stand alone, or running on their own, not even connected to a network. He could access any system that was drawing on power."

Roger was so astonished at this, it caused him to fall back into a desk chair and stare at his father, his mind racing with ideas and questions.

"So imagine what the possibilities are now, with access to the cruiser and if we had it, the network insertion module. The government must be going crazy knowing that someone out there has this type of technology, just waiting to tap into their systems. Somehow I think they found out about it and that Randy designed it. Imagine if this fell into the wrong hands son. Someone could get access to the military nuclear missile systems, access to the air traffic control systems, or even access to the stock market on the Wall Street network systems. You could do anything you wanted, or access anything out there!"

Roger had a major headache now with all of this information his father had just dropped on him. It was like his dad was unwinding at a shrink's office and unloading years of secret burdens in one night.

"Did Randy show you how to access that system he made?" he asked.

"Not all of them. He had only recently discovered it and was fine tuning the program for the network module. He had just told me about it one night in the shop after he returned home from a *cruiser ride*. That is what he used to call his excursions across the city on the power lines. He loved to take them."

His father looked down at the floor and said with tears in his voice. "The next night he was dead, we didn't get to talk about his latest discovery in too much detail. He was out testing it that night and when he returned home he appeared a bit shaken up. I really didn't pay much attention to it. But I'm a dad, I know when something is bothering one of my kids. I had planned to talk to him the next night at dinner after work, but," and he stopped talking and stood deep in thought.

"So do you think he hid the program or information about it somewhere?" asked Roger.

His dad snapped out of the stupor he was in and looked up at Roger. "I thought so son, I searched everywhere in this lab and in the house. I have searched all of his computers down here and all of the files I could find to see if there were any clues but I couldn't find anything."

"There must be somewhere you missed!" He exclaimed.

"Of course I did, I know Randy and he always had a backup plan and hidden locations for his secrets," replied his dad.

His father looked at the clock on the wall, "Holy crap look at the time! Its past 1AM already." They both stood up, Roger with his giant headache and his father feeling concerned about giving him too much information and responsibility. "I think we need to get to bed, we can discuss more of this in the morning,' and then became very serious. "I don't want you to tell Aaron and Max about this lab just yet. OK son?" his dad said.

"OK, I won't mention it until you tell me I can," replied Roger.

His dad turned and he motioned to Roger to head toward the stairs.

"What about Servo?" asked Roger as she zoomed up toward them both and headed with them up the stairs.

"Let's keep her in the house for now and out of sight. I don't want the neighbors seeing her buzzing around the house. You can show her to Aaron and Max tomorrow," said his father.

As they started up the stairs Roger turned to his dad,

"Wait, you never told me where you hid Randy's Ducati cruiser," and he stopped at the bottom of the stairs looking at his dad.

"I have that in a nice secret place at Grandmas house," smiled his father.

"Grandmas? You have got to be kidding me!" he shrugged. "Is there anyone in this family who doesn't know? Even my grandma knows, *wow.*"

Roger motioned to Servo to land in his hands with a little whistle. Just like a pet bird, she zoomed over and nestled in and appeared to power down and Roger put her gently into his pocket. His father reached up taking hold of each of Rogers's shoulders, turned him around facing the stairs and gave him a little push from behind to start the climb. He flipped off the light switch as he left the lab following Roger and Servo up the stairs. Calvin turned the signal jamming device hidden in the record player off and they both went to the house and immediately up to bed. Roger was sure he wouldn't sleep at all that night but he quickly fell asleep shortly after his head hit the pillow.

Chapter 13

Searching

That next morning Roger slept until noon. He was totally exhausted from the brain overload of all the information his parents had given him. It was now Sunday and after Roger opened his eyes, he lay there for a few moments and just stared up at the ceiling going over the past two days of his life and how quickly it had changed. The new information he had learned about Randy and the amazing list of his inventions, thinking about some of his own inventions and the involvement in their lives from the government before and after Randy had died.

Roger sat up on the edge of the bed, picked up the window remote from his bedside table, pointed and clicked. The windows to his bedroom automatically opened to let in the fresh air.

"I love this invention" he thought to himself, as a cool morning breeze softly blew into his room, with it, the smell of a fresh morning rainfall. He inhaled a slow deep breath with his eyes closed and began to take in that smell of cool air from wet rain that was filling his room from the weather outside.

Once out of bed, he walked over to the window and looked out to observe wet ground and the view. He looked over toward the shop and stood there reflecting about the newly discovered secret lab in the basement, trying to comprehend all that his father had shared late last night.

As he stood there looking out the window he noticed something that he had never paid much attention to before. He was focusing on a very tall electrical tower. It was a high voltage power line tower that was located a few hundred feet away from the back end of their property. It was one of many in a chain of towers stretching across the small valley. The trail of towers that were all strung together were used to carry the power lines from the hydroelectric dam located up the canyon 40 miles from his house. The lines stretched all the way into town to a power substation where they would then distribute the power to the rest of the Belford residents.

But the particular tower he was focused on had some sort of platform built on it. None of the other towers he observed had platforms like this built on them. It was like a small deck shape, located about ten feet below the lowest set of wires that were directed by this tower. He looked closer and he could see a small set of stairs that were in a zig-zag style leading up one of the massive legs of the tower. These stairs stretched from the ground up to the deck platform and they were enclosed by an apparent locked gate with some apparent caution signs hanging on it. They actually were too far away to read, but he had seen signs similar to them on other power equipment when he went to work with his dad at the power company. He had the opportunity at times to accompany his dad on small tasks for his job and was allowed to drive around with him in the cool work truck. He continued to gaze at the platform and wondered how it appeared to most people. Most would just see it as part of the normal tower, but from what Roger had just learned last night about his brother, he had different thoughts about the platform. Roger immediately knew that this tower must be one that Randy had obviously used for his testing and experiments for some of his cruiser rides. His dad must have had a crew build the platform or worked with his friend Jake to build it. He made a mental note to ask his dad about that tower platform later when they talked.

As Roger walked lazily into the kitchen he saw Jenny seated at the table, in front of her on a plate was a delicious half eaten peanut butter and red raspberry jam sandwich, accompanied by a glass full of ice cold milk.

"*Morig seepy head,*" mumbled Jenny with her mouth full of a fresh bite of sandwich.

"Morning," replied Roger as he reached into the cupboard taking out a box of cereal. Then he took a seat across from Jenny and poured himself a bowl.

"Where are mom and dad?" he asked Jenny.

"They went to the diner for breakfast," and she looked up out the window as if to see them in the driveway, "but they haven't come back yet."

"Did you ever find the missing missile for your remote controlled helicopter?" asked Roger.

"I did," she replied. "It was in the living room under the coffee table. I had taken a few shots in there trying to hit mom as she walked by me the other day."

Roger smirked with his mouth full of cereal, let out a single mini laugh, "Hah" he mumbled, chewing with a smile.

The outside door to the kitchen opened and Aaron came trotting in with his usual big grin and crooked glasses. "Hey guys," as he adjusted his glasses on his face. "What's for lunch?" he asked as he walked over to the pantry to begin a search for something that looked appealing to eat.

"What are your plans for the day?" asked Roger.

"This looks yummy," said Aaron as he turned to face Roger, holding a banana and a bag of Cheetos. "I have no idea," he quickly muttered and looked around the kitchen.

Roger noticed him scanning the living room and knew what, or *who* he was now eagerly looking for.

"She's not here yet," said Roger.

Aaron turned and with a sigh, "She said she was coming over today," he muttered.

Roger spoke to Jenny, "When we were at the diner yesterday, Laura said she was coming later tonight," and reached across the table as Aaron sat down with a disappointed face and gave him pity pat on the shoulder.

"Laura is coming today?" said Jenny with a smile on her face.

"Yeah, she is coming over later to say hi to mom and dad and *YOU*," Roger said to Jenny.

The kitchen door opened and in walked Max. She was dressed in workout clothes, a nice pink and white sweatshirt with knee length workout pants, and her hair in a tight pony tail. She had just returned from her morning gymnastics practice.

"What's up?" asked Jenny and crossed the room to give her a hug.

Max returned the hug and came over and took a seat at the table where they were all eating. She reached over and broke off half of Aaron's banana.

"Hey, get your own," said Aaron.

Max gave him a glare that said 'shut up' without having to say a word.

Aaron caught on quickly and decided to end the issue for his own safety. He slid his bag of Cheetos over to his side out of Max's reach, just in case.

"How was practice today?" asked Roger.

"It was a tough one for us," said Max. "Coach Geiger really worked us hard. With the meet coming up Tuesday she really wanted us to push hard."

Max is on the high school gymnastics team and is one of the best gymnasts in the school, in fact the best gymnast in town. Coach

Geiger was the coach at their school and worked very hard with her. Coach Geiger had already contacted some colleges for her and they had even sent scouts to watch her at some of her meets. One college already made a scholarship offer for her to come join their team when she graduated high school.

"You guys coming to my meet on Tuesday?" she asked.

"Of course," they all answered. Then Jenny piped up, "Mom is checking me out of school early so I can come too," she announced.

"Is your mom going to be back in town for the meet?" asked Roger.

Max's face saddened, "No, she'll miss it, *again*," she said. "Mrs. Jenkins called her yesterday and chewed her out, telling her she shouldn't miss them, but she didn't seem to care."

"I'm excited to see you win first place *again*," said Roger. "You're always great. Don't worry about your mom not being there. You will have all of my family there cheering you on."

"Hey, what about me?" said Aaron. "I'm always there too."

Max laughed. "Thanks guys, that sounds great, I like to be cheered on."

"I'm outa here," said Jenny. And she got up from the table, placed her dirty dishes in the sink and headed to the living room to chill and watch a little TV.

Max and Aaron watched as Jenny left the room, waited just a moment and then quickly turned to face Roger. "OK, what gives? We're dying to hear about what your dad talked about yesterday when you went to your grandmas house?" said Max.

Roger felt like he was in a pickle. His dad had asked Roger not to tell them about all of the details just yet. But these were his best friends and besides, his mom already spilled the beans so they already knew most of the story. He decided to tell them and had just started when he heard his parent's car pull into the driveway. His parents were just getting home from their morning breakfast together.

"Oh man, my parents are home."

They turned and looked through the window and saw his parents getting out of the car.

"Listen guys," he said, "I promised my dad I wouldn't tell you this yet. Keep quiet, I'll tell you after they aren't –"

"Hello there," sounded his father's voice from the door as he walked into the kitchen behind his wife to see the three of them sitting at the table.

"How was breakfast?" asked Roger.

"It was very good," said his mother Alicia. Then she asked the three them what their plans were for the day.

They all had a small visit then separated. Rogers's parents went upstairs to relax while Roger, Max and Aaron went outside walking toward Max's house.

"OK, continue the story," said Max as they all slowly walked to her house.

Roger filled them in on every detail that his father had shared and showed him last night pausing during their walk and stopping numerous times to answer their questions.

"You gotta show me that little flying robot "Servo" said Aaron excitedly. "That is the coolest thing I have ever heard, I gotta see that little guy."

"I will, I will," said Roger. "But, it's a she. Now listen, you can't tell this to anybody, I mean it," he said in a very serious voice.

"We have the government after us and they are trying to get Randy's inventions to use for some bad stuff. We have to be even more careful from now on, OK," he said firmly.

Max and Aaron agreed and promised that no one would hear the secret from them. After a few minutes they arrived at Max's house and went inside to hang out for a while to discuss what they had just learned in more detail.

Chapter 14

The Visit

As they all sat down at their usual places in Max's living room, they were still discussing the details about the lab and the project that Randy was working on. They were going over step by step the story Rogers's father had told him that night and were trying to piece together some possible clues.

"That code name that they gave the project is pretty cool," said Aaron. '*Lightning Strike*', sounds like a James Bond film."

"I know, it is pretty cool," replied Roger. And he stood up and walked around the living room, deep in thought.

"We need to figure out the rest of this project and find out where all the pieces are hiding," said Roger. "I know the main cruiser is hidden at my grandmas house somewhere. My dad knows where it is but didn't tell me yet."

"Do you think that he will show you soon?" asked Aaron.

"I'm sure he will sometime," said Roger as he turned to face Aaron. "He mentioned to me that he needed to fix some more things at Grandmas house in the next few days. So maybe before that he will talk to me."

"Well you should tag along, probe him for more clues and information." said Max.

She got up and went into the kitchen to get a bottle of water from the refrigerator. She quickly returned and was carrying a couple of extras and tossed one to Aaron and the other to Roger, then she dropped herself back into the sofa, propping her feet comfortably on the coffee table.

"Roger, where do you think Randy hid the cruiser at your grandmas?"

"I have no idea, I've been thinking about it. I'm sure I've probably come close to it without even knowing it. Jenny and I are always exploring the place and checking out all of her and grandpa's stuff."

Aaron was leaning back in his chair and quickly sat full upright in his seat. This startled Roger and Max. He had just spilled water from his bottle all down the front of his shirt while trying to take a drink. But he was leaning back too far and missed his mouth with the bottle.

"Oh man, not again," he said leaning forward to try to let some of the water drain off his chest.

Max and Roger were laughing at him, when they heard a woman's voice come from behind them, "You three are always having a good time."

With startled faces, they quickly turned to see Mrs. Jenkins in the kitchen walking toward them. She had just entered the house quietly through the back door on her visit to check on Max and see how things were going at the house.

"*Hey there Mrs. Jenkins,*" said Max as she gave her a soft hug.

"Hello sweetie," replied Mrs. Jenkins and she turned to see Aaron flapping his shirt trying to air dry it a little. She gave a small grin and took out some tissues from her purse and started dabbing them on Aaron's shirt to get him dry.

Aaron stood there like a little child letting her finish her routine to clean him up. He knew from earlier experiences of spilling on himself around her, that it was worse to try to stop her when she did her mothering and it was easier to let her have her way and finish what she was doing.

"There now," she said, stepping back admiring her work on the shirt, it was still showing a wet mark but the sogginess was now gone.

Roger was watching her dry Aaron's shirt as he stood there like a wet little boy and then jokingly said *"Such a big boy now,"* as Aaron glared back at him.

"OK, OK," said Mrs. Jenkins as she looked at Roger.

"Stop being a wisenheimer or I will turn you over my knee," she said with a cute smile.

Mrs. Jenkins turned to Max, "I spoke with your mom this morning. She called me after she tried your cell and you didn't answer."

"I know she called me, but I didn't want to talk so I ignored her call," said Max.

"Maxine, you need to answer her calls. It's hard for her to be gone and she misses you," scolded Mrs. Jenkins not pausing for her response. "She told me to tell you that she is stuck at work a few more days and asked me to come over to check on you and to see how your practice went this morning."

Max was angry and appeared to be sad at the same time.

"Like she cares how my practice was, I bet she didn't even ask you that," she snapped at Mrs. Jenkins, "you probably told her I had practice to remind her, didn't you?"

Mrs. Jenkins looked like a loving mother, "Sweetie, she loves you, she feels bad she is not here very much."

"Yeah right she does," said Max in an agitated voice and turned throwing her half empty water bottle at the sofa in anger.

The jolt of the bounce caused the bottles loose cap to come off as it rebounded from the couch and took aim directly at Aaron. His eyes widened as he saw the water now starting to spill out of the top, approaching him quickly. As the bottle bounced off his chest, Aaron stood motionless. Water splashed him in the face completely soaking his shirt. He looked down to see the bottle bounce on the floor, then looked up at Max.

It took a few seconds for the scene to register with Max and Roger. They started laughing at the look on Aarons face, a mix of embarrassment and frustration.

Aaron watched as Max began laughing and her anger quickly melted away. He was glad he could cheer her up even though it meant getting soaked again.

"Thanks a lot for the shower, *Maxine*," he said, a smile now on his face.

"Oh dear," said Mrs. Jenkins as she quickly jumped up and hurried back into mother mode. She grabbed a towel quickly from the kitchen and set work again in her routine, drying off Aaron.

"Maxine," said Mrs. Jenkins, "Look what you did to this poor boy," and chuckled a little as she removed his glasses and toweled his face. Aaron stood there letting Mrs. Jenkins finish her duty. She was actually a better mom for Max then her own mother had been the past years since her parents' divorce. Her father had transferred with his job to Chicago right after the divorce and she rarely saw him. She kept her pain inside, but Roger and Aaron both knew that it hurt her greatly so they rarely discussed it, not wanting to upset her.

Max went to her room and came back carrying a sweatshirt. "Here you go bud," and she tossed it to Aaron to replace his soaked T-shirt. But without his glasses he didn't see it coming. He caught it as it fell after bouncing off his face.

"Thanks," said Aaron and he changed shirts and put his glasses back on and smiled.

Mrs. Jenkins took his wet shirt and went off to do a load of laundry.

"Feeling better?" smiled Aaron. "I hope I gave you enough laughs to get you out of your funk."

"Much better," chuckled Max.

Roger turned to both of them, "You guys want to go for walk?" he asked, "I want to show you something."

Aaron and Max looked up at him and replied, "Sure, where are we going?"

"Follow me," said Roger and proceeded to walk out the front door.

"We'll be back later!" hollered Max down the hall toward where Mrs. Jenkins was doing laundry.

"OK Sweetie," sounded Mrs. Jenkins motherly voice from the laundry room and they followed Roger out the door down the steps and walked back toward his house.

Max was rolling along next to Roger and Aaron on her long board as they walked. Instead of going to Roger's house they turned down a different street by Aaron's house and headed out toward the open valley behind Roger's house.

"Where you taking us?" asked Max.

"I noticed a place this morning and think there might be some clues located there," said Roger.

He started explaining to them about the power line tower that he had noticed earlier behind his house and that it was the only one that had its own platform. He explained that he thought it was the tower that Randy had used to launch his cruisers from and that it might be the one his dad may have built.

"Are you serious?" exclaimed Aaron.

"Listen," said Roger, "My brother had to connect his cruisers to the power lines somewhere and his lab is hidden under the shop in the back yard. Look," he said pointing in the distance toward the tower and then over toward the shop. "Look how close it would have been to the high power lines from his lab."

Max picked up her longboard as they climbed over a small barbed wire fence. They walked a short way into the open green field at the end of the street and stood in the short green grass. From where they were standing, they could see Roger's house in the distance to the left. Over to the right, the giant metal tower Roger was taking them to. While they continued their walk, they heard behind them the sound of small engine coming their way. They turned and saw a man on a motorcycle heading toward them on a small trail that had been worn into the field from constant dirt bike riding. The dirt was being stirred up behind the motorcycle as it approached them. Roger looked closer and saw that it was his dad. He recognized the blue helmet and red motorcycle as he drew closer.

The three of them stood still as Calvin continued toward them. As he approached he slowed down the motorcycle right next to them doing a sharp turn, slightly leaning and coming to a cool skidding stop, spraying the path with dirt and pebbles. His dad turned off the engine and removed his helmet. "What do we have here?" he asked and he put the kickstand down and climbed off the motorcycle. He stood leaning with his back against the motorcycle looking quite casual with his legs slightly crossed as he stared at the three of them.

"That was a cool skidding stop," Aaron told Calvin, holding out his fist for a knuckle bump. Calvin did not return the knuckle bump and he continued to look at them. He then looked at Roger, not saying another word. The look his father was giving him felt like he was peering into his soul. Roger looked down toward the ground. His father knew his son very well. They spent so much time together and Calvin sensed that Roger was guilty of something.

"Where are you three going?" he asked.

"Dad, I'm sorry, I couldn't help it," blurted Roger.

He was never very good at keeping secrets from his parents. His dad could always see right through him. Now his sister Jenny, she was a pro at keeping secrets from their parents. Roger was jealous of how she could keep her cool and not give up any information when she was being interrogated by mom and dad. She was a rock under pressure and never cracked. Roger however, was hopeless at keeping secrets.

Calvin folded his arms and looked at the three of them, then asked, "How much did he tell you?"

Max and Aarons faces were transparent. It was clear to see that Roger had told them everything about Randy and the information his father had shared with him last night.

As they stood there facing Calvin they saw his face go from firm and tough, to an inviting friendly smile. This grin made them both relax, then their mouths opened and spilled their guilt. They both instantly started blurting out at the same time their stories. Both of them were firing words at Calvin so fast and over each other as each tried to explain. Calvin stood up tall and raised his hands in the air trying to stop them both from bombarding him with their stories.

"OK, OK, that is enough you two, slow down, one at a time," he loudly said over the two of them as they continued blurting out their stories and rambling on and on.

He then held up both hands in a stop motion with his palms facing Aaron and Max, raising them up and down signaling them to slow down to a stop. They both quickly slowed the words down that were coming out of their mouths, then both went silent.

"You're not in trouble my friends," said Calvin, "I knew Roger wouldn't be able to keep what I showed him a secret very long. It would have killed the poor guy," and he turned to Roger reaching out taking him into his arms, pulled him close and gave him a short hug and release.

Roger looked up at his dad with a smile, a feeling of relief for betraying his father's request not to tell Aaron and Max about the lab and Randy's work. He knew his father's hug and words were his forgiveness and that he wasn't mad at Roger and most importantly, he wasn't in deep trouble or grounded.

"Dad, I noticed that tower this morning when I was looking out my window. I figured it might have been involved in Randy's cruiser project. It was the only one with a platform and stairs that led to the high power cables. So, I was taking Max and Aaron down to check it out. I wanted to ask you about it this morning but you were out with Mom getting breakfast."

Calvin looked over at the tower then back at Roger, "Impressive, you figured that out pretty quick," he said.

"We were just headed over to the tower to check it out and have a closer look," said Roger.

"Do you mind if I join you?" asked Calvin.

"Not at all," replied Roger.

"We're glad you are coming with us Mr. D," said Aaron.

They all turned to walk toward the tower. Calvin climbed back onto his Suzuki motorcycle, started it up and slowly drove it next to the three as they continued their walk to the tower.

Chapter 15

The Tower

The walk to the tower from where Calvin had joined them on his motorcycle was brief. They were just past the halfway point from where the three of them originally climbed the fence to begin the short journey into the green field. As they approached the tower Roger remembered the times he was with his father at work and they would drive up to these massive structures. They always looked so small in the distance, but when you were standing next to them they appeared to stretch way up to the heavens.

Calvin decided to take this time as they stood at the base of the tower to give them a quick lesson on power lines and safety. He parked his motorcycle and turned to face Roger and his friends.

"This tower is actually called a pylon. It holds the high voltage power lines that are used to distribute electrical energy and carry it across long distances."

He went on to describe the power grid that connects the entire United States and the distance that power lines travel. He went over the same information he told Roger in the lab about the power grid and how Randy used the power lines as a track to drive his cruisers on. He went on to discuss some of the dangers of electricity and how deadly it would be to their bodies if they touched the lines or came into contact with them.

"In my job with the power company, Eagle Pass, I was able to help Randy in the design and testing of his first cruiser." He said, "The system Randy designed and created to harness the power and tap into the high voltage cables was pure genius. He understood how power worked and that the energy could be harnessed. He developed his first cruiser and had tested it multiple times successfully on some older lower hanging lines that were scheduled to be removed after the new and improved pylons were installed. I decided to build this platform on pylon number 460." And he pointed up to the pylon where there was the number 460 painted part way up the tower. "Each pylon had a number so they could keep track of them for maintenance and the power company knew where every single one was located."

"I made the platform on this pylon with my best friend Jake. He knew all about Randy's cruisers and inventions and came to the inaugural launch and most of the test runs."

Roger cut in- "You guys knew Jake. He was my dad's army buddy and helped him build the lab under the shop," Roger said to Max and Aaron.

"Of course we did, we saw him here all of the time with you guys," replied Max and Aaron. "He was a good guy, it sucks that he died," said Max.

His father continued, "Jake loved to watch Randy test the cruisers on the lines. We would bring him up to the platform where he would connect the cruiser and do what we would call his *test flights*," he said with a proud smile.

Calvin then walked up to the locked gate at the base of the stairs that led to the platform above. He took out his keys and proceeded to unlock and open the gate. He stood in the gate and looked up the stairs to the platform that he and Jake had built.

"I haven't been here in almost a year. I remember the last time I was here with Randy," he said, "He was testing a module for his latest digital mapping for the cruiser, it was an amazing one. He called this version "Lightning.""

"Cool name," replied Aaron.

Calvin reached over to small locker inside the gate, flipped through the combination, opened the door and took out some blue hard hats that were stored there for the power company workers. He handed one to each person and shut the locker. They all put on their hard hats and started the walk up the stairs to the platform.

When they reached the platform and looked down, they could see how high they were in the air.

"This pylon stretches up to 185' feet, this platform we are now standing on is about 120' feet above the ground," said Calvin.

The pylon was a double pylon that had a set of power lines at 130 feet and the other set were located at 170 feet high. It was massive and amazing to be standing on the platform where his brother once stood with his invention, not to mention that the view from it was spectacular.

Calvin pointed to a small engraving on the pylon. "This marks the maiden voyage he took with "Sparky," he said.

"Sparky?" asked Roger.

"That was the name of his first cruiser." his father chuckled, "I know, pretty funny name, but it was a good invention and led him to his latest improved cruiser."

Calvin told them that if you were an electrician and worked mainly with electricity you were referred to as a "sparky". The name came about because if an electrical circuit was wired incorrectly or had any problems, the circuit always produced a shower of sparks when it would malfunction. Randy had created lots of sparks while inventing his cruisers, so the name stuck.

Roger was looking at the engraving and noticed a strange marking just below the inscription that caught his eye. It was the shape of an eagle with its wings outstretched and had two lightning bolts coming out from behind it diagonally upward. It was completely black and looked like it was burned into the metal like a hot branding iron had made the mark. He was reaching up to touch it when a loud sound startled him. He quickly spun back around with his heart racing, looked and saw that the sound was Aaron. He had tripped and fallen because his foot had caught the small edge of a lift in the center of the platform.

"Are you ok Aaron?" asked Calvin.

"Yeah," he mumbled as he was getting back to his feet. "What the heck is that thing that tripped me?" he asked.

Roger handed Aaron back his hard hat, it had fallen off and slid across the platform when Aaron face planted after tripping.

Calvin stepped over to him, "You tripped over the lift platform," he said. "It's the piece that the cruiser would rest on over there by Max," he pointed across the platform to where she was standing, "Right next to Max are the controls that engage the lift and it would raise the cruiser up to the cables so that it could be connected to them just ten feet or so above our heads," and pointed up above their heads to the spot where Randy would attach the cruiser to the cables.

Max turned to examine a small box mounted to a short pole. The box that Calvin pointed to had a latch on the side. She reached over and flipped the latch. Immediately a control panel and keyboard began to fold down from the panel.

"Hey this is pretty cool," said Max.

There were blinking lights, a bunch of buttons, switches and a small joystick controller. It looked like it was powering up as it came down into position. When it came to a rest a small click sounded from the panel and a mini screen instantly lit up and was displaying some information about the system.

Calvin stepped over to Max and was joined by Roger and Aaron. He began to show them what it did and how it operated. He used the control joystick to raise the lift and turn it around, back and forth. He demonstrated how it would lift up and how high it would go. He then hit a button on the panel that did the coolest thing Roger had ever seen. There was a sound of a flock of birds zooming over their heads. The area all around the platform was immediately covered with a type of camouflage. The entire platform that they stood on was completely encircled like they were in a tent.

"This was for privacy so that people would not be able to see us up here on the platform with the cruiser, or see us doing test launches or working up here," said Calvin.

Calvin pressed the button that retracted the camouflage covering and with a sound of a flock of birds, it had quickly folded up and disappeared.

Roger butted in front of his dad, "Let me drive the lift," and with a hum, the lift hydraulics began winding down and he controlled it back to its starting position.

Calvin reached over and hit a red button on the corner of the panel and the lights on it went dark. Then he closed the control panel back up and latched it shut.

"So what do you think?" Calvin asked with a big grin.

"This is so awesome dad!" replied Roger. "I know, this is so sweet," exclaimed Aaron while he stood looking around.

"I really love the view from up here," added Max.

"I'm glad you all approve," said Calvin. "Let's go back to the house so we can talk and I will give you a tour of the Lab."

"No way," squawked Aaron, his voice crackling like a chicken. "Sorry," came the crackling voice again, "My voice does that when I get excited."

Calvin laughed and then directed them all to the stairs so they could leave. They went down the stairs, returned their hard hats to the locker and Calvin locked the gate behind them as they filed out and stood by his motorcycle. Max picked up her longboard and they started the short hike over to the house. They heard Calvin fire up the motorcycle and he came zooming past them and hollered, "Meet you in the shop," as he drove through the field heading back to house.

"I can hardly wait to see this lab," Aaron said excitedly. "But I am even more excited to see that cool little flying robot named Servo you are hiding in your room!"

"Me too," echoed Max, as she moved along quickly walking toward the house with her two best friends.

Chapter 16

Gorgeous and the Lab

When they arrived back at the house after their short trek across the green field, they noticed a car parked in the driveway as they approached the house.

"Oh dear," said Aaron as he started to move about excitedly, "She's here, she's here." Max rolled her eyes as she turned to show Roger her disgust in the way Aaron was acting. *"Stop acting like a sissy school boy!"* demanded Max, *"Laura is not going to marry you or be your girlfriend!"*

Aaron continued to shake Rogers arm in excitement, "I don't care, she still is so gorgeous," said Aaron, "I can still dream about us, *so don't crush my dream!"* He barked back at Max.

"Fine, fine, go ahead," she said sarcastically as she stepped aside at the bottom of the stairs by the back door of the house. Then she motioned, after you, waiting for him to pass by heading up to see his *dream girl.* Max took the opportunity and gave him a hard punch in the arm as he bounced up the steps in front of her to see his love. But he didn't even respond or flinch to her dead arm punch, obviously because his heart was all fluttering in love and only Laura filled his head.

The three of them entered the kitchen, Max and Roger trailing behind Aaron. They saw that Calvin had arrived and had taken a seat at the table next to his wife Alicia. Across from them sat Laura with Jenny sitting glued to her arm with a huge beaming smile.

"Look who came to visit," exclaimed Jenny, pointing at Laura.

"Hey Laura," said Max and Roger as they approached the table and were pulling out chairs to have a seat.

Aaron stood next to Laura, eyes wide and flittering in love. He reached out taking her hand softly, giving a gentle kiss to the back of her hand and then letting go. *"Hello my love,"* Aaron said in slow voice with a huge smile.

Laura looked back at Aaron with big eyes, pretending to be in love and slowly leaned toward him. She took one of his hands and placed her other hand on his shoulder pulling him in next to her to sit by him. She leaned over to him and whispered in his ear in a seductive manner, *"Oh my Love where have you been?"*

Aaron's eyes widened in shock and he turned to face her. He thought to himself. "Is this it, no way, she loves me," his mind racing quickly with these new thoughts flooding into his head. She was actually starting to pucker her lips and lean into Aaron like she was going to kiss him. Aaron closed his eyes in surprise and he slowly leaned toward her for his dream kiss.

She then instantly and quickly shoved him off the side of the chair sending him tumbling to the kitchen floor. Laura started to laugh, *"not a chance kid',"* she said to Aaron over the laughter filling the kitchen.

Aaron, red faced and ignoring the laughter, picked himself up off the floor and looked back at Laura. With big wide eyes and a look of longing on his face plead to her, "One day my love, one day you will miss me and come running into these arms." And he held both arms out toward her as if waiting for big hug. They all began to laugh harder and louder at him and the way he was behaving.

"One day," he said, "You just need some time to let my love sink in." The laughter slowly came to an end, as Aaron took a seat at the kitchen counter.

Earlier, Roger's mother had set out a plate of cookies on the table in front of Laura and Jenny to snack on. Max and Roger sat at the table and began to help themselves to some of the delicious homemade oatmeal cookies.

"How long have you been here?" Roger asked Laura.

"About an hour," she answered.

Roger's mom leaned in to take a cookie from the plate, "Laura is going to be leaving us," she said in sad voice, looking over at Calvin.

"What do you mean leaving us?" Calvin asked Alicia.

Laura cut in to answer as Calvin now looked over at her, "I'm going back to school to finish what I started." She explained to Calvin that she was going to Illinois State in the next couple of weeks. She told him she was leaving early to settle in, get an apartment and find a part time job.

"We are all going to miss you very much," said Calvin as he reached over taking her hands in his from across the table. "Promise us you will stay in touch, we love you very much young lady," said Calvin in a loving voice.

"I will," replied Laura looking back at Calvin with a soft smile on her face. "I promise."

Alicia spoke up to break the silence that had filled the room after the announcement of bad news. "I wasn't expecting you until later," she said to Laura, "you're welcome to stay while I finish getting dinner ready."

"I really need to get going. I have so much to do before I leave, but thanks for the invite to dinner. I should have planned better before I came over. But I have other plans for later. I'm so sorry," replied Laura as she got up from the table.

"That's fine dear," replied Alicia.

They all stood to give her hugs before she left. There was a feeling of sadness in the kitchen now. One by one they all gave Laura a hug and when it came to Aarons turn, he stood there with his cheesy smile. He reached up straightening his glasses that always seemed to be crooked because he needed a new pair, then said to Laura, "Don't worry babe, we can make this long distance relationship last."

Laura rolled her eyes along with Jenny and Max and pulled away, not giving Aaron a hug or any verbal response to his comment. She then turned to walk out the door with the small group of them following her out and down the steps to her car.

"Call me if you need any help getting packed up sweetie," said Alicia to Laura as she was getting into her car.

"I will," said Laura. "You have been so good to me," she said smiling back up to Alicia, as she shut the door and started the car.

As the car rolled backward leaving the driveway, they all turned and walked back to the house, except for Aaron. He stood there watching his love drive away. Laura noticed that only Aaron stood watching her leave. She looked at him and smiled, then blew him a kiss from inside of her car. He pretended to reach for the kiss and caught it, then turned toward the house and held her kiss in his hands up against his heart with sadness. Then he turned around and walked into the house to join his friends.

As he came back into the kitchen he heard Roger's mom tell Jenny to set the table and that dinner was nearly ready. She had put a nice turkey in the oven for Sunday dinner earlier that day. Aaron had now just noticed the delicious smell of the turkey roasting in the oven as the aroma had filled the kitchen.

Roger's mom turned to face Max and Aaron, "Would you two like to stay and join us for dinner?" she asked.

"Of course we would and thank you for the invitation," said Max.

"Thanks Mrs. D," said Aaron. "You know I would, I just need to call the folks to tell them where I'm at." And he walked over to use the phone on the wall in the kitchen.

They all took their seats around the table. Calvin said grace and they all filled their plates and then began to fill their bellies. The meal was delicious, 'You are the best cook ever Mrs. D," said Aaron as he continued to fill his face with mashed potatoes.

"Thank you Aaron," replied Alicia.

"He's right mom, you are the best," said Jenny, quickly followed by Rogers comment, "Great meal mom."

"They are all correct dear," said Calvin, "you are a magician when it comes to cooking, you make the most delicious meals for us, we are all very grateful for you."

Alicia blushed as she thanked them for making her feel good and their gratitude toward her for the time she spent cooking meals for them all to enjoy. After dinner Jenny said she was tired and went to take a bath before bed. With her now absent, they were able to sit at the table and discuss the lab and the visit that Calvin had promised them earlier.

"Let's go see the lab?" whispered Aaron across the table to Calvin as he was chewing a delicious taste of pie.

Calvin glared at him as he held a finger up to his mouth, signaling Aaron to keep quiet and turned to motion with his head at his wife who was filling the dishwasher with dishes from dinner. Aaron saw this and quickly understood that Mrs. Dexter was not aware yet that he and Max knew about the lab.

Alicia came back to the table to get another handful of dishes and asked them all to help clear the table. They all quickly got up and proceeded to help clear the table of dishes. After the dishes were gone and placed in the dishwasher they all took seats around the table. Calvin looked over at his wife Alicia,

"Dear, I have something to tell you," he said slowly as if trying to find the words. "These three kids here are very special to us and I have shared something very special with them," said Calvin. Alicia put down the cup of tea she was sipping and looked at Calvin.

"What did you do Calvin?" she asked.

Calvin sat up, looking at his wife, "Well, Roger had already spilled the beans to them about the lab," he said, "And I just happened to stumble on them as they were approaching tower 460."

Alicia looked over at them shaking her head, as Calvin continued, "I gave them a tour of the tower and platform this afternoon." When he finished he prepared himself for the scolding that he thought he would receive from his wife, only she didn't get upset or angry with him at all. There were no verbal explosions of anger from her.

"It's my fault too, Calvin," she said. "I gave them some information about Randy and his death. I'm afraid I'm to blame for them starting to put the pieces together about Randy and our family. I was so tired of holding that secret in. I needed to talk to Roger about it, he was starting to ask questions and I wanted to him to know the truth." She explained. "Roger had found the silver box at your mother's house and I thought it was a clue to find Servo," she said with a smile.

"Yeah-" cut in Aaron, "I am dying to meet that little thing, go get it Roger!" he said.

"You will soon," said Roger with a smile, "But Jenny doesn't know any of this yet, we need to keep it secret ok?" he told them.

"OK," said Max and Aaron.

Then Aaron sat up and quickly began rubbing his hands together quickly, *"So, let's see this lab,"* he said with grin.

"As soon as Jenny goes to bed, we'll take a tour," said Calvin.

Mrs. Dexter replied, "That's right, so go and keep yourselves busy until she finishes her bath and goes to sleep."

The next hour was brutal for Aaron while they watched TV in the living room, he was dying to see the lab and the thought of playing with a flying mini robot was killing him. The three of them sat discussing the information they had learned the past two days and were debating their next move, which was to find the cruiser hidden at his grandmas house and taking it for a run. Roger had access to his brother's secret lab. And he knew that hidden inside were the directions for driving the cruiser and everything he needed to know for piloting it across the power cables. The three of them were discussing the destination of the first flight they wanted to take across town and to get familiar with the controls. Then discussed future trips to Las Vegas or Chicago. Anywhere could be their possible destination and their heads were racing with ideas.

Calvin came into the room, "It's time guys," he said and motioned for them to follow him.

They passed Mrs. Dexter in the kitchen, "Are you coming mom?" asked Roger.

"No, I need to be here in case Jenny wakes up. I wouldn't want her to panic if she couldn't find anyone here," she explained. "But have fun," she said and gave them a wink. "And remember you three, this is more than a secret and *NO one* can know about it," she said pointing sternly at the three of them.

"We got it Mrs. D," replied Aaron. "Me too," said Max.

"OK then," said Calvin and then pointed at Max and Aaron, "You two, follow me," and then pointed at Roger, "son, go to your room, get Servo and meet us in the shop."

"Got it," replied Roger and he turned and sprinted up the stairs, taking the steps two at a time, at the same time the others headed out the back door.

When Roger reached the top of the stairs and was almost to his room, he heard a humming noise coming from behind the closed door.

He looked down at the bottom of the door and he saw a dim light shine through the gap near the floor and then it was gone. He leaned against the door with his ear to listen for any clue about whom or what was inside his bedroom making the humming noise again. He reached down taking the door knob in his grip and slowly turned the handle to open the door. As he leaned against the door he slowly took a peek around the edge of the door into his room. Instantly two little bright headlights were right up in his face and he could hear the hum of Servos engines as she hovered there.

"Servo, how did you get out of my closet?" he asked. She zoomed quickly around his room, headlights shining and then quickly came back to a slow hover in front of his face looking at him. She just hovered rising slightly up and down in front of him, like a small puppy waiting for a tennis ball to be thrown so that she could zoom over and fetch it.

"Have you been waiting for me?" he asked her.

Servos headlight's looked up into his face and she then tilted up and down, like she was saying "Yes" nodding her whole body. Then she took off again and buzzed around the room twice before coming to stop above Roger's right shoulder. She looked like a parrot resting on his shoulder as he turned around to face the door. He went down the stairs, Servo hovering close, passing by his mother in the kitchen and out the back door heading toward the shop. When they passed by his mother in the kitchen, Roger thought he heard Servo make a small noise that sounded like she said "hello" to his mom. Servo dimmed her lights as she hovered while he trotted across the back yard into the shop to meet the others.

As Roger was going across the back yard to the shop he was briefly out in the open. He didn't see the dark black car parked across the street from his house. The very dark tinted windows were all closed except for the driver's side window. A man sat behind the steering wheel holding a pair of binoculars that were aimed directly at Roger and followed him and little Servo moving quickly across the yard to the shop where the door was now closing. The man watching them had a long scar above his left eye that was a few inches long. As the man sat in the car on his stakeout, he was smoking a partially burned cigarette hanging out of the corner of his mouth as he peered through the binoculars. The man slowly took the binoculars down and placed them on the seat next to him, took out his cigarette, flicking the ashes from it and picked up a cell phone. He dialed a number and placed the phone to his ear.

"It's me," he said in a very deep voice. "I can confirm that they have the key."

On the phone a woman's voice, with a deep Russian accent replied, "Cooper, are you sure?"

"Oh yeah, I am sure," he replied back to her, "I saw it flying around the boys bedroom and follow him across the backyard."

He paused, listening to the Russian woman's voice on the other end of the call, apparently giving him some instructions.

"OK, I got it" replied Cooper.

He lowered the cell phone, pressed the END button and tossed it over onto the seat next to him, right by the binoculars. He took a last drag on his cigarette, flicked the butt out of the window onto the road below, rolled up the window and started the engine to his car. The car pulled forward as the headlights came on, did a U turn and headed down the street, disappearing into the darkness of the night.

Chapter 17

The Eagle

A dark haired attractive woman, Natalia Ronavich came walking down a wide hallway and into a large elegant office. She looked around the room searching for her boss. She was dressed in a black business dress. Her ponytail swayed as she walked around the office and placed a few papers on a huge polished desk. She stopped by the windows looking out over the city skyline, taking in the view of the city lights. Her reflection was gleaming back at her in the window. She peered at herself and adjusted her dark eye makeup.

"Natalia, is that you?" came the deep voice of Roman Volkov from the adjacent room.

She turned around and walked over to a large door partially open on the side of the office from where she had entered. She pushed the door without stopping as she walked into the huge changing room. She continued through the large tile room toward a hot tub located in the center. A small set of stairs led up to the hot tub, surrounded by comfortable lounge chairs. A dark haired middle-aged man with a black and grayish goatee was leaning back, his head resting on a folded towel with his eyes closed. He held a glass half full of ice and Vodka in one hand as he sat soaking motionless in the hot tub with small trails of steam rising from the bubbles surrounding him. He heard the steps from Natalia's heels clicking as she approached.

"Yes, it is me Volkov," replied Natalia with her Russian accent. She came to a stop and took a seat on the edge of one of the lounge chairs, perched sitting straight up.

His voice also bore the Russian accent, "Natalia, do you have news for me?" he asked, sipping the Vodka.

"Volkov, we have found The Key," she replied.

He instantly opened both eyes and stood up in the center of the hot tub in his swim trunks.

"Where is it?" he asked anxiously, as he took another sip and put the glass down on the edge of the hot tub.

"I told you Volkov, we found it, I did not say we had it in our possession yet," Natalia replied.

Volkov scowled. "What am I paying you for if you don't have *The Key!*"

"We will have it very soon, I promise," she replied in an apologetic voice.

"I don't like this plan of yours Natalia. I have not liked it from the start. I have been waiting for *a year* for you to bring me that key."

She looked at Volkov standing there. He was slowly moving to the edge toward the steps to climb out of the large hot tub. But instead of walking up the stairs he began to hop on one leg as he held the hand rail. He was hopping up the steps because he only had one leg. His left leg was completely gone up to the middle of his thigh. Natalia watched him briefly struggle out of the hot tub and stand up fully to face her. He picked up his large white robe while balancing and put it on covering his body. He took a towel from a table next to him and began drying his face and hair.

"Volkov, I have told you before, we need to be patient and let the boy and his father figure out the devices," she said as she approached him around the hot tub. "We lost the last one when the older brother was blown up in his lab and my associate Cooper was injured. I need the young boy alive. He is part of the key to operating the system. My spy told me the dead boy Randy had something hidden that only his little brother would be able to use. The father is showing the young boy these things now. The more his father shares with him, the better it is for us when we take the boy."

She was standing next to Volkov as he sat down in a large padded chair and looked up at her. She got his drink from the edge of the tub and handed it to him. He took another sip, closed his eyes and leaned his head back resting in the chair.

"Be patient, you have waited this long for my plan to work, it is nearing completion," said Natalia.

"I trust you Natalia."

He put down his drink and wiped his head again with the towel that was wrapped around his shoulders. As he drew the towel away there was an emblem on the left side of the robe near his chest. It was an eagle with two lightning bolts coming up from each side.

Volkov sat up and took off his robe and laid it down on the chair behind him. He continued to towel himself off. After he was completely dry he reached over to a small silver box on the table next to him and lifted the lid. A soft blue glow of energy could be seen inside the box as he reached inside taking out a small device that had a strap attached to it. He wrapped the strap of the device around the thigh of his missing leg, just above where his leg had been removed. After he secured the strap he stood up fully on his one leg, stretching out his back taking in a deep breath. He then reached down and pressed a button on the small cell phone sized device. Instantly a small amount of energy trickled down to the floor from the device strapped to his thigh. The green and blue energy field appeared to be dripping a watery substance. It continued to grow making small sounds of crackling and buzzing. His face cringed momentarily as the energy began taking the form of a leg. It quickly sprouted a foot and then five toes, resting firmly on the ground supporting him. Volkov now stood on two feet like a whole man. This new energy leg supported him fully and worked just like a normal flesh leg as he took a few steps and retuned back to the table where he shut the lid of the box that held the device. He did a little dance-like move with his new and fully operational electric leg.

"How is the device working for you now?" questioned Natalia.

"It is working very well," he said, as he danced over to the bar and took another glass, added some ice and poured some vodka for Natalia. He picked up his glass and danced back over to Natalia, handing her the drink he just made. He held out his glass as she stood up and they chinked their glasses together. "Cheers to your plan," he said with a smile taking a drink. She followed and took a small sip from her glass.

"My people tell me there has been activity again at the pylon tower. It won't be long now," she said.

"Good," smiled Volkov, then took another long drink from his glass.

"Now if you will excuse me, I have some work to do," said Natalia as she put her glass down and turned to leave.

"Thanks for coming to me personally to deliver the news," replied Volkov.

"You're welcome," she replied as she left the room.

Volkov took another drink, finishing his vodka and placed the glass on the table. Then he danced over to a door that led to another room in his penthouse, a little zip now in his step as he left the room closing the door behind him.

Chapter 18

Fits like a glove

Roger turned around after he pulled the shop door closed and saw his dad closing the lid to the record player. It contained the jamming device that was blocking the hidden microphone that had been placed in their shop. Aaron was staring at Roger in amazement but his eyes were focused on Servo hovering over his shoulder like a parrot. He approached Roger to get a closer look at the little flying robot. As he drew closer to Servo, her headlights turned bright, shinning into Aarons face. She appeared to be scared of him as her defense mechanism kicked in, the bright lights shining at him as a possible threat.

Aaron was shielding his eyes with his hands as if he was outside in the bright sunlight trying to see around the blinding light. "Argh, those are some bright little high beams she has."

Roger turned his head and looked at Servo hovering over his shoulder. She appeared to be shaking like she was nervous. It was interesting to see her little personality. The fact she was scared by Aaron was intriguing to him.

"Hey girl, it's ok, Aaron is a good guy," Roger said to Servo in a soft voice.

She looked over at Roger blinding him with her high beams, back at Aaron, made a little beep as if she was saying, 'OK' and her headlights dimmed back to a soft glow.

"That's better," said Aaron rubbing his eyes, "So you have your own personal bodyguard now?"

"I guess so," Roger replied. "She seems to like me."

"*Wow, she is so cool*," said Aaron as he stood close to her, taking in every small detail of the little robot as it hovered next to Roger.

As Aaron slowly reached up to touch her, she lurched instantly at his finger. A little arm quickly popped out of her side and a spark zapped him.

"Aahh!" screamed Aaron and he leaped backward away from her. "She bit me!" he said in a high pitched voice, putting his finger into his mouth for comfort.

"You're such a little baby," laughed Max as she approached Servo, pushing Aaron to the side. "She barely got you." She had been watching the interaction between Servo and Aaron from a short distance away. Max approached Servo and held out her hand, "Come here little girl," she said in a motherly soft voice to Servo.

Instantly Servo zoomed over to Max, circled her head twice in excitement then pressed her tiny robot body up under Max's chin giving a little hum. It was a cute little robot type of hug she was giving Max. She turned to face Aaron, Servo still clinging to her neck in a long hug making a purring noise like a baby kitten.

"We girls know how to get along," she said sarcastically, smirking at Aaron.

"Girls!" said Aaron, shaking his head left to right.

Servo let go of Max and slowly approached Aaron with headlights glaring at him, her headlights tilted inward, looking mad. She made a high pitch short beep and zoomed at Aaron a few inches in a fast burst of movement. This sudden start and stop made her look like she was preparing to charge him again.

"Aahhh!" Aaron screamed again and jumped back taking shelter behind Calvin who was bursting with laughter.

Calvin stood between Servo and Aaron, "OK, OK you two, let's just get along." He turned to Roger, "I can't believe I'm trying to parent a robot," he said shaking his head.

Servo quickly obeyed Calvin and returned to Roger, hovering over his shoulder at what was quickly becoming her normal spot. The funny thing about this scene was that you would have sworn Servo was staring over at Aaron as if she had a beef with him about something and was giving him the stink eye.

Max, Roger and Aaron turned around after they heard a locker door being opened from the back corner of the shop. Calvin had opened the locker and pulled up on the hook next to the garden tools that hung in the cabinet. It was the secret lock to open the door to the hidden lab. Calvin pushed the door open and stepped back.

"This is it," he said to Aaron and Max, "The secret lab we told you about."

Max and Aarons eyes lit up as they approached the secret door and let Roger take the lead into the dark door way. As soon as Roger entered the doorway into the darkness, two tiny headlights brightly shone from above his shoulder. Servo was lighting the way as they all walked down the stairs into the lab. When they reached the bottom of the steps Servo zoomed over to the wall. Her tiny arms were now protruding from her sides and she reached over with her tiny little hand and turned on the lights to the lab.

Instantly the lab was fully lit. Max and Aaron were turning a slow circle, taking in the entire lab, their mouths hanging open in amazement.

"This place is amazing," uttered Aaron as he came to a stop, facing the table with Randy's first cruiser sitting in pieces.

"I know," drawled Roger. "I know."

"What's with all these monitors?" asked Max.

She was standing in front of the wall that had nine large flat screen monitors arranged in a giant square. They were all turned off as she looked at them. As she stood there she noticed a little shelf like area to the side of the monitors that had different types of computer ports and connectors on it.

Roger came over and stood next to Max looking up at the monitors. She turned to see him standing next to her and saw little Servo hovering in her new claimed territory above his shoulder, two little headlight eyes staring back at her.

As she was looking at Servo, she noticed the tiny light eyes staring back at her and then Servo's eyes lifted up looking over her shoulder behind her at the monitors on the walls. A small noise came from Servo that sounded like she said the word "Ohh."

This sound got the attention of Roger and Max, they both looked at her as she slowly rose into the air a few feet and then moved toward the wall of monitors. Her little headlights turned and scanned across the small shelf that was located on the side of the monitors, with a little burst of movement she started to slowly move forward toward the shelf.

"Dad!" said Roger. His father and Aaron turned to see why Roger called.

They all stood there watching little Servo moving toward the shelf, it was like something was pulling her toward it. As she drew closer, now in a slow hover, a few blue lights appeared near the front of the shelf and small section opened up. It was like a mini landing pad for Servo. At the same time a small drawer opened up on the bottom of the shelf revealing a black glove.

Servo turned around in midair, facing the room, her lights softly shining on the four of them staring at her in amazement and watching what was happening. She then turned and slowly lowered onto the landing pad.

Her headlights went out and she powered herself down to recharge.

"What is-" Roger was cut off instantly as the wall of monitors turned on and began to get brighter as they came to life in front of them.

A large symbol was now showing on the screen, it was an eagle in great detail. The symbol of the eagle stretched across all of the screens and was very large. The wings were outstretched and the eagle image had two purplish lightning bolts that came up from behind it, both heading different directions.

"I have seen this symbol before," whispered Roger.

"I know, it was on the platform this afternoon, engraved on pylon 460," said his father.

"What does it mean?" Max asked Calvin.

"I'm not sure," he replied.

Then he stepped up to the little drawer that had opened under Servo's shelf and cautiously looked inside at the black glove. Roger approached him and also peered in the drawer with Max and Aaron behind them standing on their tip toes trying to get a peek.

Calvin reached in and took out the glove, then walked over and sat the glove down on a workbench. The other three joined him, all staring at the glove. It was encased in a hard plastic like material and had a small type of display screen that was built into the back of it. It had an area past the wrist that was longer than a normal glove and extended all the way to the elbow of the person who would wear it. There were numerous buttons all around the sides and below the display on the back, was a tiny glowing keyboard.

Aaron stepped forward, reached down and picked up the glove and began to put it on his hand. As soon as he put on the glove and started to wiggle the fingers, across the room Servo's eyes quickly opened up and small red light came out on the top of her head. The red light was flashing like a police siren and made a small alarm noise.

"Take it off Aaron, quick!" said Calvin.

A voice sounded from the glove that was a mix between a computer and a woman's voice. It loudly announced, *"ACCESS DENIED!"*

Instantly, a shower of sparks emitted from the glove as Aaron was ejected from it. The glove fell to the ground and he was knocked backwards across the lab a few feet.

"Aahhh!" came the familiar sound of Aarons scream as he crashed to the floor knocking over a couple of stools.

He got up, his hair emitting small puffs of smoke from the ends with burnt pieces that were standing straight up from the electrical surge that had just gone through his body.

"What is wrong with your brother, Roger?" he asked, trying to catch his breath and running a hand over his burnt hair, trying to get it to lie back down. "He loves to shock me with his stuff. He is dead and still pranking me."

Max and Roger were laughing at the scene they had just witnessed of Aaron getting shocked yet again by Servo.

"I told you to take it off," chuckled Calvin to Aaron as he patted him on the shoulder.

"The control glove has biological sensors built into the finger tips, so only people with access are allowed to wear it," explained Calvin.

He was sliding the glove on his hand as he turned to talk with the three of them, looking curiously at the glove. "This is the main controller and key for the computer system on the cruiser. It can't fly without it, but looks a bit different from when I last saw it. It looks like

Randy may have made some changes to it," he said as he scanned over it.

As soon as he had the glove on and adjusted for a good fit, the familiar computer woman's voice sounded again, only this time *"Identity confirmed"* and lights started blinking on the glove as the system powering the glove started to come alive. The small screen lit up, showing the same symbol that was showing on the wall of monitors, the eagle with the two lightning bolts, only it was a lot smaller because it was being displayed on the four inch screen located on the back of the glove. Words started scrolling by as the operating system was quickly loaded. The keyboard had lit up dimly and the small lights that were flashing on the back of the glove all turned green, signaling the system had finished starting and was online ready to go.

Roger's dad wiggled his fingers and slowly waved the glove back and forth,

"Ah," he said drawing a breath, "still fits like a glove-." And he held it up still wiggling the fingers as he smiled at the three faces looking at him.

"Oh man, that was cheesy Dad," laughed Roger and Max.

Calvin smiled, "Get it, the glove fits like a glove." Roger rolled his eyes back at him.

"OK, follow me, let me see if I remember how to use this thing," and he walked over to stand in front of the monitors on the wall, looking up at them. The monitors turned a light blue color, flickered and the words Cruiser 5.0 appeared on the center of the giant screen. As they stood there looking at the wall of monitors, the eagle symbol slowly faded and was replaced instantly by a logon screen. It was waiting for a username and password for verification. Calvin held the glove up in front of his face hand outstretched. A small wave of light shone across his face and appeared to be scanning it. Calvin spoke out of the side of his mouth as they stared at him,

"Security measures, its scanning my retinas for confirmation," he explained as he tried not to move his mouth while speaking.

The light disappeared and the monitors flashed the words "ID Confirmed," then a soft woman's voice came from the glove, "Hello Cal, how are you doing today?"

"I'm doing good Tory," replied Calvin.

"*I don't think so*," replied the voice. "I just scanned your vital information and you apparently have not cut back on your cholesterol intake, plus your blood pressure is a little high." Tory sounded like she was scolding him.

Calvin rolled his eyes as he turned to face the group, "I never did like that feature Randy installed in the glove," he went on to explain, "Randy added the medical check software to work with the glove. After the glove verifies your ID with your fingertips, it scans your vital information and tracks your heart rate, blood pressure and numerous other pieces of medical data of the current user. It keeps track of your health history and your condition while you wear it in the cruiser and travel on the lines. Your medical condition could be tracked to see how your body would react to the cruiser at high speeds and turns during your line travel mission." Then he continued, "I always hate being told I eat too much junk food by a computer."

He turned back to the monitors, "Never mind that Tory, can you please pull up the power grid?" he asked.

"I would love to sweetheart," replied Tory and the screens changed to a large map of the city of Belford.

"Hey dad, does mom know about your girlfriend Tory?" asked Roger snickering.

His dad turned to him smiling and then his face went to a stern fatherly glare, signaling Roger to zip his mouth and keep quiet. Rogers smile immediately left his face and he was instantly quiet as Aaron stepped up next to him staring at the giant map.

Aaron turned to Calvin, "So sweetie, what are we looking at?" as he burst out laughing, causing Max and Roger to join him.

"OK, OK, that's enough." said Calvin, but the three of them continued to laugh a few moments longer and then went silent as Calvin glared at all of them.

"Are you finished?" asked Calvin sternly. They all answered with a soft "Yes, sorry," and then Aaron couldn't help himself and softly added, "Sorry, sweetie," and emitted soft sounds of laughter with his mouth closed, snorting through his nose trying to hold in his laugh, attempting to get Max or Roger to join in again.

Aaron wasn't looking at Calvin, who had just lowered the glove and was aiming it at his rear end. Instantly, a small lightning bolt shot out from one of the fingers, zapping Aaron on the left butt cheek.

"Aahhh," blurted Aaron with a jump, both hands now clasping his butt cheeks.

"Do I have your attention now, *Sweetie?*" asked Calvin.

Aaron turned, quickly apologizing for his comments and stood there with full attention on Calvin and the monitors.

"What you are looking at is a grid map of our entire city and surrounding areas," said Calvin, as he typed on the small keyboard on the back of the glove. Instantly on the map all of the electrical pylons appeared. They saw the river and the hydroelectric dam with the trail of power lines from it leading all over the map. More detail was appearing as Calvin continued to type on the glove. Pylon 460 appeared to be highlighted on the map. This was the large power pylon in their back yard.

"You can see that this map shows all of the large pylons as well as every power line that is connected to any power pole. If you look you can see the power lines that are actually buried," and he pointed to the map and showed them how to tell the difference between power lines that were buried and power lines that were connected to power poles. Buried lines were dotted lines colored blue and overhead lines were solid red. He showed them the locations where the power cables would transition into the ground from aerial to burial cable.

"These are dangerous areas, because they transition underground. You will get pretty messed up if you tried to go down underground obviously." He explained, "Randy was working on a way to make the transition to be able to travel underground."

"What, No way!" They blurted out. "How can you go underground without getting killed?" snapped Aaron.

"Yeah dad, how the heck can you do that?" questioned Roger.

"Listen, Listen," hushed Calvin as he quieted them down. "Just let me explain ok."

The three were quiet as he pressed a few keys on the glove. A highlighted route lit up on the screen, it started at pylon 460 and stretched up north to the edge of town where it stopped at a location Roger could tell was the hydroelectric dam.

"This is the last route that Randy took the day before he was killed. His flight started from the lab at Bell Grove University and he went to Canyon Lake Dam up north about 50 miles and then returned."

Tory announced, "Randy was testing his latest software updates, the file is called "Cruiser 5.0." She took over the monitors and was now displaying a list of files. They all looked up at the list and one file folder name in particular stood out to Roger, '*Test Flight Videos.*'

Roger pointed up and anxiously tapped on the screen pointing on the folder, "Dad, open that one," as he was pointing to it.

Calvin spoke, "Tory, open the folder '*Test Flight Videos.*'

The folder opened and now displayed numerous files, all video files with different numbers.

Roger spoke out loud, "Tory, please play the file number two hundred-twelve."

The woman's voice announced, "Voice print not recognized," and continued "Please confirm Identity."

Then the glove made a beep and Servo zoomed over to Roger looking at his face. Her lights quickly scanned his face and retinas, then Tory announced, "ID confirmed," and the file opened, the contents displaying on the monitors.

"How the heck did she know my ID?" asked Roger.

As Roger's dad started to answer him, "I don't know-, "he was cut off by Tory.

"Randy added user 'Roger Roy Dexter', on May 9th. He performed your retina scanning to create your user account while you were sleeping." said Tory.

"Your brother was a sneaky one," said Max.

"*If only you knew*," replied Roger.

Chapter 19

Cruiser 5.0

The sound of Randy's voice caught everyone's attention and they looked up at the monitors to see Randy standing on platform 460. He was standing next to the lift that was used to raise his cruisers to the power cables. He was wearing a cool looking flight suit with black gloves. On one of his hands, he had on a similar glove as the one Calvin was wearing. The suit Randy was dressed in looked like a streamlined astronaut's suit, sleek and light.

Resting next to him on the platform lift, sat something they didn't recognize. It didn't look like the cruiser that they all had seen sitting on his work bench in his lab that was now sitting in pieces. Randy stood next to the strange looking object. It looked like a large white football. The numbers GX-460 were painted in black letters on the side of it as it sat resting on the platform lift.

The video was being filmed by something hovering in front of Randy and moved around him with a smooth flow.

"Servo, zoom in on this right here," said Randy, as he pointed at the device.

"Servo is doing the filming for him," whispered Aaron.

At the sound of her name, Servo's headlights came on in a soft glow as she sat next to all of them in the docking station facing them.

Randy continued, "This part of my new cruiser is the most advanced of any hardware on the planet," and he pointed at the football looking device as Servo zoomed in closer showing what looked like a white egg resting on top of the device. It was labeled UGM1.

Randy continued, "This is the underground module version 1. This is my first test flight with it. This module will allow me to transition as I travel above ground, to be able to travel on a power cable as it goes down underground. It will allow the cruiser to transform and protect the pilots as they make the transition underground. It forms a protective shell around the pilot as it performs a molecular realignment of the pilot's body into fine matter. It alters the cruiser and the pilot's physical mass which converts them into tiny particles of contained matter, allowing them to pass through the smallest of spaces, spaces so small they are practically thin as air. The pilot has to be wearing this," and he pointed to himself as Servo zoomed in on him. He was pointing to his special flight suit. "This has to be on the body while you are inside this new model cruiser."

Servo filmed Randy standing there, looking buff in his tight suit and zoomed in and slowly began panning from his feet up to his head to show the helmet that he held under his arm. The camera then panned over the football shape and the small egg shaped device on top.

"My newest Cruiser 5.0 is created by pure energy. When activated, there is a protective force field that will encircle the pilots and protect them at the same time with the new module transforming them and protecting them. It is a powerful force field of energy that the pilots are surrounded by and control from inside the cruiser," described Randy.

Servo then backed up from Randy as he raised his helmet up and put it on his head. With a small click, the helmet was now secure. A small green display flashed and was showing across the inside of the face mask of the helmet on the lower right side.

Randy's voice was a little muffled while he continued to talk inside the helmet.

"This is my heads up display," as he pointed at his face on the screen on the lower right. "This is a digital display of the cruisers systems status and controls. It is more advanced than military fighter jets and allows me to control the cruiser with my eyes and voice to get an instant status of the systems without having to look down at the flight controls."

Randy lifted up his right gloved hand, the glove with all of the controls and pressed a few buttons and typed on the keyboard. He walked over, climbed up on the lift that Servo had raised up a few feet for him. He stood there above the small football device resting below him on the lift. A low hum came from the cruiser and small ball of lightning now appeared in the center of the white football shape that was resting on the platform. The ball of power started to grow larger. It looked like a miniature lightning storm of red and blue bolts of energy as the ball grew larger. With a sudden crack, there was a flash of light and a huge ball of glowing energy was sitting before them resting on the platform, with Randy now sitting in a pilot's seat inside of the sphere shaped ball. The cruiser had transformed into large oval shape of glowing power. The edges glowed and rippled like the surface of a lake and looked like smooth rippling water. Every few seconds little sparks were emitted from the water-like-surface similar to a small Fourth of July sparkler, spitting off sparks. A very low hum was coming from the cruiser as it hovered on the platform with Randy sitting comfortably inside on one of the four seats that were available. He was sitting in the left seat and could be seen pulling on his five point seatbelt harness.

"I always hate that part of the power up sequence." Randy said," It makes your stomach a little queasy when the flight suit connects and links the bio data to the cruiser systems. It makes me queasier still when the UGM1 comes online. That transformation always seems to make me sick. I have found, however, that the best way to counter its effects are to drink a soda loaded with caffeine before I fly," and he pointed over to the control panel on the platform that operated the lift. Servo panned over with the camera to show a Mountain Dew soda can resting on the panel.

Roger looked over at his dad, "Did you ever go for a flight in that cruiser?" he asked.

"Yes son, I went a few times in that model. But I never went with the UGMI model underground. Randy had told me he was working on the latest version of it and that it would be amazing. He was going to show it to me, but had the accident before I could see it."

His dad continued on, "I have his older 4.0 model hidden at Grandmas house. I will show you that one at a later time."

They heard Randy's voice continue on with his video segment about the Cruiser 5.0, "Servo, come on and take a seat."

The video shifted to a different angle and it appeared to be coming from another camera that was stationed on the tower. It was being shot from a stationary camera that was filming and was showing Servo as she circled around the cruiser a few times scanning over its surface.

"She does a preflight check before each flight," explained Randy, "She checks everything over in fine detail, searching for any flaws and records the sphere for my analysis. I review the video back in the lab after the flight."

Servo then flew up to the top of the sphere and slowly docked with the UGM1 module. As she docked with it, a small shimmer of energy slowly encompassed her until she was blanketed by it. A small circular opening appeared at the top of the larger sphere that Randy was seated in. Servo was in the module she had docked with and was lowering slowly down into Randy's sphere through the opening. She then came to a rest in her smaller sphere right on top of the flight controls inside of the larger sphere.

As soon as she docked and made contact with the module she was now resting in, more sounds of deep humming were heard and the whole sphere now turned to a transparent ball of energy. It was difficult to see Randy and Servo inside of the sphere, they were slowly disappearing and getting harder to see in the small ripples of energy as they appeared to fade away.

"The Cruiser 5.0 is now fully armed and ready for travel," said Randy from inside the now invisible sphere of energy.

"Let's take the Eastern route today Servo," said Randy.

Servo responded with a couple of small beeps and you could hear her saying "Chicago," before she slowly began to increase the power in the sphere. The energy noise began increasing higher and higher as the power increased.

The video segment changed to a view being recorded from inside of the cruiser so you could see Randy and Servo.

"Punch it girl!" said Randy. The sphere blasted away at the speed of a bullet, leaving behind a flash of sparks as it sped down the power lines.

Inside of the sphere Randy was holding a joystick control with his left hand and pressing buttons with his right hand on the flight control panel. One display showed a scrolling GPS map and the route he was traveling. A second display was showing the power line grid giving his current location. The grid map showed upcoming pylons, the cable routes and where they branched off to other nearby cities and destinations. The grid looked like a spider web of lines practically everywhere.

"You can go anywhere you want in the country," said Randy. "I love to go to Chicago, I want to show you something special," he said.

The control panel showed the power levels and other digital readings that no one but Calvin could understand, except for a speed odometer that they could see was displaying "105". They understood it to mean, one hundred five miles per hour.

"We are really moving now, Servo," Randy was heard saying. Then he went on to describe the flight controls and the colorful displays on the flight dash, giving a thorough overview of how this cruiser operated. "There are some pilot operating manuals I have made that are hidden in the lockbox in the lab. They describe everything I am showing and telling you and contain a special chapter on navigation. In fact, I made a small simulator program and have it installed inside of Servo, so you can hook up a game controller to her and drive the simulator for practice on a TV somewhere in private. It is a good training tool for a pilot that wants to learn to fly this thing."

As the cruiser raced down the lines you could see a blur of trees and towns as they raced above them. The sun was setting and darkness could be seen creeping across the sky. It was a bit overwhelming to see and hear his brother again. Roger glanced over at his dad. He was staring at Randy with a longing face, a few small tears appearing, rolling down his cheeks. Roger knew his father felt the same way he did, seeing his brother in the video again. They both missed him terribly. Roger reached over taking hold of his father's hand. His father felt his grasp and looked down to see Roger looking up at him also with teary eyes. With a side hug they both leaned into each other and continued to watch Randy on the screen as he cruised through Iowa.

"OK, here is the area I wanted to test." He approached an area where the power lines transitioned underground. On the computer map, blue dotted lines appeared up ahead a short distance away and he began slowing down. "Servo, activate UGMI," said Randy. He let out a moan mumbling "This gets my stomach cramped," as the sphere shrank in size. The sphere quickly collapsed into a thin long mass with Randy and Servo still inside as it stretched and wrapped around the power line. The sphere, in its new compact form, followed the power lines underground. "It appears to be working perfectly," said Randy. The next few moments the sphere traveled underground and then emerged, traveling back above ground and up onto the high wires of the towers. When it reached the towers, it picked up speed again and followed the power lines as they stretched over a large canyon. "The cruiser transition went perfectly," said Randy. Then he had Servo deactivate the UGMI and the cruiser 5.0 transformed instantly back to its regular size and shape.

"Well Servo, we can check that one off our list now," laughed Randy. "Let's slow down a bit," and the cruiser slowed down as they began to approach an enormous city in the distance. It was very bright with lights and the skyline as tall buildings glowed in the darkness like giant beacons. It was downtown Chicago and they were slowly approaching it. Randy reached down pressed some buttons on the control panel and the map of power lines zoomed in on their current position. The destination showed a large letter "C" on the map.

"No way," said Roger, "he's not going there, no way!"

Max asked, "Where are you talking about?"

Randy's voice echoed "Servo, take us to the far light tower at the stadium."

The cruiser was making turns and banks as it glided along the power lines of downtown Chicago. Roger knew where his brother was headed. He was going to stop at the Chicago Cubs baseball stadium, the home of their favorite baseball team.

From inside of the cruiser you could see the stadium lights glowing in the distance. There was a baseball game going on at that moment. The cruiser arrived at the stadium on the light tower he mentioned and came to stop. The video segment flashed and was being shown from Servo's camera again. She hovered around outside of the parked cruiser. Her video showed the cruiser as the power sphere was collapsing into a smaller ball. Quickly the ball of energy deceased until the small football shaped sphere sat powered down back in form, resting on the ground.

Randy was sitting on the top of the Chicago Cubs baseball stadium at the base of a giant light tower that was supporting the high towering wall of lights. They were shinning down on the baseball game below. Servo came to rest by Randy as he unfolded a chair that was stashed on the roof top by the light tower. He had obviously been here before. He had stashed the chair in an earlier visit along with a jacket in a small backpack. Randy reached over and put on his team jacket, proudly displaying the "C" for Cubbies and he took a seat in his chair. The view was spectacular from way up where he sat watching the game below. Servo quietly rested next to him videotaping him as he relaxed. He looked down at the scoreboard below checking the score. Sadly he discovered the Cubbies behind by 3 runs in the 7th inning. "There is still time to come back, they have done it before Servo," he said, looking at the camera. "This is one of the benefits of line travel,' he said with a smile. "I'm going to head downstairs, get a hot dog and soda then come back to enjoy the rest of the game."

The video screen went dark and the symbol of the eagle with lightning bolts appeared on the screen.

"No way, that is so cool," exclaimed Aaron. "I know, "said Max, "that is so amazing."

"That explains how he always had new "Cubs" memorabilia in his room all of the time," said Calvin.

Roger laughed at his dads comment.

"He was so cool," said Roger as he smiled at his dad. "I wish he would have taken me there."

"I know," laughed his father. "He never took me and I was his dad!"

Calvin began to pace the floor, he reached down to the glove he was still wearing, pressed some buttons and spoke, "Tory, where did Randy hide Cruiser 5.0?"

Tory answered, "In the lockbox sweetie."

"And where is the lock box?" asked Calvin.

The sound of gears turning and clinking behind them made the group jump and turn. They quickly scanned the back of the lab to see where the noise was coming from. They saw an old water cooler rising up, being lifted into the air. It was resting on an odd box that was beneath it. Calvin walked over to the lock box and opened a latch on the side and pulled it open. Inside was a very large suitcase that appeared to be from the 1950's. Roger walked over, picked up the suitcase, brought it over and placed it on one of the lab workbenches. With two clicks he opened the suitcase to view the contents hidden inside. The others gathered around him as he lifted the case open. Inside were two helmets along with two flight suits and the pilot manuals that Randy had spoken about, along with a couple of smaller boxes.

"Where is the cruiser?" asked Aaron.

Roger took out all of the contents of the suitcase and placed them on the workbench.

"It's not here Dad," said Roger.

"Take a closer look son."

"Dad, it's not here," he said as he held the suitcase upside down and began to shake it, hoping for something to appear or to fall out.

"Come on you three, it's right there," he said.

Roger's dad looked amused at the expressions on the faces of the three perplexed teenagers. "Look, it is right over there," he said still smiling and pointed at the water cooler that lifted up when the secret pod came rising up from the floor.

They all looked at it and it now made sense. The water cooler was in fact, not a water cooler at all. The top of the cooler was disguised to look like a full water bottle. Inside of it sat the football shaped cruiser that they were looking for. The bottle only appeared to be full of water, but was really empty on the inside and had only the illusion of a shimmering full bottle of water on the outside.

Max reached over and lifted the bottle off of the base. She examined the top and found the latch to open the bottle, which she did and removed the fake top cover. She removed the sphere and carried it over to the workbench and sat it down, the rest of them looking at it. The words GX-460 in chipped paint stretched across the side of the football looking sphere.

Calvin approached the sphere and examined it closely.

"Where is the UGM1 adapter, the one Servo docks with to enable underground travel?" he uttered to himself.

Roger heard his comment and then wondered the same thing. "I'm curious too, where did he hide it?"

"Tory," sounded Calvin's deep voice, "where is the underground module for the cruiser?

Tory responded, "In the lockbox sweetie."

"WHO ARE YOU CALLING SWEETIE?" sounded another woman's voice loudly. This caused them all to jump and look toward the stairs. Alicia stood there at the bottom of the stairs laughing at how she had just scared them all so badly.

"Calvin," she said, as she stared at Roger's dad, both hands on her hips with a stern look. "Who is calling you sweetie?" she demanded, but it was obvious she didn't really care, she was just having fun messing with Calvin, making him squirm after another women was talking fresh with him.

Calvin stammered for words, "Dear, Sweetheart," he cried, "Listen, it's not what you think." Her stern look crept into a smile and then a laugh. "I know who it is dear."

"Hello Tory, how are you doing tonight," Alicia asked the computer.

"I am doing well Mrs. Dexter." It is so nice to see you again," Tory replied.

"Mom, you startled me," said Roger.

"Sorry Son, I couldn't help it. I heard Tory talking to dad so I wanted to scare him." Alicia turned to face Calvin, "I was wondering what you all were up to, so I came to see for myself."

Calvin told Alicia everything they had been doing and learned the past couple of hours and showed her the new cruiser.

"We need to find one more piece," said Calvin, "The UGM1 module that attaches to the top of the cruiser for Servo to dock with."

He then showed her the video segment that showed the module and what it looked like. She immediately burst into tears when she saw her dead son Randy and heard him talking to the camera.

After she had calmed down and wiped the tears from her eyes, Calvin again asked Tory where the UGMI module was and Tory again replied that is was in the lockbox.

They looked and searched the lockbox under the cooler again. "There it is." said Max and she reached into the box and took out the module. The module had fallen out of the suitcase somehow and was resting at the bottom of the box in a dark corner.

All of the pieces of the cruiser now rested on the workbench in front of them. The flight suits, helmets, cruiser, module and a black flight glove. One other glove was still on Calvin's hand.

"Well" said Calvin, "Let's take this thing for ride. Who's first?" he asked.

"Calvin Dexter!" scolded Mrs. Dexter. "It is way too late to take them out for a joyride. It is nearly midnight! Luckily, I was in the house and spoke with Aaron's mother when she called around 10:00 asking if Aaron was still here. She hadn't heard from him since he asked to stay for dinner. I told her he was helping *you* and Roger in the shop and that I was sorry that we hadn't noticed the time. So I asked her if he could spend the night. She wasn't too happy with him sleeping over on a school night, but agreed to let him stay. So I think it is best to get them to bed right away."

Alicia turned to Max, "Maxine, I spoke with Mrs. Jenkins and told her you were going to be home late and that there was no need to wait up for you because *Calvin* would take you home."

Both Max and Aaron told her thanks and apologized that they had completely forgotten to call home.

Alicia turned to the three frowning faces and pointed to the stairs. "Bed time," she said as she pointed to the stairs leading out of the lab.

Grumpily, the three stomped up the stairs in disappointment followed by Calvin. He left Servo resting on the docking platform station next to the monitors and told her to "stay" until tomorrow. Servo looked at him and made a small "Beep," that he understood to be "OK."

Calvin put the control glove on the shop table by the cruiser pod and walked to the stairs to close up the lab and turned off the lights. He noticed the glow of the monitors that were still left on.

"Tory," he called, "Please power down the system."

"Anything for you darling," replied Tory, as the monitors turned off. He rolled his eyes at her flirting comments as he left the lab heading up the stairs. When he was in the shop he disabled the jamming device and locked the shop doors for the night.

Calvin walked Max to her house. She lived across the street and down a short distance. It was cool outside and very late. As he was returning home he looked over the valley behind their house. The moon was full and he could see some storm clouds in the distance. Flashes of lightning briefly illuminated the night in the distance as a storm slowly rolled in. He came up the driveway to the rear of the house and walked up the back steps and into the kitchen. His wife was sitting at the table sipping a cup of hot tea. She had just put the boys to bed and they had looked exhausted.

"Have a seat dear," said Alicia and she motioned to Calvin to sit. He took a seat at the table as she poured some hot water over a tea bag into a mug for his nightly tea.

"Thanks honey," he said as he took the spoon and stirred his tea bag in the mug, poking it a few times. He took a small sip, testing the temperature of the hot beverage.

"Aahhh, that is perfect," he said as he sat back comfortably in his chair. "So what do you think about us spilling the beans to our three musketeers?" he asked his wife.

"I think it is great to finally let someone know what is going on. No matter how young they might be," she replied. "I am excited and scared at the same time for them. I think they can learn so much from Randy and what he was trying to do for our family and for our community," she commented as she added a spoon of sugar to her tea.

Calvin took another sip of tea, then added, "I know, I feel the same way about it. I am very nervous to tell them all I know. I have so much more to add, more than they can even imagine right now, but in due time and as they get older, I can explain more to them."

"What do you think about the threats the government made to us, about not telling anyone what Randy was working on?" she asked.

"I really don't give a hoot what they told us last year. I'm just mad at myself for letting them pressure me like that and most of all, I am more upset for believing they would do something like that," he said a little angrily. He quickly calmed, "Besides, we have access to the cruiser now with all of the bells and whistles," and with a smile, he took another sip of tea. "Let's see them try and stop us now."

The rain from the storm was now arriving over their house and started to splash on the kitchen windows as it fell. They sat at the table watching the storm outside, finishing their tea as the sound of rain grew louder on the rooftop.

After they finished, Calvin took their empty mugs and placed them in the sink.

"Tomorrow is a big day for all of us. I get to take the three amigos for a ride in the *cruiser*," he said with a smile.

"Not until after school, of course," she reminded him.

"Of course dear," he said as he pulled her into a nice hug, holding her gently pressing his lips to hers, softly kissing her. Then they both released each other and turned out the lights, leaving the kitchen heading off to bed for the night.

Chapter 20

Bullies and Gymnastics

The next day at school it was very hard for Roger to focus and keep his mind on his classes. Unfortunately in the bird man, Mr. Wilkins class, Roger had not been focusing on the lecture and when he was asked a question by Mr. Wilkins and not hearing his name called, he was left to take the abusive and derogatory comments thrown at him again for not paying attention. It was humiliating the way this teacher seemed to enjoy bringing down Roger every chance he could get. This day was no exception. Making matters worse, Roger did not study for today's test that he knew about on Friday. His weekend had been filled with so much new information that any thoughts of school had fled his mind. All he could think about was the cruiser and the chance he was going to have tonight to go for a flight.

Mr. Wilkins had finished grading their vocabulary tests by the end of class while they all read an assignment. He placed the tests under the stuffed pigeon paperweight on his desk and read a few notes. After he finished reading, he took the opportunity to hand the tests back in front of the class before the bell rang. He had an evil smile as he stood at the front of the class, calling each individual up as he held up their tests, displaying the grade they received in bright red sharpie. Rogers face reddened in anger when his name was called because Mr. Wilkins beamed and proudly announced that Roger had received a bright red letter F. It was marked on the test as he proudly displayed it for all of the class to see until Roger came up to claim it and return to his seat. Roger sat there glaring at Mr. Wilkins with angry eyes and a mean stare. He only received the bad grade because one of the essay questions on the test was about pigeons. Roger wrote a paragraph how useless the birds were and that he hated them. Apparently his teacher did not find that amusing and the grade he received proved it. Finally, the bell rang releasing Roger from this dreaded class.

At lunch Roger sat by Max and Aaron, discussing the events that happened last night. They were so pumped up and excited to go on a cruiser flight that the recent humiliation in English class couldn't upset Roger anymore. He was happy to be sitting outside in the sun, enjoying the company of his two best friends. While sitting and leaning against a tree eating his sandwich, he reached down to pick up his bag of chips. As he reached for them, a large foot came pressing down on his hand and chips, crushing both and pinning his hand to the ground.

Roger yelped in pain as the giant foot belonging to Gary Crawford smashed his lunch and chips, showing no sign of being pulled back.

"What do we have here," sneered the bully, as he looked down to see his foot on top of Rogers hand. He gave a smirk and looked back to Roger, now cringing in pain.

"Get off of him" screamed Aaron as he started to rush Gary.

A few steps before Aaron was going to make contact with Gary, the large kids head whipped backward sharply from a large orange bouncing off of his forehead. He tumbled backward and fell on his rear end, facing Max who had just thrown a fastball right at his forehead. Aaron stopped his approach and looked over at Max with a huge smile. She had nailed Gary right between the eyes with the large orange that she was just getting ready to peel and eat. Roger jumped up holding his crushed hand close to his chest and stepped over to stand by Max.

One of Gary's henchmen, David, approached Max with an angry face and she did the most amazing thing ever. She burst into one of her gymnastics moves, flipping over backwards. As she did so, her feet came up and caught David's chin as he was about to grab her. His head jerked backward and he toppled over flat on his back, out cold, a small trickle of blood appearing where her shoe had caught him on the chin.

Gary had jumped to his feet and was rushing over to punch Max. Immediately she saw him and she did another amazing lightning quick maneuver. She dropped to the ground into the splits as his punch sailed over her head, completely missing her. She then kicked around into a roundhouse spin move and her Converse shoe caught him behind the knees, causing him to buckle to the ground. As Gary struggled to get to his knees, he was bent over cussing at Max, telling her how he was going to beat her up. Suddenly from out of nowhere, Aaron kicked him in the face with a perfect upward shot, stunning him. Gary fell over onto his back, dazed and staring up at the sky, a stream of blood now emerging from his lip and nose.

As Gary lay dazed on his back, Aaron was so mad and frustrated at him that he leaned over Gary's limp body on the ground and screamed into his face," I hate bullies!" He continued to scream at him, "Why do you and your friends pick on us, you jerk!" he then slapped him across the face with the back of his hand. "Stay away from us from now on, you hear me, Stay Away From Us!" as he back slapped with the other side of his hand in a reverse mode, making a second loud smack on the other side of Gary's face.

Ben, the school security guard arrived on the scene and stood next to Aaron. They both looked down at Gary laying on the ground.

"What the heck did you do?" asked Ben, as he turned his head sideways to look at Aaron.

"Uh-uh, he tripped" stuttered Aaron," I saw him running and," he was now joined by Max, "Yeah," said Max, peering over at Gary and his bloody nose.

"We were sitting here eating lunch," said Max, as she started in on a story. "We saw Gary and David running, so we said out loud to them, *you better not run in the lunch area, you might trip and have an accident.*"

"Yeah," said Roger looking down at Gary lying there dazed on his back, now holding his nose.

"We all said out loud, *"Gary and David, you better slow down,"* said Max. And then Aaron and Roger both nodded their heads in agreement, "Yup," they both said at the same time.

Roger then said, "They both slipped after stepping on my lunch, smashing their heads together," then pointed to his crushed lunch that lay scattered about over by the tree.

Ben stood up fully and looked at the three of them with piercing eyes and a stern look. "Uh huh," he said in an unconvinced tone. "If they slipped on your lunch way over there," he pointed over to the tree and lunch mess on the ground, "Then how in the heck did they end up so far apart and not even near the lunch you say tripped them?" asked Ben.

They all three looked at each other, when Max quickly answered, "They were running *real fast Ben, really fast.* We told them to slow down or they might get hurt. *And now look what happened,"* she motioned with her hand at the scene, "they biffed it."

Ben looked at them and smiled, "OK then, serves them right. They should read the signs," as he pointed to the sign that said, "No Skateboards, Running, or Bicycles Allowed" clearly posted on the outside wall of the cafeteria.

"That's right," said Max.

Ben helped Gary and David to their feet and began to escort them to the school nurse. The other three turned and started to vacate the area, picking up their trash and smashed lunch bits scattered about. They quickly tossed it in the garbage and left in case Ben called them back for more questioning.

While retreating from the scene, they turned into one of the hall ways. "That story was brilliant Max," said Roger, "even though I don't think Ben believed any of it!"

"I know it! *I'm so glad you are my friend,"* said Aaron, as he hugged her tight for a second. She pushed him back and punched him on the arm. "Get off of me dude," she said, then turned to Roger, "How is your hand?"

"Sore, it's starting to throb now," said Roger. "That guy is such a jerk!" he exclaimed. Then he laughed out, "Did you see his face when that orange nailed him? It was classic, his head just jerked back with the stunned look on his face!" They all broke into laughter again just as the bell rang.

"Ok, see you guys later," said Roger, "Meet at my house after school," he told them both.

"I'll be there after practice," replied Max.

"Ok, see you later," they all said to each other and went different directions to their classes.

School had just ended and kids were filing out of the school. "Hey Roger, wait up," called Aaron as he jogged up next to Roger to join him in the walk home. They decided to skip the bus ride and walk home instead. Aaron saw Roger rubbing his hand, it was very red and a little swollen after Gary had smashed it.

"How is your hand?" asked Aaron.

Roger smiled, "It probably feels a lot better than Gary's face does right now," he said, as they both began to laugh and went over the details from their lunch time brawl.

They continued walking discussing the upcoming cruiser flight and decided to take the route home that would bring them to their neighborhood park. It was the coolest park. It had a small creek flowing through the center of it. There were a lot of pavilions nestled in the trees for families to eat and cook food for gatherings. Tennis, baseball and soccer fields were located on the far end by the pool. Their favorite hangout at this park was an old steam train engine and coal car that were laid to rest next to the playgrounds. The train was put there in the 50's after it was retired by the local power plant. The plant workers wanted the train engine to be on display at the park and for their children to be able to play on. Every kid from the town of Belford had hung out on that train and had climbed over every inch of it during their childhood. It was the best train for a game of tag. Kids would run and fall off trying to get away, climb on top of the smoke stack and slide down the coal car trying not to overshoot the small landing and see if they could keep from crashing to the ground below. It was the best. The giant black train stood there, always inviting for kids to climb aboard and have fun.

They both sat on the front of the train and took out homework. It was a quiet day at the park that afternoon. They didn't have a lot of homework, but it was always fun to hang out on the train and work until it was time to go home. There was something about being outside on this giant beast that made it easier to do a little bit of studying.

Aaron and Roger sat on the front of the train talking and hanging out for a bit, noting the time to make sure they would arrive home when Calvin returned from work. They got an ice cream from the vending machine in the park then left heading for home. They parted ways once they arrived at their street and went to their own houses agreeing to meet back up shortly at Roger's house.

As Roger came up the walk to the house he looked in the wide driveway and noticed his dads work truck was not home yet. He went into the house to get another snack and wait for his dad to get home from work. He walked in the door to see Jenny eating a sandwich at the counter and watching cartoons on the small TV.

"Hey girl," he said.

She waved her hand, not making eye contact, or saying a word, her mouth was full of food and her eyes stayed focused on the TV.

Roger grabbed a granola bar from the pantry and a little pack of goldfish crackers and headed up to his room. He entered his room and tossed his backpack on the chair next to his desk. Then he fell forward onto his bed like a dead body, bounced a couple of times on his stomach and lay there with his face buried in his pillow, resting from the school day.

Chapter 21

Partners

The sound of a truck pulling into the driveway woke up Roger from the after school nap he hadn't intended to take. His head quickly popped up as he listened closely to the sound just to be sure. It was his father's truck. He was just getting home from work.

Roger jumped to look out his window and saw the truck coming to a stop in the driveway. He saw his dad climbing out of the vehicle, but then on the passenger side of the truck, he saw someone else getting out. He looked closer and saw that the man getting out was a lot younger. He was a nerdy looking guy with big glasses and messy hair. His father appeared to be talking to him, pointing around the yard and discussing something with the man.

Who is that guy and what is he doing here- wondered Roger.

Roger's dad looked up at the second floor window and saw Roger peering down at the two of them. He gave him a friendly wave and a smile and motioned for him to come down stairs. Roger politely shook his head up and down, turned and headed down stairs to meet his father to see what was going on.

As he came down into the kitchen Jenny was still there watching TV at the counter with both of her hands holding her chin with her elbows resting comfortably on the counter.

"Hey Jenny, do you know that guy out there with Dad?" as he pointed out the window of the kitchen to his dad and the man standing there talking in front of the shop.

She turned her head to peek out the window, looked at him for a few seconds, then turned back to watch her TV show, her hands still holding her head under her chin.

"Well," said Roger impatiently, "Do you know him?"

Without turning to look at Roger she slowly answered, "That's Jeffrey. His name is Jeffrey Taylor."

Roger looked out the window again, "Oh yeah," he said, "You're right. I remember that guy. He's the goofy nerd who played on dad and Jake's company softball team a couple years ago. Thanks Sis," Roger said to Jenny, then he reached up and turned off the TV she was glued to as he was leaving to go out the door.

"Hey!" she yelled as she turned to glare at him.

"Come back to earth, you TV junkie," he said as the door closed behind him.

He could hear her calling him a name through the closed door but couldn't quite make out what she said, it only made him smile. He knew she would get her revenge later on him for cutting her off in the middle of her show, but it was worth it he thought as he walked down the back steps toward the shop. Calvin and Jeffrey both turned to watch him as he came out the back door and down the steps toward them. They stopped the conversation they were having as Roger approached. He caught a few words they were saying about the power grid.

"What's up," asked Roger with a smile as he came to a stop next to them.

"Roger, I don't know if you remember Jeffrey," as he gestured with his hand to his side where Jeffrey was standing.

"Course I do," Roger lied, as he held out his hand to Jeffrey, shaking hands and greeting him.

Jeffrey smiled back at Roger, "It has been a couple years since I last saw you Roger."

"I know," replied Roger." It has been a while. The last time, I think was at the company softball game." Jeffrey smiled as Roger snickered. "You took a pop fly right in the forehead during the game and got knocked out," said Roger.

Calvin let out a small laugh, "That's right, your head was split wide open, and not that it was funny."

Jeffrey now snickered with them, "You're right," he said as he lifted up his bangs and leaned forward, displaying a long scar from where he had been stitched up along his hair line, "It took twenty two stitches to close it," then continued, "but would have probably been about half of that amount if I didn't cut it worse when I hit the fence as I was falling unconscious on my face."

Jeffrey then let out a long nerdy kind of laugh that was joined by Calvin and Roger. They joined in laughing because Jeffrey's donkey sounding laugh quickly drew them in.

After the laughter died down, Calvin informed Roger that Jeffrey was not only a good friend from work, but was also a good friend of Randy's. In fact, they had been college roommates their freshman year.

Roger shook his head up and down, "That's cool. So did you have any classes together?"

"We had chemistry and computer programming together," Jeffrey said.

"Your brother was so smart. He pretty much kept to himself. He was always immersed in his studies and projects."

Rogers face lit up, "You knew about his projects?"

"Oh yeah, I knew a lot about his early projects," replied Jeffrey.

"And that is what we're here to talk about," Calvin said, as he pulled open the large sliding door to the shop, gesturing for them to enter, closing the door behind them.

Roger took on a more serious look now. His mind began to race. *What is going on, who is this guy that my dad seems to like and trust so well?*

Jeffrey stood in the shop and looked around. "Boy, I haven't been in here for a quite a while," he said turning as he scanned the shop. "I see you still have the old Ford Mustang, Cal."

Roger had noticed that most of his father's co-workers used "Cal" as a nickname for him. He kind of liked it and it didn't seem to bother his dad.

"I do, that car will be with us a long time," replied Cal as he stepped over to the counter and opened the fridge.

"Root beer or cream soda?" He asked, looking at Roger and Jeffrey.

"Sure, cream soda," replied Roger, as he took one from his dad and unscrewed the bottle cap.

Calvin handed one towards Jeffrey, but he held up his hand, "No, no, I can't drink soda," he giggled, "The little fizzy bubbles give me the worst gas," he said as he held his stomach and gave a little donkey laugh.

"Well then you definitely can't have one. I like the fresh air in here without you fouling it all up with root beer gas," chuckled Calvin.

Roger jumped and turned, startled by the roaring donkey laugh now coming from Jeffrey.

"Oh Cal, you are so funny," said Jeffrey, as the donkey laugh sounds slowly came to a stop.

Calvin smiled and walked over to the license plate on the wall. He took a screwdriver from the bench and pried the microphone out from where it was hidden in the wall. With a hard jerk of his hand, the little device and its wires were ripped from its location.

"I'm tired of the thought that someone is trying to spy on us," he said as he dropped the device and crushed it with his foot on the floor. He then turned on the jamming device in the record player, just to be sure, then took a seat on the shop sofa. Roger sat himself down on a stool next to the counter.

Jeffrey stayed standing and now faced Roger and his father, waiting for Calvin to speak.

"Roger," said Calvin, "Jeffrey has been working for me at the power company since he graduated from college."

Jeffrey took a seat at the other end of the sofa and started to speak, "I'm a computer systems engineer at the main facility-

Jeffrey was cut off by the sound of the shop door being quickly pulled open and the sound of a boy and girl arguing. They continued to banter with each other and their argument could be heard as Max and Aaron walked into the shop.

"See, I told you so, you idiot," said Max to Aaron.

They both could see Roger and his Dad seated on the couch, "They're still here, they wouldn't have gone without-"

Max quickly stopped as she now caught a glimpse of the stranger sitting on the other end of the sofa. Aaron and Max stood there for a brief moment, "Hey guys," said Aaron. "Who are you?' he asked Jeffrey.

"My name is Jeffrey Taylor," he said as he leapt up from the couch and quickly approached Aaron and Max, his hand outright ready to greet and shake. As he took Aarons hand he quickly shook it very fast, "Nice to meet you," he said, he then quickly took Max's hand and shook it very fast, like he did with Aaron, "Nice to meet you too," he said to Max.

Calvin was in the background announcing to Jeffrey, "These are Roger's best friends, Maxine and Aaron."

Aaron leaned in a little closer to Jeffrey and whispered, "I'm the number one *best friend*," pointing to himself.

This comment made Jeffrey laugh with a sudden burst of donkey laughing, causing Max and Aaron to jump.

"Whoa there," said Max, reaching out patting Jeffrey on the shoulder to calm him down, "take it easy buddy."

Jeffrey's laughter continued after her comment and then slowly came to a stop as he took his seat back on the couch. Max and Aaron pulled up stools next to Roger after getting a root beer for themselves. Calvin then gave Max and Aaron the same speech he gave Roger about Jeffrey and how he worked with him at the power company.

Jeffrey looked at Calvin and asked, "Cal, are these two OK to be here for this?"

Calvin nodded yes to Jeffrey and motioned to him to continue.

"Ok, as I started to tell you, I am a computer systems engineer at the main facility over at 'Canyon Lake Hydroelectric Dam.' I helped to create the computer systems and updated the software programs that are used to monitor the power that is being generated and distributed from the Dam. After a little while I was promoted and became the man in charge of all of the systems in the whole state." Jeffrey stood up and continued his story as he slowly paced the shop, "As the power is generated at the dam, it goes to storage and distribution systems that feed power to Belford and the cities surrounding us. That power is fed to every city and house through the power lines that Cal," he motioned to Calvin, "has installed and manages with his crew."

Jeffrey continued, "The power delivery system uses pylon towers and high voltage lines that Cal has worked designing, installing, and maintaining for years. My job was to create an updated computer system that would monitor and control how much of this power is delivered and where. The system was also supposed to monitor any issues and outages or possible dangers that might happen and if there were any problems with the delivery to the customers. The systems that I created replaced the old ones that had been in place for decades after the Dam was built.

Aaron couldn't contain himself and said in a laugh, "Those *Dam* computers must have been old, I bet it took you a *Dam* long time to replace the *Dam* things."

"Shut your *Dam* mouth," Roger said back with a laugh, "you don't know a *Dam* thing about Jeffrey."

Calvin rolled his eyes, but it was too late to stop them now.

Max joined in, "Cal helped," she said smiling at Calvin, "He was running *Dam* power lines all over the *Dam* place."

This whole exchange struck Jeffrey hard. The donkey laughs were coming in full force and his eyes filled with tears from laughing so hard. Aaron saw this and decided to take it further,

"*Dam* Jeffrey-, are you OK?" he asked.

Jeffrey looked up, laughing and said "My *Dam* stomach is killing me from laughing," he joined in the Dam talk, belted out a donkey laugh and leaned against the counter to keep his balance from laughing so hard.

It took a minute for them all to quiet down. Jeffrey's face got serious and then he spoke. "I was upgrading one of the monitoring center systems one night and I noticed it was getting some strange readings from the program. I thought it was a software bug at first, or something was wrong with my new program. After going through my program code, I realized I had found something happening along one of the main delivery lines. I was seeing little power spikes happen that seemed to travel down the lines for miles." He turned to explain further, "It is not uncommon to have these types of power spikes. They happen all of the time. But, what was not common was that the spikes always seemed to originate at the same location. I started pulling data from the previous months and found that almost every night at random times, a power spike would originate from a certain tower pylon. They all started at pylon 460."

Roger, Max, and Aaron looked at each other and then over to see Calvin smiling at them. Jeffrey continued, "I knew something was going on at pylon 460, so I went to talk with Cal. It was his department that was responsible for the pylons and he knew everything about every pylon tower that was installed in the state."

Calvin then continued. "When Jeffrey approached me at first, I didn't have any idea why he wanted to see the maps for pylon 460. He told me he was doing some research on it. I immediately got curious about his intentions with this tower because that was the tower behind our home in the field. It was the pylon that Jake and I had just built the launch platform on for Randy's test flights. I gave him the maps so he could see what he needed."

Jeffrey spoke again. "After I saw the location of the pylon from the map, I decided to pay it a visit and check it out, to see if I could figure out or get a lead on what was causing the power spikes. I didn't know that it was located right behind Cal's house until I arrived late one evening and saw the company truck parked in the driveway. I was parked across the street from your house looking at the map to verify that I was at the correct location. As I looked down again to verify the pylon, I saw two figures riding on a four wheeler quad, with a small trailer in tow," Jeffrey pointed across the shop to Calvin's large four wheeler partially covered, with the small trailer sitting next to it.

"So I climbed out of my car verifying no one else was around and secretly followed them. The sun was going down so I had the advantage of being hidden a little with the cover of darkness. The two men parked the four wheeler and one opened a gate while the other went to the trailer and started to untie a large object. At first I thought it was a bicycle, but then it took on a different shape. From the angle of the view I had I saw that it was not a bicycle at all because there were no wheels and it had an odd shape."

Jeffrey now walked to the small fridge and took out a bottle of water, took off the lid and took a drink. Max and Roger realized that they had finished their root beer while they were hypnotized by the information that Jeffrey and Calvin were giving them.

"I snuck closer to the pylon as their attention was focused on carrying the object up the stairs to a platform. I could see part way up the tower. As I got closer, I made sure to stay out of their view and hid behind some tall bushes. I stayed behind the bushes and had a perfect view of what they were doing. I pulled a small pair of binoculars from my satchel and took out my inhaler.

"What's a satchel?" asked Aaron.

"A man's purse," giggled Max.

Jeffrey continued, "The shrubbery I was hiding behind was starting to make my allergies act up, my nose was starting to run and it was getting hard to breathe. After a few puffs of my medicine I peered through the binoculars and saw that it was Cal standing up on the platform with a young man that I was sure was Randy." Then Jeffrey turned to face them all as he put the lid back on his water bottle.

"Cal was helping Randy on the platform arrange the strange object on a smaller platform that was elevated a few feet in the air. After they had the device in its position Randy took out a suit of some sort from a bag. He put it on over his shorts and t-shirt and then placed a helmet on his head and climbed up onto the platform. Cal went over, opened up a panel of some sort and appeared to be busy pressing buttons. The object had two seats side by side that were supported by a small frame.

"The object he saw was the Cruiser 4.0," said Calvin.

Jeffrey continued, "Randy sat down and fastened himself in the seatbelt then I saw the most curious thing that caused me to drop my binoculars. A little tiny space ship was flying around the object and would hover over to where Cal was standing working at the panel and then would zoom back over to Randy seated in the device."

"That must have been Servo," said Aaron, with a sneer, "that thing hates me."

Jeffrey was looking at Aaron as he spoke and then smiled, "Me too!" replied Jeffrey, "But we can share stories about her later."

He continued, "The little spaceship was unbelievable to me. I picked up my binoculars and continued to watch what was going on. Then Cal took out a suit and helmet from the bag that Randy had used a few minutes before and put on the suit and helmet and took a seat next to Randy, fastening himself in with the seatbelts."

After another sip of his water he continued. "The little spaceship flew over to the control panel where Cal had been and pressed some buttons that made the lift rise higher toward the power cables just above their heads. As soon as the large device was close to the wires, I saw a small ball of power from the arms of the thing attach to the high power cables with a few sparks falling down. The device was not actually touching the cables, but was being connected to them by this small ball of energy that was holding itself to the cables. The small robot hovered above them and attached to a part on top. A deep hum grew louder and louder and then in an instant the whole device was enclosed by a larger ball of energy. Randy and Cal were visible inside the ball of energy that was attached to the cables. Then the ball of energy encasing them moved forward a few feet and then it took off, having the appearance of a bolt of lightning shooting down the power lines until it was quickly out of sight."

Jeffrey tossed his empty water bottle in the trash. "I didn't know what to think. I was freaking out while I sat there looking at the platform where the sphere of power had just held my co-worker. It was there and then it was gone in an instant. I don't remember much after that."

Calvin stood up and chuckled, "That's because he fainted after seeing us take off. We found him lying on the ground after we returned a short time later. He hit his head on a small branch when he fell and would need stitches again. We loaded his unconscious body on the trailer with the cruiser 4.0 bringing him back to the shop. We put him on the couch and bandaged the back of his head. When he came around, we thought for sure he was going to tell others about what he saw, but he was really interested in the project. We knew he was going to stay quiet. He became the newest member of our team."

Jeffrey took a stool next to the others while Calvin spoke. "Jeffrey then went on to create software that would help us on the test flights. He was our *'Eyes in the Sky.'*

"I called the software *'Eagle,'* said Jeffrey.

"He became our own *line traffic controller*," said Calvin. "His software for the power grids proved invaluable. He would help route us if there was construction on any power lines, or reroute us around power outages etc. We had radio communications that he and Randy made that could use the power lines as large antennas so we could broadcast and talk around the country."

"So here we are," said Calvin, "I spoke to Jeffrey about what happened this past weekend and he was excited to help us with test flights of the new Cruiser 5.0."

Calvin took out the operating manual that they had found yesterday in the lock box that Randy created for Cruiser 5.0.

"I read this today at work," as he held up the thick manual. "It was a slow day so I had plenty of free time. Randy really outdid himself on this model 5.0. I knew how to fly 4.0 pretty well, but this one has been impressively improved."

They all jumped, completely startled as the metal cabinet door to the secret lab loudly and instantly burst open. They watched a little hovering robot come zooming into the shop and make a flight around the large shop looking at each of the occupants.

"Servo," exclaimed Jeffrey, "It has been a long time little girl, since I saw-"

Servo sped over to Jeffrey and hovered in front of him. She was face to face and glared her headlights angrily as she hovered up and down.

"You're not still mad at me are you?" he asked.

She turned around hovering in front of him now showing him her back side and her little robot arms folded. She was pouting.

"I'm so sorry for spilling my energy drink on you in the lab, that was a long time ago," he said apologetically.

Servo's headlights then went from a mean slant and brightened a little bit. She appeared to have forgiven him for his clumsy act. She then zoomed up to him under his chin giving him a little love hug, one little arm tickling his chin.

"Stop it," he laughed and shrugged, softly pushing her away from his chin.

She made another sweep of the shop then came to hover above Rogers shoulder in her claimed spot.

"She snuck up on me once while I was working in the lab one night tracking Randy on a test flight. She startled me making me jump. I spilled my energy drink all over her, causing her to short out and fall to the floor in a shower of sparks," he explained. "She seems to flash back to it every time she sees me. So I have to apologize again to her when she flashes back to that day. It must have been very traumatic for her."

"I have no idea why she hates my guts," said Aaron, as he walked over to where Servo was hovering by Roger and reached out to her attempting again to start a friendship with her. "Hello sweet, pretty little robot," he said in a tender voice. His hand was now ready to pat Servo on the head when a sudden burst of electricity in the shape of a small lightning bolt shot out from her little hand, zapping Aaron on the shoulder.

"Aahhh," sounded a startled scream from Aaron as he fell to the floor, being tazed by the bully robot. Laughter filled the air as Aaron lay on his back resting on the floor, shaking a little, with a small black hole burnt in his shirt. "I am beginning to hate that little bug zapper more and more," he whispered as he slowly pulled himself up from the floor.

Calvin stood up and pulled Aaron to his feet brushing him off and patting him on the back.

"So that is the short version of how Jeffrey was shanghaied into working with us on Randy's projects."

"Did you bring your gear?" Calvin asked Jeffrey. "I think it is time to prepare for a flight,"

"Of course, let me get it from my car," replied Jeffrey.

He pulled the shop door open and hurried to his car to get his gear, leaving the door open.

As Jeffrey trotted to his car he didn't notice the dark black car parked across the street. It was dark outside and the street light that the car was parked under was broken. The orange glow of a cigarette shone for a brief moment as the man inside watching Jeffrey was inhaling. The driver's side window was partially open to allow the smoke to escape as he continued to watch Jeffrey rummage through his car. He picked up a camera from the passenger's seat. The camera had a telephoto lens that he focused on Jeffrey, snapping numerous photos. He took some of Jeffrey's car and his license plate. He then focused the camera on the open shop door. He saw an object inside the shop that was hovering above a young boys shoulder. He was taking numerous photos but the last few were cut off as the door to the shop was pulled closed. Jeffrey had returned with his gear to start preparing for the launch of Cruiser 5.0.

He took one last puff on his cigarette, tossed the butt out the window and started the car. With a satisfied smirk he pulled onto the street, did a U turn and drove off down the road in the dark. As soon as the car was a short distance away he turned the headlights on to light the way back to where he had come from.

Chapter 22

Cleared for Takeoff

Jeffrey returned with his gear and the whole group headed down the secret stairs to the lab below. Jeffrey was busy, taking laptops and a headset out of his bag and connecting them to the wall of monitors. He had pulled a small table over in front of the monitors and was now seated, typing on the laptop preparing the systems.

"Hello Jeffrey," spoke the familiar Tory.

Jeffrey's head quickly popped up to see Tory's pretty face looking back at him from the wall of monitors. Her hair was blond and she had big dark eyes. She was a computer generated image that looked real and perfect.

"Hello T-T-Tory," he stuttered.

She smiled back at him with her big beautiful lips and perfect teeth, fluttering her eye lids at him. *"I have missed you,"* she drawled, *"I'm so glad you came to see me,"* she flirted.

Jeffrey went a darker shade of red then looked away, embarrassed. None of them had seen what Tory looked like. They had only heard her voice yesterday.

Max stepped over by Jeffrey and smacked him on the arm with the back of her hand getting his attention, "Dude, she's not real, she's a freaking computer," she said in disgust.

Max turned after she finished scolding Jeffrey and saw that Aaron and Roger were staring up at Tory with twinkling eyes, obviously taken by her beauty. She shook her head and stepped to face Tory, who peered down at Max from her monitors.

"Well hello there little girl," said Tory as she gave a condescending smile to Max.

Max pointed up at Tory and angrily said, "You listen here you bimbo, stop flirting with all of the men in here!"

Tory's face now changed, a hurt look spread across her face as Max continued to scold her.

"And another thing, I'm going to be sixteen years old in two weeks, so knock off the *'little girl'* comments!" she yelled at Tory.

Tory's eyes welled up and tears started to roll down her pretty face, making her makeup run as she started to cry.

Max rolled her eyes at the crying computer. She looked over her shoulder at Jeffrey who had a stunned look and saw the others watching her. She looked at Roger and mouthed the words, "She is a computer," as she pointed up at the monitors, then she turned back to face Tory. "Pull yourself together Tory," Max said in a softer, friendlier voice.

Tory was wiping the tears away from her cheeks and dabbing at her eyes with a tissue, so that she didn't smear her makeup. She looked down at Max.

"I'm sorry I yelled at you," apologized Max,

Tory smiled and her face lit up with happiness, *"Thank you,"* said Tory.

Jeffrey spoke, "Tory, we need to prepare the grid and a launch sequence for a test flight with Cruiser 5.0 tonight."

Tory instantly went into processing mode and her face disappeared from the screens and was replaced with a large detailed map of the city and power pylons and cables. On a lower section of the monitors new details appeared that made sense to Jeffrey. The status of the power grids levels along with other data was scrolling on the screen as Jeffrey focused on the main display of information.

"I have access to all of my systems at the power company from here," he said. "It is part of a module I was working on with Randy before his death. We can tap into the network at the power company from the power connections here in the lab. There is a lot to it, but you need an encrypted key that we hid in Servo to get through the security firewall to gain access to the system," said Jeffrey. He pointed to Servo who was hovering over Roger's shoulder while Roger stood there watching Jeffrey work. "Servo, I need you to upload the key please.

Servo made a small beep that sounded like an "OK," and she zoomed over to the shelf that was next to the monitors and landed gently on the docking port. Small lights on the side of her body flashed purple and orange as she uploaded the key into the system for Jeffrey.

"She needs to generate a new encryption every time she connects to the system for accessing the power grid and getting through the network firewall. We created the method as a security measure in case the technology fell into the wrong hands. Inside of Servo is an encryption program that is hard coded to her memory. When she connects it to the systems it allows her to generate the encryption keys that match our power grid systems. This allows us to access everything on the network. We actually could access any computer system in the world with the program and computer chip inside of her," explained Jeffrey.

The map on the wall of computers showed a test flight route start to stretch across the map, the color green showing the path that was best for them to take tonight.

"Ok, here we go," said Jeffrey.

Servo had finished tapping into the network with the encrypted key and sat in the docking station. She was waiting for the route they were going to take to get downloaded into her flight systems when Jeffrey was ready. They all looked up to see the green path stretching across the map of power pylons.

"There is some construction going on south of here so I am routing you around it. You need to be careful in case there are line men up there working while you come zinging past in the cruiser. You could zap them or cause them to get hurt when you pass by," said Jeffrey as he continued to type on the laptop and upload the map to Servo.

Servo was in the docking station and flashed a bright blue light through her headlights as the upload came to her systems. Then she undocked, flew up and hovered by Roger.

Jeffrey noticed that Servo always seemed to hover by Roger. He took a second glance at her and said, "She is like your own little personal bodyguard."

"I can confirm that," said Aaron as he rubbed his shoulder, the one with the burned black Taser hole from earlier.

"Ok Cal, all systems are good to go," said Jeffrey.

Calvin took one of the helmets from the workbench and put it on as Jeffrey put on his headset.

"Radio check, one, two, Bravo, Charlie," said Calvin inside the helmet.

"Loud and clear," replied Jeffrey.

Calvin took off the helmet then put on a cool flat black flight suit that was folded on one of the workbenches. "Ready guys?" he asked the three amigos.

"Let's roll," said Roger in pure excitement, followed by Max and Aarons shouts of excitement.

"OK Jeffrey, we're heading out to the platform," said Calvin. He took the football shaped cruiser while the others scooped up the rest of the gear, the flight suits and helmets and packed them in black equipment bags and left the lab.

Once outside, they loaded the equipment into Calvin's truck and he drove them down to the tower. On the way, Calvin called his wife's cell phone and left a message that they were going to look for fishing worms. He smiled and told them this was a code that they used for the night time cruiser flights. Alicia was not home he explained. She had taken Jenny to a movie so she wouldn't find out about their flight plan for the night.

They arrived at the base of tower 460 and climbed out of the truck in the dark. Calvin took out a small flash light to see and unlock the gate for all of them to pass through. Aaron, Max and Roger escorted by Servo, carried all of their gear up the platform. He then went over to the control panel by the lift and turned on a light that gave the platform a cool, light blue glow so that they could see where they stood. He then pressed the button to activate the camouflage net that he had shown them the other day. There was a zipping noise as a curtain quickly encompassed the platform, hiding them from anyone on the outside.

Calvin unzipped one of the equipment bags and pulled out a flight suit and helmet and handed it to Roger. He put it on and noticed that it was just like the suit his dad was wearing, the same cool looking flat black color.

"Roger, you are nearly the same size as Randy so his suit looks like a fine fit for you."

Calvin took out two more suits, bright white with cool red stripes on the sleeves. "Max and Aaron, put these on," as he handed the suits and helmets to them.

"This might be a little bit big on you Aaron so you can roll up the sleeves and legs if needed," instructed Calvin.

A few moments later they all stood on the platform dressed and ready for the flight, helmets and all. Aaron had the sleeves rolled up to fit his arms and after a little fidgeting he looked ready to go.

Calvin and Servo were busy moving around the platform preparing for the flight. Calvin had his helmet on and was talking to Jeffrey through the radio. While waiting for instructions Aaron, Max and Roger were goofing around with the radio intercom system built into the helmets for communication.

"Radio check, Bravo Alpha," said Max.

"Roger," replied Aaron, "I hear you loud and clear."

"What do you want? You called my name," echoed Roger on the radio.

They all caught on to the game.

"Do you hear my transmission," asked Max again, "Radio check," she announced over the system.

"Roger that," replied Aaron, "I read you-

"What do you want?' cut in Roger, "you called me again," he laughed.

"OK, OK," said Jeffrey across the radio. "*And you guys thought I was a nerd*" he laughed.

"OK," announced Calvin, as he stood near the platform holding the large football cruiser under one arm getting all of their attention. He stepped forward and placed the oval cruiser on the platform, then stood up.

"Everyone over here and stand by me, facing forward, Roger you are next to me on my right, Max and Aaron take a position behind us."

"Home base, are you ready?" he spoke into the radio mic in his helmet.

"We are good to go," Jeffrey replied back in his earpiece.

"I don't understand Dad," said Roger, "We can't *all* fit in the cruiser, why are we all standing here?"

"I told you son, I read the manual and Randy's notes today at work. I also loaded the simulator software on my laptop and practiced some flying at lunch. *This Cruiser 5.0* is a large improvement to what we have seen in the past," said his father.

Then Calvin put on the main control glove and several things started to happen at once. The glove powered itself on after verifying his ID and Servo began buzzing around the flight platform like a hummingbird. She was making beeping and humming noises as she whizzed by going from one side of the platform to the other preparing for takeoff. She then buzzed over to the control console, pressed some buttons and then hovered over next to the small football shaped sphere.

"OK, hold on to your lunch," Cal said. He then pressed some buttons on the glove and typed a few key commands on the small glowing keyboard. Instantly a small glow started to come from the sphere beneath them. They heard the noise it was making as it was growing louder and the ball of energy it was creating beneath them seemed to grow faster and larger, reminding them of the sound a helicopter makes when it starts to power up. The ball seemed to expand another few inches and then a bright flash of light was emitted from the sphere that engulfed them all. Instantly they were all sitting in flight chairs facing forward, hovering inside of the giant sphere, floating up and down ever so softly, like a small boat floating on a lake.

"How is everyone doing?" asked Calvin over the helmet radios.

"Doing great Dad," said Roger smiling back at his dad as they looked at each other.

"A little nervous," replied Aaron.

"Great," responded Max.

The control panel came to life in front of Roger and Calvin and finished the startup process. A large display in the center of the console was showing their location on a big map and several other digital windows filled the display with few smaller displays on the sides of the main large one. The dashboard was lit softly so that the glow and glare from the panel lights didn't make it difficult to see outside.

"It feels like we are in the car going for a ride," said Roger.

"Yeah, but I have never been in a car like this before," replied Aaron as he and Max sat in the back seats looking around in amazement.

"I'll show you what these displays and controls are all for later. For now I'll just show you a few on this maiden voyage," said Calvin.

"OK, the flight path is clear to go," Came Jeffrey over the radio.

At this announcement, Servo approached the sphere as it bobbed ever so softly. As she was approaching the top of the cruiser where she was to dock, the platform lift rose slowly up higher toward the power cables above. Just before it made contact with the power cables, Servo successfully docked into the module and the cruiser sides, ceiling and floor appeared to ripple out of sight. They were now all concealed in the cruiser and not visible from the outside even if someone happened to be looking at them.

A deep humming of the energy they were contained in was now softly in the background as Calvin pressed a few buttons on the dashboard and told them all to fasten their belts. They quickly put on their five point harnesses and gave the all clear.

"Hold on," announced Calvin, as he took the joystick controller at his left and pushed a power lever forward with his other hand.

The energy hum grew louder as they slowly moved forward off the platform and away from pylon 460, slowly heading down the lines.

"Just taking it easy for a minute until I get the hang of this new cruiser," said Calvin.

"Holy crap," said Aaron. He had looked down and could see the ground far below as they moved down the cable slowly, they were up very high.

"It's ok," assured Calvin, as he moved the throttle forward increasing the speed a little more.

'We are actually moving down a power cable suspended by a ball of energy.' Roger's mind raced at how this was impossible. But it wasn't, he was actually doing it. He was line cruising with his dad and his best friends.

"OK, let's go!" Calvin announced. He then pushed the throttle full forward.

With a loud crack, they took off like a speeding bullet hurling down the cables, their heads all slammed backward into their flight seats and they felt the g-force of the sudden burst of speed pulling on their cheeks.

Sounds of excitement filled the intercom system as they all let out small comments, "Oh Yea," and "this is so awesome," as they sped down their path.

Roger looked down at the speed and saw the digital screen that displayed 100. His eyes widened, "Dad, how is this possible?"

Max let out a scream of enjoyment as they saw the houses and buildings zooming by.

No comment had come from Aaron.

"Hey Aaron," Roger asked but there was no answer.

Then he heard Max laughing on the intercom, "He passed out."

"What?" gasped Roger, "What a dork," as he joined in with her laughing.

Calvin looked concerned and reached down pressing a few buttons on the dash board. A picture of a body with the name "Aaron" above it came on the screen. It was diagram of the human body showing Aarons heart rate and vital information about him. "Everything checks out good, he is fine," said Calvin.

Jeffrey came on the radio, "I show him fine as well on my systems, the poor kid just passed out. I know that feeling all too well."

"Too bad," said Max, "he is missing the best ride EVER!"

Jeffrey came on the radio again, "Ok guys you are at the halfway point of the flight, you need to turn around and head back."

"Aw," cried Max and Roger, "we are just getting started."

"Roger that," said Calvin. Then he pulled the throttle back to idle causing them to slow down.

His dad maneuvered the cruiser off the main power lines down onto a smaller set of lines, crossing low near a city street, then back around and up another set of power lines heading back the way they had just come. As they rose up the line to the higher lines and back onto the main route, Calvin punched it again. They were pressed against the back of their seats as they shot down the lines heading back home to pylon 460.

A few minutes later they heard a voice come from Aaron as he gained consciousness.

"Huh, what the, where are we?" he muttered.

"We are heading back home buddy," replied Roger.

Max punched him on the arm, "You passed out when he took off like a bat out of hel-

"I know," Aaron said. "I couldn't help it. This sphere thingy makes me feel a little sick in my stomach."

"It's ok," said Calvin as he laughed a little. "You're not the first one to pass out taking their first cruiser ride."

"I hold the record for passing out six times," they heard Jeffrey reply with a donkey laugh over the radio.

They all laughed, even Aaron when they heard the donkey laugh of Jeffrey's over the radio.

As they headed back into town and slowed down, Roger looked down and over at a particular house that was lit up from the street lights around it. He saw a man in the back yard that had a familiar build and he was looking up at a flock of pigeons circling his back yard. Roger recognized the man. He was Mr. Wilkins, his mean English teacher. He was herding in his prize pigeons for the night.

"Hey dad, circle around this area on the lines again and make a high speed pass by that house down there on the left, ok," Roger asked, as he pointed down at Mr. Wilkins house.

"What for son?" questioned Calvin.

"I want to say hello to those pigeons that are landing on the power lines," replied Roger.

"Son, you know what will happen to those pigeons if we speed by the power lines they are resting on, right?" asked Calvin.

"*Yes I do*," sneered Roger with an evil smile, '*Oh yes I do.*"

Calvin agreed and turned the cruiser up and around the power lines that ran above the houses.

Roger whispered over to Aaron and Max, "That is Mr. Wilkins house down there," as he pointed downward.

Both Max and Aaron knew who he was and his love for pigeons. They both snickered at the plan Roger had in mind. As they approached the spot where the pigeons were comfortably resting, everyone in the cruiser was anticipating what was about to happen to Mr. Wilkins birds.

Mr. Wilkins heard a little cracking from where he was standing in his backyard by the pigeon cages and looked up at the power lines to see a strange surge of energy coming his way directly at his pigeons. His eyes widened when he looked up and saw the ripple of energy from the sphere on the power lines as it hit his flock of pigeons. Each bird instantly burst into small puffs of feathers as the sphere plowed through them leaving a blizzard of feathers in its wake behind. Everyone in the cruiser looked over their shoulders to see the cloud of feathers and could hear the screams of the man cursing at the energy ball that just incinerated his precious prize pigeons.

"That was awesome," laughed Roger, along with Max and Aaron.

"You should be ashamed of yourself for that," scolded Calvin, but he couldn't hold back his laugh and joined in with the others.

"Nothing like fried pigeons for dinner," laughed Aaron, making them all laugh harder as Calvin turned the cruiser back on course heading back to their house.

"OK, you are coming up on final approach Cal, slow her down," said Jeffrey.

As they slowed down, Roger was able to see the numbers on the pylons they were passing. He saw 470, then 469, 468, as they drew closer to pylon 460. Calvin brought the cruiser to a stop right above the platform lift then pressed a few buttons on the console initiating the power down sequence.

Servo disengaged herself from the module on top and the view from the sphere started to go fuzzy. They were now visible again from the outside. The sphere detached itself from the power cables as the lift began to lower. Servo had initiated the controls to bring them down and begin the power down sequence of the system.

"Get ready to dock and power down," said Calvin. The lift came to stop and they were now docked on the platform.

The hum of the sphere started to get quieter as the sphere started the sequence. Then in an instant, the sphere compressed down to the shape of a football. Calvin knew this was coming and dropped his feet down fast enough to catch him while he went from sitting in a flight seat to having no seat beneath him as the sphere rapidly disappeared.

Max, the gymnast with fast reflexes, was able to react fast enough and get her feet down. There was a thud, the sound of flesh smacking metal and the air rushing out of Aaron and Roger as they hit the ground, their reflexes too slow to catch themselves.

Calvin and Max each reached down grabbing the hands of the boys and pulled them to their feet. Max had to laugh a little at the sign of them rubbing their sore rear ends, as she took off her helmet. They followed Calvin as he moved over to the edge of the platform to talk. Servo pressed a button on the control panel and the camouflage screen quickly swished closed.

Chapter 23

Flight School 101

"So, what did you think of the flight?" asked Calvin.

"What flight," replied Aaron, "I missed it." he said sarcastically. *"I might as well have stayed home."*

Calvin reached over to Aaron giving him a soft pat on his shoulder, "There will be plenty of other flights to come," said Calvin, assuring Aaron.

Roger and Max stood there smiling the biggest of grins.

"I call shotgun next time," said Max, claiming a seat up font for the next flight.

Servo came hovering in close and circled the group. The lift was now fully retracted and she was busy securing the platform getting ready to leave and go with them back to the lab.

"It looks like she is ready to go home," said Calvin as Servo hovered over to Roger taking her place quietly at his shoulder.

After securing everything they all left the platform and climbed inside of Calvin's truck. He drove them all back to the shop and joined Jeffrey back down in the Lab. They removed their flight suits and took seats scattered around the lab.

"Next week we'll go up again. Before the next flight I want you three to start doing some homework," Calvin said as he handed them each a copy of the flight manuals that Randy had created.

"You are now officially enrolled in Cruiser 5.0 School. I need you all to get very familiar with those manuals. You are all going to have to know how this cruiser works and how to fly it. I will be training you all to pilot the cruiser on how to use all of the controls and instruments. Congratulations my student pilots," he said with a cheesy teacher like grin.

"We have our own air force now," said Jeffrey, a little donkey snort came out as he smiled at the three happy faces with enormous smiles shining back at him.

"*Congratulations on joining the team*," said Tory.

They all smiled, "Thanks Tory."

Max leaned over to Jeffrey and asked him, "So, who created the computer Tory?"

Jeffrey smiled, "Oh-, Randy and I created her in college when we were roommates. We were taking the same programming class together. The teacher assigned us to be partners and gave us an assignment for our final project. We had to create our own artificial intelligence program. Randy, was girl crazy and wanted to make ours a woman. So we incorporated all of the women we dated on campus into her personality. We studied their emotions, behaviors and quirks then programmed them all into the system," he explained.

Max held up a finger, "Wait a minute, *you dated a lot of women in college?*" she asked Jeffrey with doubt in her voice.

"Oh yeah", Jeffrey replied with a crooked smile, "you wouldn't *believe* how many hot college chicks would go out with me once they found out I was a computer genius and that I could hack into the school records to change their grades," he laughed.

Max's face turned sour, "*That is horrible!*" she exclaimed. "You were taking advantage of those girls."

"No-no," his face was a little scared as Max started to scold him, "I didn't do it for that, honest," he exclaimed.

Max stood there frowning at him taking a motherly stance as he looked back at her,

"Randy was the womanizer, he had dates all of the time, I just tagged along. Also most of the personality traits of Tory are from the girls *he* dated," then he waved his finger in the air, "so technically its Randy's fault that Tory is so emotional."

Max rolled her eyes and prepared a retort, but Calvin interrupted their discussion. "Ok, let's get back to the business at hand."

Roger looked confused as he was flipping through the pages of the manual while his dad was speaking. The words on the pages were all scrambled, it was just a bunch of letters filling the pages and he couldn't make out one word in all of the jumbled letters.

"What's with this manual?" he asked looking up at his father, "I can't make out a single word in this thing," as he held up the book. Max and Aaron began flipping through theirs as well and quickly discovered that their manuals were also unreadable.

"Mine is messed up too," said Max.

"Mine three," joined in Aaron.

The three of them looked at Calvin, hoping for an explanation.

"I know," replied Calvin, "you need to know how to decode the pages. They are made with encrypted print that Randy created."

"Encrypted print!" snorted Jeffrey, "That's impossible Cal, there is no such thing."

Calvin held up his hand to stop all of the comments coming at him, "Just listen to me, let me explain," he said calming them down.

He looked over at Servo, who was hovering over Rogers shoulder staring back at him.

"Can you go get the pink case in the lockbox?" he asked her. She then zoomed off to fetch a small pink case that Calvin had placed there earlier.

She quickly zoomed back to Calvin and dropped the case in his hand and returned to her post at Roger's shoulder. Calvin opened the case that contained a few pair of reading glasses. He handed a pair to each of them, instructing them to put them on.

"All of your questions will be answered," said Calvin.

"These glasses," he explained, as they all put them on, "will let you read the pages of your manuals. The glasses are used to decrypt the print so that you can read it." The group gave a sound of acceptance as they looked at their manuals, now being able to read the once jumbled print.

"I need you all to have these read by Friday if you are expecting to take another flight next weekend," Calvin said firmly.

"Jeff, do you have any plans next Friday night?" asked Calvin.

"No," Jeffrey answered shaking his head from side to side, "I would love to be here to help," he said enthusiastically.

OK, then," said Calvin, "Get studying and don't lose those glasses!" he ordered them. "Keep them safe and protect them."

Calvin then stood up tall, everyone was watching and listening to him closely as his voice turned sincere. "Listen guys, we have got to be very cautious about this cruiser project. There is probably someone watching us, wanting to get it."

He had their full attention as he stressed the importance of secrecy. He reminded them of the hidden microphone and most importantly, the threat the government had made to Calvin and Alicia to stay quiet and not tell anyone about what Randy was working on when he was killed.

"You all need to be very careful and use your cell phones to call me if you see anyone strange, or have anything out of the ordinary happen to you, OK?" he told them sternly.

They all agreed, looked down with their new glasses and continued to flip through the pages of the flight manuals that Calvin had just entrusted to them.

"I need to be going," said Jeffrey, "My mom will be upset that I am out so late, I have work in the morning."

"*Your mom will be mad?*" replied Max with a laugh, "How old are you?" she asked Jeffrey

"I am twenty five," he replied back, with a look of arrogance in his expression.

"*And you still live with your mom*my?" teased Max.

"So what if I do," snapped Jeffrey, "She is older and needs my help, so shut up!"

"*Time to get your own place little boy,*" said Aaron under his breath to Roger. They both snickered to each other.

Jeffrey didn't hear their comments as he gathered up his equipment to leave the lab. The others took their manuals and headed up the stairs to leave with Servo close behind.

"Goodnight Tory," said Jeffrey, as he turned to leave the lab with Calvin, who had just secured everything back in the lockbox for the night.

"*Goodnight boys,*" she replied, then went into system standby mode as they left.

When they were upstairs in the shop, Calvin asked Roger and Aaron to walk Max home and told them when they returned that he would drive Aaron home in the truck. He really just wanted to talk with Jeffrey alone for a minute and this would keep the three busy and away for a moment.

Aaron and Roger left to take Max home while Calvin stood by Jeffrey's car talking.

"Cal, are you sure you want them to know how to fly the cruiser?"

"I am," replied Cal. "These are some very bright kids and I hope they will be able to pick up and continue the research Randy was doing and finish his projects someday."

"Do they know about all of the stuff he was working on?" asked Jeffrey.

"No they don't. They are still too young to know what he worked on for the military. I don't want them to know all of that yet, but in due time I plan to share it with them."

Calvin turned his head and looked in the distance to see the three of them walking away together, "Unless they figure it out for themselves," commented Calvin.

"Don't worry Cal, I am here to help you if you need anything. I was deeply involved with a lot of the programming Randy did. We worked together a lot in school and again after you recruited me to help on the cruisers. I really got to know about what Randy was working on and he shared his designs and plans with me," remarked Jeffrey.

"He really must have trusted you Jeff," said Calvin.

"He really did, we were great friends, we go way back," said Jeffrey. "In fact, I am the one who introduced him to Laura."

This comment had Calvin's full attention, "What was that?" he asked Jeffrey, "You knew Laura first?"

"I did," he said, "She came to me about changing her grade in her chemistry class. So I helped her go from a D to a B overnight," he giggled, "*and not by studying*," he grinned, "and in return, you see, girls were always so grateful to me after changing their grades, they were so grateful that they would-

"OK, OK!" Calvin interrupted him. "That is too much information Jeff, I get the point," he exclaimed holding up his hands, "apparently it does pay to be a criminal," he laughed.

Jeff continued, "So, after our date that night, Randy came home from the lab just as Laura was leaving our dorm room. I introduced them and they hit it off. She invited him to a Karate class she was teaching that night. So he went to her class, got beat up by her and they fell in love after that."

"I wonder why I never knew that about Laura and Randy."

"It was no big deal," said Jeffrey.

Roger and Aaron were returning after walking Max to her house.

"OK," said Calvin, "Thanks Jeffrey, for the help tonight."

"No problem," said Jeffrey as he got into his car and rolled the window down. "See you guys later." Then he drove away.

"Let's go, you two," said Calvin, as they climbed into his truck and he drove Aaron to his house.

Chapter 24

The Baby

The next few days passed uneventfully. Roger never seemed to come out of his room except for school, meals and bathroom breaks. He was studying his flight manual every moment he could, trying to learn the controls and how to operate the cruiser. He even started using the simulator program that Randy had programmed in Servo. He hooked her up to his computer monitor and used her for training. It was a fun simulator and he was getting pretty good at it. It was more interesting than reading. Studying the manuals was very hard and sometimes he would get dozy and find himself at his desk, surrounded by his messy piles of half-finished inventions fast asleep.

Roger was studying in his room this particular night and just started to doze off again when a 'Zap' of electrical current went shooting through the back of his neck causing him to violently wake up.

"What is your problem!" he yelled at Servo behind him.

She had just zapped him awake so he could continue to study his manual. She hovered around in front of him and was glaring at him with her little robot eyes.

"If you zap me again I will disconnect your battery," he exclaimed, shaking his finger at her.

She made a few sharp robot beeps and sounded like she was scolding him for falling asleep and not studying as much as she thought he should. She then turned around and retreated to the other side of the room to the work bench that had some parts scattered across it.

This caught Roger's attention so he continued to watch what she was doing at the work bench. She was working on something and looked very busy. Roger got up and walked over to get a closer look and see what she was up to. She had Jenny's tiny remote control helicopter on the work bench. Servo's little robot arms were briskly moving between some old laptop parts and broken cell phone pieces. She was hard at work building something out of the toy helicopter.

"Oh man, Jenny is going to be mad at you for breaking her helicopter," he said to Servo.

Servo spun around and looked at him for a quick moment, made a beep, then went back to work busily on her project.

"OK, whatever," said Roger.

He picked up his door remote and clicked the door open and headed toward the kitchen to get a drink and a snack. He clicked the remote again to close the door behind him and put it in his pocket.

Roger had just opened the refrigerator when he heard the kitchen door open. He looked up to see Max walking in the back door. Max was dressed in her exercise clothes and she was just returning from her daily workout.

"Hey there," said Roger.

"Hello, toss me a water bottle please," she said to Roger as she pulled out a chair at the counter.

Roger tossed her the water bottle and she opened it taking a long drink.

"That was a great gymnastics meet yesterday," he said to her.

"Thanks," replied Max.

She had a meet that Tuesday and their team had won by a landslide. She performed a flawless routine on the beam and on the uneven bars. She was very talented and competition seemed to bring out the best in her. She was still very mad at her mother for missing the meet, but Roger and his family went and cheered her on, along with Aaron and Mrs. Jenkins.

"So how is your cruiser study coming along?" Max asked.

"Not bad, only I have this small problem."

Max tossed her now empty water bottle into the recycle bin and turned to give Roger her full attention.

"If I am tired and start to slack in any way, Servo is there to electrocute me and forces me to keep studying," he explained. "It's very annoying."

Max laughed as Roger explained to her what the little robot was doing to him. Then she said, "This gives a whole new meaning to the word "cyber bully."

"That is so dumb," said Roger as they both laughed.

They both quickly turned their heads to look out the window of the kitchen. The sound of truck doors closing in the driveway had caught their attention. Through the window they saw Calvin getting home from work. The other door they heard close was Jeffrey getting out of the truck. Jeffrey was holding a small bag that looked just like the same one he brought the other night that held his equipment and gear.

"I wonder what's up," said Roger as he continued to watch the two of them.

"Let go see," said Max as they both walked out into the yard.

"Hey," said Jeffrey as they approached him and Calvin.

"How is your homework coming along?" asked Calvin with a smile.

"*Shockingly well,*" replied Roger with some sarcasm in his voice and a smile from Max.

He then explained to Calvin and Jeffrey how Servo was shocking him during his homework if he got tired.

Calvin laughed and then was joined by Max and Jeffrey.

"We are going to be in the shop working on the Mustang. We want to check if Randy programmed any additional data into it," said Calvin.

"Can we come along?" asked Roger.

"You need to get back to studying the manual, we have a flight in 2 days," answered Calvin.

"Ya, we know. Can't we take a break? We have been studying day and night," Roger complained.

Calvin looked at him sternly. "You need to study son."

"OK, we'll get back to the books," said Roger, as he and max turned to head back in the house.

They could hear the shop door rolling shut as they entered the kitchen.

"I want to give the simulator in Servo another try," said Max, "I am getting better at it. Then I can give Aaron grief about being a better pilot than him."

Roger let out a little laugh as they discussed a simulator fight they did last night.

"I'm going home to take a shower and then get back to reading the cruiser manual," said Max. "I'm still sweaty from my workout and I want to get cleaned up before I can relax and study."

"I guess I'll get back to it too." replied Roger. He reached into the fridge to get a soda to take with him. *"Servo will probably be looking for me soon anyway."*

Max grabbed her longboard that she had leaned against the wall by the door when she arrived. "See you later bud." And walked out the door headed toward home, thinking to herself, "I hope Mrs. Jenkins saved me something yummy to eat, I'm starving!"

"Talk with you later," replied Roger as he headed up the stairs to his room.

As Roger came up the stairs and was now on the landing, he heard a very strange noise coming from inside of his bedroom. He leaned against the closed door and pressed his ear to it, trying to hear what could be making that new sound he heard. It was not the familiar sound that Servo usually made. He took the remote from his pocket and clicked open his door. He peered around the edge of the door and into the room, scanning from side to side to try for a glimpse of the sound. He took a small step forward into the room and stopped suddenly when a speeding object came quickly up to him making a sudden stop, hovering a few feet from his face, then began slowly approaching him.

His mouth dropped open in awe, he was looking at Jenny's little red and white toy helicopter hovering a few inches from his face. It had two small headlights on the front of it just like little eyes, similar to the headlight eyes that Servo had. It was flying all by itself. The tiny helicopter headlights scanned his face and made a small beep. Instantly Servo came zooming up next to it, hovered and made some beeps back to the helicopter. They exchanged beeps of different tones back and forth a few times between each other. They were communicating in their own robot language. It looked like Servo was giving the helicopter some motherly instructions. The little helicopter then zoomed around Roger's bedroom a couple of times and came to hover right beside Servo. Then Servo's two little tiny hands clapped together, like she was proud of the helicopters performance. Her little headlights were beaming with happiness.

Roger came into his room and quickly closed the door. The two little robots backed up and hovered in the center of the room facing Roger.

"Did you just create a baby?" he asked Servo.

Servo's body tilted happily up and down, confirming to Roger that she just turned Jenny's toy helicopter into her little baby.

"*No freaking way!*" exclaimed Roger, "you made a baby out of Jenny's helicopter and brought it to life!"

Servo came up close to Roger, her new little baby helicopter hovering at her side. Servo's little hand motioned over to the helicopter and she spoke the word in a small computer voice, *"Sparky."*

The little helicopter continued to hover and a very tiny computer tone came from it that sounded to Roger like it just said the word "*Sparky*" to him.

Rogers face lit up with pure joy. Servo had just introduced her new creation to him.

"So your name is *Sparky*?" he asked.

The little helicopters motor sped up excitedly and it took off making a speedy flight around his bedroom. It then came back to a slow hover in front of him and tilted up and down in a yes motion.

"I am losing my mind," Roger said to himself grabbing his forehead with his hand.

"Servo is now a mother."

He turned and looked at Servo, *"I guess Sparky is a little girl?"*

Servo tilted up and down confirming "Yes."

"This is crazy," he mumbled to himself. "Servo actually turned my sister's toy into a mini robot."

Roger's eyes were glued to the two little robots as they continued to fly around his bedroom, zooming like they were playing a game of tag. After a few minutes of this game, it looked like little Sparky was very tired. She appeared to be slowing down. She slowly flew over to the work bench and made a soft landing, her headlight eyes looking very sleepy and droopy. Her helicopter blades stopped spinning as she sat exhausted on the work bench. Servo came hovering up next to her and landed gently at her side. She reached over and took a small cable that looked like a cell phone charger in her little hands and plugged one end of it into the battery charger port on the side of Sparky and then the other end into a power strip on the workbench. A soft purr like a baby kitten was now coming from Sparky and a small glow from her head lights while she sat resting, getting charged back up.

"Amazing, truly amazing," commented Roger as he sat down taking in the scene, wondering how he was going to explain what he just witnessed to his Dad, his mom and friends.

He walked over to his desk by the window, sat down and continued to study his manual. He had read through the entire manual twice so far and was now just skimming, taking notes on some of the systems he wanted to try on the next flight. An hour or so later Roger was distracted by the sound of the large shop door rolling open. He looked out of his window to see his father and Jeffrey emerging from the shop. They had been down in the shop for a couple of hours researching the Mustang.

"I'll ask dad later if he found anything," Roger thought to himself. He looked down and continued to read his manual as his father and Jeffrey climbed into his dad's work truck and drove away.

"Roger, Jenny!" came his mother's voice from the kitchen, "come and eat."

Roger took off his encryption glasses, put them away and hid his manual. He then went down stairs to eat dinner with his mother and Jenny.

He came into the kitchen at the same time as Jenny, they looked at each other, paused and then sprinted for the same favorite spot. There was competition for this particular seat that they both liked at the table. Jenny beat Roger and quickly sat down before he could get to it.

"Ha," crowed Jenny, "beat you to the spot," she said with a victorious grin.

"Next time you are going down!" He repeated, *"Next time, girlie!"*

Alicia placed the bowl of spaghetti on the table and took a seat with her kids.

"Where is dad?" asked Jenny.

"He took Jeffrey back to the office so he could finish some work and then get his car to go home," replied Alicia, "Dad will be back shortly.

The three of them enjoyed each other's company as they ate dinner that evening. After they were finished, Jenny and Roger set aside a plate of food for Calvin, cleaned up the kitchen and the dishes with their mom before heading off to shower and get ready for bed.

Roger had just finished his shower and was heading back to his room to check out the new little baby sister robot that Servo had built.

"Roger."

His dad's voice from the stairs caught his attention. Calvin was walking up the stairs still eating from a plate of dinner they had saved for him when he called Roger's name.

"Holy crap dad, you scared me," said Roger.

"Sorry son, I just got back from taking Jeff to the office," Calvin replied, as he shoveled a fork loaded with food into his mouth.

Roger was standing on the landing in his robe just outside his closed bedroom door while he talked with his dad about Jeffrey and what they were doing in the lab. His father told him they didn't find anything new in the Mustang.

"Dad, *I have to show you something*," said Roger in a strange tone.

The way he said this captured his dad's curiosity. He stood there holding his now empty plate, looking at Roger curiously.

"*What is it Roger?*"

"Something very strange dad, I have to show it to you because, *you wouldn't believe me if I told you.*"

Chapter 25

The Eagle Plan

Volkov stood at the head of a very large conference room table slamming his fist down hard on the polished wood.

"I am tired of waiting!" he yelled to the small group of men and women seated around the large oval table.

The glass conference room they were all in was located in the top corner of a high rise office building. The tall city skyline surrounding the building they were in could be seen through the large glass windows of the room.

The people in attendance were paying close undivided attention to Volkov. He stood there angrily in an expensive handsome suit and tie. He kicked a small chair in anger with his electric leg sending the chair sailing across the room hitting the far wall. A small hum of sizzling energy buzzed from his leg and then was silenced. They all flinched from the chair and heard his leg buzzing and were aware of his electric prosthetic leg. None of them wanted to be close to him in case he was to get angry and kick one of them.

"*Volkov, I told you we are very close to taking them,*" said Natalia in her thick Russian accent. "My best man and his people are there keeping a very close eye on them. He is the very best and will not-

"Natalia," he cut in, "you have been promising this for over a year now!" he said angrily. "I need to access the military's computer systems very soon in order for our plans to come together." He turned and looked out the windows of the large conference room down at the city below. "You know how much we have at stake here Natalia." He turned to face her and the faces of the other scared people also seated around the table.

"Volkov, I will have it in the next few weeks," explained Natalia.

Volkov held up his hand to silence her as she tried to explain her plan to him.

"I will give you three days Natalia," he said, his face glaring and serious as he stared at her. He held up three large fingers, "Three days, or else your team will end up like the older brother," he said with a crooked smile.

Natalia looked at one of the men seated at the table across from her. She was looking for his permission to see if the new three day time table was acceptable. He slowly nodded his head yes to her. She then turned to face Volkov, took in a deep slow breath as she rose, standing up straight and confident in her high heels and tight blouse.

"Fine Volkov, I will go meet with Cooper and his team. We will move in shortly and take the boy and his family along with the robot key. We will move them to the secret facility in the mountain and find out what they know. This time we will not be so easy on them. When Randy died we knew they didn't tell us all that they knew about his work."

Natalia was not happy with Volkov as she turned and started to leave the room, her slender hips swaying back and forth as she walked away. The rest of the people seated at the table jumped up and quickly started to follow her out of the room.

"Nikolay," said Volkov to one of the men following Natalia. "Please stay for a moment. I need a word with you alone."

Nikolay was the man who nodded to Natalia that they could make the new three day deadline to kidnap Roger's family and Servo. He was a handsome man with dark black hair and a strong build. He was the same height as Volkov, very healthy and physically in shape.

Natalia slowed her pace as she was leaving the room for a moment and looked back to see Nikolay as he stopped and turned back to speak with Volkov. She wondered to herself what Volkov was going to be discussing with her second in command and was very worried about the new time crunch that they had just been given to finish their mission.

The door to the large conference room made a small click as it softly closed shut. Volkov was facing Nikolay as they both stood by the large glass windows. Volkov turned back to the conference table, reached down and took out two cigars from a small wooden box on the table. He offered one to Nikolay who took it, bit off the end, spitting the cigar chunk into the garbage can by the table. He put the cigar in his mouth and Volkov lit it for him with his small silver lighter. As Nikolay puffed twice to get the cigar lit, he looked at the lighter Volkov was holding. On the side of the lighter was a detailed insignia etched into the silver. It was an eagle with two bolts of lightning rising from behind, the apparent symbol Volkov was using for his establishment.

After Volkov lit his own cigar he stood with Nikolay and slowly exhaled a puff of smoke, "We are good friends Nikolay. I trust you, my friend, with my own life. Our friendship goes back to when we were younger boys growing up in military families. We met that cold day at the base in Leningrad in our youth. We both share the same goal Nikolay. We are going to take over the military with the regime I am creating. We need the boy. I want his father and their technology so that we can access the Russian military computer systems. We have been paid a lot of money we used to finance that boy Randy to develop the systems. I must have them very soon. The time is drawing close for us to gain access so that we can collapse the financial and defense capabilities of our enemies and take control of them."

He then turned to Nikolay, "I want you to make sure Natalia is successful on this mission," said Volkov.

"I will be there for her," replied Nikolay as he let out the puff of smoke he just inhaled.

"If she gets harmed on this mission, I will hold you responsible," Volkov said as he flicked his cigar above an ash tray. "I want you to personally go with her and give her anything she needs to complete this mission," ordered Volkov.

"I will be with her my friend. You can count on me," said Nikolay as he took another long inhale on his cigar.

"Thank you Nikolay, I care deeply for Natalia," said Volkov," I need her to be safe."

Nikolay turned to Volkov, "Most fathers do care for their daughters Volkov," he said with smile. "I will protect your daughter, my friend."

Volkov returned the smile, "Thank you Nikolay," and gave a hug to his friend as they patted each other's shoulders. They turned with their cigars in their mouths and Volkov proceeded to escort Nikolay out of the conference room.

Chapter 26

The Family

Roger stood just outside his bedroom door with his father right behind him. He knew that Servo and Sparky were zooming around his bedroom because he could hear the small sounds of their engines behind the door. It sounded like they were both very busy at something in the room.

"That sounds a little like Servo," said his father. He could also hear the excitement and small engine noises coming from inside of Roger's bedroom.

"It is," replied Roger, "but that's not all. Have a look." As he opened the door and started to walk into his bedroom.

"Look out!" shouted Jenny from inside of his room.

Servo came rocketing at the open door right at Rogers head, Sparky right behind and following fast. They both zoomed over Roger and Calvin's heads as they ducked down. Then the two tiny flying robots continued out into the hall-way making a fast, speedy circle around the large open landing. Calvin's eyes were wide in amazement. He was at a loss for words as he watched the two robots zooming around in a tight formation.

"They are playing tag," laughed Jenny, smiling and giggling as she watched Servo and Sparky zoom back into the bedroom, doing a few fast circles around the room.

"Jenny, what are you doing in my room?" said Roger, frustration in his voice, but then quickly ducking again as the two robots buzzed by his head low and fast.

"I was walking by your door and heard a very strange noise coming from you room so I opened the door to see what it was."

She stood up and pointed at the two robots as they made a flyby. "When I opened your bedroom door, my remote control helicopter almost took my head off!" exclaimed Jenny.

Calvin was watching the two robots with great interest. "Where did the helicopter come from Roger?" he asked.

"Servo built it today while you were gone with Jeffrey," said Roger.

"Truly amazing, she made a baby," Calvin said bewildered.

"What did you do to my helicopter?" asked Jenny.

"I-I didn't do anything to it. *She did it,* " replied Roger as he pointed at Servo.

Jenny also pointed at Servo as she tore by. "What the heck is that thing?" she asked.

Calvin interrupted Roger and Jenny and spent the next few minutes talking with Jenny, explaining where Servo had come from. He told her a few basics and just the stuff about Servo and Randy. Nothing about the lab, but he explained Servo and swore her to secrecy and kept reminding Jenny how important it was to keep the whole thing very secret.

"This is so cool," she said, "I can't believe she was that little silver box thingy making the beeping noises on your nightstand the other day."

"Yep, there she goes again," Roger said, as Servo chased Sparky out the bedroom door, around the landing, returning back to the bedroom.

"What is going on up here?" asked Alicia as she entered the room.

She let out a small scream as two tiny robots took aim, shooting straight at her. She ducked as they both narrowly missed her and continued to fly by, circling around the room again.

"Be careful dear," said Calvin, "we have another baby in the house."

"A what!" shouted Alicia.

Calvin then explained to her where the tiny helicopter robot had come from. She watched it zoom around the room and remembered the crazy ninja robot Randy made several years ago and how it would attack her randomly.

Sparky was now showing a little slowness and looked like she was tired. Her headlight eyes were slightly drooping as she appeared to be coming in for a landing on the work bench.

"*Aww,* she must be low on energy," said Jenny.

Servo hovered in next to little Sparky and she plugged the cell phone power charger into a port on her tiny body. Her headlight eyes closed and she looked like she was now fast asleep, purring like a baby kitten.

"If that little thing attacks me like Randy's old robots used to, then I won't hesitate to lock it up!" declared Alicia.

Servo looked at her, making a beeping noise, showing concern in her headlight eyes.

"I'm sure you will be fine. Aaron is the one I'm worried about being attacked," laughed Calvin.

Roger laughed at his comment and the memories of Aaron getting shocked again.

"So Jenny," said Roger, "whose room does Sparky get to sleep in tonight?"

"Mine of course," replied Jenny, "after all she was made from *my* helicopter."

Roger nodded in agreement, reminding her to keep these new little family members a secret.

The next morning was dark and raining. It was a little chilly and Roger remembered that today he needed to take his CUBS power jacket to school to show his electronics teacher Mr. Moody. It was time for it to be graded for his final project in class. Max and Aaron came by to take the bus to school together. Roger took Max and Aaron to his room to show them his new baby robot, Sparky. They stood in amazement as she zoomed around the room after meeting them both. Aaron was very uneasy about getting close to Sparky. He had been shocked too many times by her crazy mother Servo for some unknown reason.

"Don't be a chicken," said Max as Sparky was zooming around her head, apparently very pleased to meet her.

"OK," said Aaron, "Here goes nothing."

He reached up to Sparky as she hovered looking at him. He held his hand out stretched and open, so she could land in his palm. He looked very tense and nervous and prepared himself for a possible shock from the little helicopter looking into his eyes, his big crooked glasses staring back at her.

Roger, Max and Servo were glued to the scene, waiting patiently to see how Sparky would accept Aaron. The little headlight eyes flickered at Aaron like she was blinking and wondering what to do. She looked down at his hand and then back up to Aaron's face, made a small beep then softly landed in his palm, accepting him as a new friend.

Aaron's face was beaming. He looked over at Max and Roger as he held Sparky gently in his hand. She slowed her spinning helicopter blades to idle and sat purring in his palm. She really liked him.

Servo instantly zoomed over to hover next to Aaron and Sparky as he held her. Her face looked like she disapproved of Sparky's choice to be Aaron's friend. A few beeps came from Servo like she was scolding Sparky for this apparent betrayal. Sparky beeped back at Servo apparently standing by her decision as they had a robot argument.

Max, Roger and Aaron all gazed at each other and smiled at what they were witnessing. Aaron became too confident that he had Sparky on his side and turned and said to Servo, *"Ha, she likes me. So you better get used to it."*

That comment was big mistake. Instantly Servo shot him with a small shock of energy from her little arm, blasting Aaron off his feet, sending him tumbling backward bouncing off the bed and into the wall. When Aaron was blasted away, little Sparky instantly started to hover where she had been resting in his palm.

Max and Roger were laughing so hard they had to sit down. Aaron just lay on the floor, trying to calm down and rest a moment while he waited for the pain to slowly leave his body.

"I hate that little toaster," Aaron softly whispered.

Little Sparky slowly hovered over above Aaron to see if he was alright. He looked fine and showed signs of life so she zoomed over to where Servo was hovering and started beeping wildly, scolding her mother for blasting her new friend.

The school bus pulled up outside and sounded the horn for pickup. Roger quickly grabbed Aarons hand and pulled him up off the floor to his feet and helped him straighten his crumpled shirt. Roger put on his CUBS jacket as they all headed outside to the bus covering their heads with their arms from the rain as they ran. They were greeted by the bus driver Darin as they climbed on the bus and found seats together.

Chapter 27

Got an A

Mr. Moody, the electronics teacher was a shorter man. He was wearing Roger's CUBS jacket as he stood in front of the class. He was impressed with the small display that Roger and Aaron were showing him in the demonstration. The display was showing the system power at 100% as the jacket announced the same.

"This is really amazing," said Mr. Moody. "So what else does this thing do?"

Roger stepped over and showed him the small button that made the power rod come springing out of the jacket sleeve. The sudden appearance of a glowing blue rod shimmering with a few sparks startled Mr. Moody.

"Whoa, this is so cool," said Mr. Moody.

Roger explained how it was like a cattle prod and a very strong electric shock could be sent from it. Mr. Moody was waving his arm around with the glowing rod in slow movements. He wasn't paying attention to his arm movements and how close he was to Aaron standing there.

"So how bad does this thing shock-"

Roger and Mr. Moody both jumped as they heard Aaron scream in pain and shoot back a few feet slamming into the chalk board then falling to the floor.

Mr. Moody had accidentally touched Aaron on the thigh with the fully charged rod, instantly sending a powerful shock with sparks through his body launching him backward.

Roger and Mr. Moody had turned quickly to see Aaron falling to the floor. He had just bounced off the blackboard. The erasers and chalk fell down on him, lightly dusting him in chalk powder.

"I'm so sorry Aaron, I wasn't paying attention," said Mr. Moody trying to hold in his laughter as he went over to him.

The class was fully engulfed in laughter at the sight they just witnessed. Mr. Moody was trying to get them to quiet down as Roger helped Aaron to his feet. Roger brushed the chalk dust from Aarons face and shoulders.

"I am so sick of getting shocked," he moaned to Roger quietly, "I have lost count now between the robots and now this."

The laugher from the class was slowing down as Roger powered off the jacket, taking it off of Mr. Moody.

"Well that is definitely an "A" for the two of you," exclaimed Mr. Moody to the boys. He was helping Aaron now and checking him out to make sure he was ok.

"Yes," they both said and reached to each other giving a high five.

The class started to giggle again when they high fived each other and the chalk dust that covered Aaron puffed from their hands in the air.

"I give you a perfect score of "10" for the dismount from the chalkboard," said Max. She held up both hands gesturing a perfect score and then clapped a few times.

She was standing in the doorway to the electronics class and had witnessed the gymnastics tumble that Aaron performed after being electrocuted on accident by his teacher.

"What are you doing here?" asked Roger as the bell ending class rang.

"I was on my way to the front office and was passing by your class and saw you both up front giving your jacket presentation, so I stopped to see how it was going. Then I saw Aaron get zapped," and she laughed again thinking of the startled look on Aaron's face as he was blown backwards.

Max reached up patting Aaron on the shoulder, "You ok, bud?"

"Yeah, I'm just a little fuzzy in my head," he replied.

"We did it," said Roger, "we got an A," he said with a big smile. They were all walking down the hall after the bell rang to get their stuff and leave for the day.

"So Max, why are you going to the front office?" asked Roger.

She had a huge smile on her face as she responded excitedly, "OK, so this morning at gym practice, a coach from Bellgrove University was here scouting us with her assistant. They were very impressed with my routine and performance. They talked with me and Coach Geiger for a while and wanted to meet with me and my mom after school to talk about a *possible scholarship.*"

"No way!" replied Aaron.

"I know. Can you guys believe it!" said Max as they walked down the hall toward the front offices. "I didn't think colleges would be scouting me this early."

As they turned the corner, outside of the front school offices was a very pretty blond haired slender woman. She saw them, waved and smiled as they approached her.

"Maxine," she called out to her daughter as she took a step to her, embracing her in a tight hug.

Roger and Aaron stood watching Max and her mother embrace. Max rolled her eyes while in the hug. Obviously she was still upset with her mother for missing her gymnastic meet the other day.

"I was just returning from the airport, heading home from my business trip when I received the call from your principal Mr. Tolman. He told me the wonderful news about the scholarship," said Max's mother.

Max stepped out of the hug and stood by her two friends.

"I am so proud of you sweetie," her mother said as she beamed at her.

Max had a cold look on her face. Roger and Aaron could sense the frustration with her mom.

"You are proud of me," snapped Max back at her mother, "but not proud enough to make it to any of my meets!" she said angrily.

Her mother's face was sad and hurt, "Sweetie, I am sorry I can't always be there, but I have to work since your father left us," she tried to explain.

"I KNOW!" Max replied angrily, "It still makes it hard on me mom."

"Listen honey, can we talk about this at home?" she asked, trying to calm Max down.

Max had a lot of hurt after her parents' divorce. She was angry at how it messed up their family's happy life. She seemed to always vent the anger on her mother when she returned home from a long business trip.

The Principals office door opened and Mr. Tolman stepped into the hallway greeting them all. He was in his early 30's and a very handsome man. Mr. Tolman was one of the youngest principals in the school district. A lot of the girls in the high school had crushes on him.

"Hello, thank you for coming in on such short notice," he greeted Max's mom Jessica, shaking her hand politely.

"*Anything for you Mr. Tolman*," replied Jessica, still keeping a hold of his hand and looking into his eyes.

Jessica had a very noticeable issue of flirting with every man she came in contact with. It drove Max crazy the way she always seemed to flaunt her perfect figure and large cleavage that was always on display from her very low cut blouses.

Max reached down and rescued his hand away from her mother's flirty grip, glaring at her.

"Come into my office," said Mr. Tolman as he stepped aside gesturing Max and her mom into the office.

"See you guys later tonight," said Max to Aaron and Roger as she stepped into the principal's office, following her mother.

As Max and her mother came into the office they saw Coach Geiger visiting with an exotic looking woman and a handsome man. The woman had her hair in a ponytail and was dressed in athletic gear, with a red coach's polo shirt and jacket from the state college. She was very fit looking and had a pretty face with dark eyes. The man was large and strong, dressed in athletic clothing with a jacket also showing the state college cougar mascot on the front. They both stood up to greet Max again and Jessica as they entered the room while Mr. Tolman shut the office door.

"Hello Mrs. Smith, it is pleasure to meet you," said the visiting coach as she took Jessica's hand greeting her.

"My name is Natalia Ronavich. I am the gymnastic coach from Bellgrove University." She turned to introduce her assistant coach gesturing over to the man standing there, "This is Nikolay Novikov."

"It is a pleasure to meet you both," said Jessica. They shook hands and were seated across from Natalia and Nikolay. Mr. Tolman sat down next to Max and Coach Geiger, all of them seated in a circle facing each other.

Mr. Tolman began speaking, "Natalia and Nikolay saw Maxine's team win last week at the gymnastics meet and asked to attend the practice today to observe her. They have been following young Maxine and her performances for a while now."

"Yes-" interrupted Natalia in her Russian accent. "We wish to have Maxine join our college team when she graduates from high school. We are prepared to offer her a very lucrative scholarship with world class training."

She stood up and pointed to Nikolay. "We both are from Russia and have trained numerous gold medalists there. We were hired by the university here to work and to train talented young gymnasts for their program. Max will be getting the best training in the world and the best news is, she will have it paid for with a scholarship."

"That is so wonderful," replied Jessica, as she looked at Max with a prideful smile.

Nikolay now spoke, his deep voice had less of a Russian accent. "We would like her to come to the University for a tour this weekend to show her our gymnastics facilities, if you are available, of course."

"I would love to come tour the University facilities with my mom and Coach Geiger," replied Max.

Natalia clapped her hands together in excitement. "That would be wonderful," she replied. "We shall send a car for you on Saturday to pick you up and bring you to meet us."

"I'm afraid I have a prior appointment and won't be able to make it at that time," said Coach Geiger, "but I could possibly meet you there a short time later."

Max looked happy that she would be there. "Ok, I guess I will still come to visit," said Max.

"That is great news," exclaimed Mr. Tolman. He was excited to see one of his students being sought after by a University.

They exchanged information and Natalia and Nikolay answered question's Coach Geiger had for them. They discussed and made the arrangements for when the car would be coming to pick them up on Saturday. They stood and were preparing to leave when Nikolay spoke, "I have a question for you Mr. Tolman."

"Yes?" said Mr. Tolman.

"When Natalia and I first arrived at the school today, I was speaking with your electronics teacher in the hall. Mr. Moody, I believe was his name."

"Ah yes, Mr. Moody," replied Mr. Tolman.

Nikolay continued, "Mr. Moody told me about an invention that two young boys had created in his class and had just shown it to him today. It was a jacket of some sort that could electrocute people and was a means of protection. "

Mr. Tolman continued to listen to Nikolay.

"These two boys sound truly remarkable and talented. I wonder if you could arrange for them to also come with Maxine on Saturday to join in the tour of the University. We have a very popular science department there and I would like for them to bring their jacket to show our electronics professor. It would be a great opportunity for them to speak with a professor and show some of their work."

"I think that is a spectacular idea," replied Mr. Tolman. "I will speak with Mr. Moody to find out the names of the two boys it was that you were discussing. Then I can contact their parents tonight about the university tour."

Max's eyes lit up because she knew who the two boys were that he was talking about.

"Mr. Tolman, those two boys are my friends Roger Dexter and Aaron Cate," said Max.

"That is wonderful news," said Nikolay with a large smile. "This is such a funny coincidence that all of these talented individuals are friends and know each other." He and Natalia both turned to leave the office.

Nikolay took Jessica's hand as he was leaving. He looked into her pretty face and gently kissed the back of her hand as she held it up to him. She was flirting with him, looking into his handsome face.

"I see where your daughter gets her beauty," he said as he smiled back at her and released her soft hand and left the office.

"We will see you on Saturday," Natalia said to Max as she followed Nikolay out the door of the office where she paused and said with a smile, "I hope your two inventor friends can join you for the visit."

Max returned a smile but the thought she was having about the visit quickly fled her mind when she saw her flirty mother holding her hand up to Mr. Tolman for him to kiss it goodbye.

"Let's go mom," said Max as she pulled her mother away before her hand could be kissed, then gently pushed her mother out the door.

Later that night Max met her best friends at Roger's house to talk about the day. Roger and Aaron's parents had been contacted by Mr. Tolman and had been told about the trip to the University on Saturday. The teens were so excited to go check it out. They were feeling proud that their jacket invention had gotten noticed by a university.

"Wouldn't it be cool if we all got scholarships and went to college together?" asked Aaron.

"It would be a blast," replied Max and Roger.

Roger's dad entered his room as the three of them were sitting lazily. "I am so proud of you three," he said, "A visit to a university at your ages." He then changed the subject, "So how is the cruiser manual studying coming along?"

"Very well," answered Roger, "I'm good to go."

"Me too," replied Max,

"Me three," replied Aaron and giggled.

Aaron's comment caused Calvin to roll his eyes then he spoke, "Tomorrow is another big day. We are going to go out again on the cruiser and test some new features that Jeffrey and I discovered the other day."

Just then the bedroom closet door flew open and two little robots came zooming in. A small helicopter was in the lead, closely followed by Servo. The small one rocketed around the bedroom, zigzagging in between the four humans in the bedroom.

"Not so close," said Aaron as Sparky cut a tight turn by his head on the run from Servo.

"Do they ever get tired of playing tag?" asked Max.

"I hope so," said Roger, as Sparky came too close to his face. A few pieces of his hair slowly rolled down the side of his face. Sparky's helicopter blades were going so fast that when she brushed his face she trimmed a clump of hair from the side of his head. "Oh man, she is dangerous," said Roger.

"That is enough!" said Calvin in a booming, deep voice aimed at the two speeding robots.

Servo and Sparky heard him and quickly slowed down and landed on the work bench.

"Ok, now back to our conversation." said Calvin. "I want to meet here at six tomorrow evening. We can eat dinner and then go for a flight together. I don't want you all to be out late and tired because you are getting picked up by the university car Saturday morning."

They all agreed and Calvin left them alone in the room, shutting the door as he left.

Roger stood in front of his mirror looking at his hair to see how much Sparky had just snipped off the side.

"You can barely tell she cut anything," said Max standing behind him watching him fidget with his hair.

"You better take it easy Sparky," said Roger as he looked over at her.

With the sound of her name, she quickly jumped onto the air, blades spinning and alert to what Roger was saying. Servo hovered in the air next to her, both of them looking at Roger. Servo hovered next to Roger, coming to a stop over his shoulder where she liked to perch.

"Who will be coming with us Saturday to the University?" asked Roger.

"My mom has to leave town tomorrow to save some big business deal in Chicago," Max said in disgust. "*So she will not be coming along.*"

"My parents asked your Dad to bring me," Aaron told Roger.

"So I guess it will just be us, my dad and Coach Geiger meeting us there," said Roger.

"It should be a fun trip," said Aaron.

Max turned to face them. "I guess so. I was hoping to spend some time with my mom. I guess I'll have to catch her later."

"Well, she better be back next week for your birthday party," said Roger, "Sweet sixteen, that's pretty cool."

Max smiled, "Yeah, I'm excited. I get my license so I can start driving us around town. I can use my mom's car all the time. *It's not like she is ever here to use it.*"

"Sweet," said Aaron, "No more having to take the stupid bus to school anymore."

The three of them laughed in agreement.

"Let's take a walk to the train park to hang out for a bit. I want to get out of the house," said Roger.

They all got up to leave. "Stay here Servo. You too Sparky," Roger ordered his two hovering pets. They both slowly flew over to his workbench and landed to wait for his return.

Chapter 28

The Plan

Natalia and Nikolay had just parked the car after returning from their visit to the high school where they had posed as gymnastics coaches from the State University. They had successfully convinced the principal and the others that they were former Olympic coaches from Russia, recently hired by the University.

"You are a genius," Natalia told Nikolay as they walked up to a small brick building. She then entered her pass code on the access panel followed by a biometric hand scan to unlock the door.

"You have all three of them and possibly the boy's father walking right into your little trap. Volkov will be very pleased with you."

"Thank you Natalia. It was a good opportunity that I had to take," replied Nikolay. "That fool of a teacher was bragging about his other two students to us. I knew who the two students were instantly when he started to describe the small skinny one with crooked glasses and then went on about his smart friend who was a natural like his brother at inventing and electronics."

Nicolay and Natalia were the only two people in the small office building. It was located at the edge of a lake somewhere in a canyon. They walked into the small kitchen and Natalia began to make a pot of coffee as Nikolay took a seat at the table.

"Call Volkov and give him an update," said Natalia.

Nikolay took out his cell phone and dialed the number and put the phone to his ear.

"The plan is in motion Volkov, we are all set for Saturday," said Nikolay.

After listening to Volkov's concerns he replied, "No, there is no need for you to come here, we will capture them and bring them to you."

Natalia took a seat at the table waiting for the coffee to finish. She was listening to what they were discussing.

"OK Volkov, good-bye," said Nikolay as he ended his call.

Natalia spoke to Nikolay for a few minutes to discuss the plan and how it was going to work on Saturday. "We will have Cooper driving the SUV to bring them to us. He will secretly gas them making them unconscious and then bring them all to our facility," Natalia said to Nikolay.

The coffee maker finished brewing and the pot of hot black coffee was now ready.

Nikolay got up and took two mugs from the cupboard. He brought them to the table and poured Natalia's coffee first and then filled his own mug.

"What about the robot key device?" he asked her. "That little robot holds the key and it is the most important piece we need."

"I have another team ready to go into the boy's house to retrieve it along with the mother and daughter if they are needed," she replied.

"Good, good," he replied. "How are the technicians coming along Natalia?" asked Nikolay.

"They are on schedule now," she replied and took a sip of coffee, stirring in some sugar. "There was a minor set-back a few days ago with motivating one of them. But he is now cooperating and back on track."

"We cannot have any mistakes Natalia," he said firmly. "Volkov is very impatient and wants this done quickly."

"I am quite aware of what Volkov wants!" she scolded Nikolay. "I am in charge of this operation and I told you that it is going according to the plan."

Nikolay sipped his coffee patiently and after a moment said, "If everything is going according to the plan, then you won't mind taking me to the technicians so I can see for myself what they have completed."

Natalia gazed back at him with eyes of anger as she took another sip of her coffee.

"Fine Nikolay, follow me to the laboratory."

She stood up and walked across the room, bringing her coffee with her. She walked into a small office supply closet in the back of the building with Nikolay following her. They stepped in and closed the door. Natalia walked over to the work bench counter that was scattered with office products. It had the appearance of a normal office supply counter with a box of paper clips, a bunch of paper supplies and some miscellaneous markers and pens. Next to the bench was a copy machine. Natalia lifted the copy machine lid and pressed the copy button like she was going to make a copy of a document. She leaned over the glass of the copy machine so that the bright scanning light passed over her face as she stood over it. After it had completed scanning her face she closed the lid of the copy machine and stood back up. A few small lights on the copy machine began to flash and there was sudden loud noise of mechanical gears instantly starting to turn.

Nikolay made a startled move to keep his balance as the room they were in began to quickly descend straight down. The elevator gears were noisy as they plummeted downward in the small elevator that was disguised as a copy room.

Nikolay looked at Natalia while she sipped on her coffee as they descended deeper into the ground in the elevator. As she finished her sip of coffee the elevator began to slow its descent. They came to a sudden stop with some clanging from the gears. Behind them the wall quickly slid open, revealing a very dim, long narrow hallway. Natalia stepped out into the hallway and as she did so the lights came on above them one by one lighting the long hallway. Nikolay looked around as he followed Natalia out of the elevator. The hallway they were standing in was actually carved deep within the mountain of solid rock.

"Where are we?" asked Nikolay.

"We are at the base of the Canyon Dam under the mountain," said Natalia.

Nikolay looked around as Natalia told him more.

"This dam we are in is the main power generating plant for the area. We have our laboratory hidden here."

She stood with him next to a giant control map on a wall. It was a diagram of the dam and showed the different levels that were down there. The diagram showed the lake and mountains with numerous underground tunnels and letters showing where they were located underground. Natalia pointed to a red dot on the giant diagram,

"This is us," she said.

Nikolay looked to see the red dot and was able to see that they were deep inside the mountain according to the map. He was able to see the long hallway that they were standing in and that there was a large room located at the end of the corridor.

"Come Nikolay, follow me," said Natalia as she turned and started to walk down the corridor.

Nikolay quickly followed her as she walked to the end of the hallway and stopped in front of a large locked metal door. Natalia slid her security card then reached over to a hand scanner. After a moment the large metal door made some loud noises as the huge metal locks disengaged. The heavy door slowly opened to reveal a large room with a high ceiling. Nikolay followed Natalia through the large door as it closed behind them.

"This is the laboratory," she said, as she motioned her hand around the room.

Nikolay turned around slowly absorbing the room. There were giant screens on one wall showing the generating status the dam was producing. A few technicians were seated in front of the large computer terminals and were busy at work. Another wall was made of a giant plate of glass. He could see through the glass into a large cavern deep in the center of the dam. There was a row of seven giant generators that were running in the distance. This was the actual generating station at the bottom the dam where the river was diverted and passed through. The water flowing from the river is what would turn the giant generators that would produce hydroelectric power to the cities in their area. There was a large deep hum in the background that was coming from the generators and the sounds from the plant.

On one side of the massive control room was a small team of technicians busily working at terminals in the area writing on clipboards. A large glass office was located in the corner of the room next to the giant glass wall. This main office was raised on a platform with a small set of stairs leading to the door. Inside of this glass office was a dark haired man with big glasses who was wearing a white lab coat. He stood at a desk facing a computer terminal with his back to the door as Natalia and Nikolay came up the steps to the office. On the glass door of the office was a clear white design etched into the glass. It was an eagle with two lightning bolts coming up from behind, the familiar symbol that was the mark of Volkov and his empire.

The man with glasses inside the office turned around to face the two visitors. It was Jeffrey Taylor. He stood looking at both of them as Natalia closed the door to his office.

"Natalia, what are you doing here?" barked Jeffrey.

"Jeffrey, this is Nikolay Novikov," introduced Natalia, "He is here to help with the mission to acquire the boy and his father on Saturday."

Jeffrey looked at Nikolay observing how muscular and strong he appeared as he stood there tall and gruff.

"Natalia," said Jeffrey, "You promised me that they would not be harmed if I agreed to help you."

Natalia looked at him with a friendly smile and walked up closer to him. She appeared to approach him slowly and friendly, then instantly slapped him with the back of her hand knocking him violently to the ground, sending his glasses skidding across the floor. She was trying to impress Nikolay so he would see that she was in charge of her mission.

"Don't you tell me how to run my mission Jeffrey!" she said maliciously as she reached down grabbing his face and squished it with her hand. She looked at him as a small bit of red blood ran from his split bottom lip.

"You will do what I tell you to do, or your dear precious mother Emma, will end up dead!"

She released his face, stood back up and looked at Jeffrey on the floor. Jeffrey got up from the floor after he found his glasses and faced the two of them. He had a scared and angry look on his face as he put his glasses back on and wiped his bleeding lip.

"Look Natalia, I beg you, please don't hurt my friends," pleaded Jeffrey, as he wiped his bloody lip again with his coat sleeve.

"I won't harm them if you continue to stick with the plan. You need to help get me the key and the boy," then she glanced sideways at Nikolay with a grin. "So tomorrow night, you will plant the tracking devices on the boy and his father when you help them take the cruiser out for another test run."

She gestured to Nikolay to give him something. He reached into his coat pocket and took out a small case that he opened displaying two small buttons.

"These tracking devices must be attached to them so that we can follow their movements during their next test flight. If you fail to do this Jeffrey," and her face went to an evil glare, "little mama Emma will have an accident."

Jeffrey's mother had been taken captive shortly after Cooper had spotted Servo at the lab while he was spying on the Dexter's house. Jeffrey was upset and his cooperation was difficult. This made Natalia start using his mother's safety to put the squeeze on him to work harder on their plan and obey her commands.

Jeffrey took the small case that held the tracking devices from Nikolay and reluctantly slid it into his lab coat pocket. Nikolay and Natalia then left the glass office.

"Are you happy Nikolay, now that you have seen the lab and the technicians?" asked Natalia when they were in the elevator heading up to the surface.

"Yes Natalia. Thank you for showing me. That is what I needed to see," replied Nikolay. "I am happy, very happy."

Chapter 29

A Shop and a Spy

Roger was sitting by Aaron on the back of the giant steam engine train at their favorite park. Max had just finished her climb up on the top of the engine above the main section. She liked to sit up there because it had a cool view from the top and had been her normal perch ever since they were small. "I am so pumped to go check out the college on Saturday," said Max, as she peeled an orange she had brought for a snack. She was tossing the orange peels down at Aaron, seeing how many she could bounce off his head while he sat next to Roger.

"Knock it off girl," said Aaron as another large orange peel bounced off his forehead.

Roger was laughing along with her when his cell phone rang from inside of his pocket. It was his dad calling him to see where he was at.

"I'm at the park with Max and Aaron," said Roger. "Ok, you can pick me up here." He said goodbye and hung up.

"It was my dad. He's picking me up to go with him to my grandmas house. He said he needs to pick up some stuff for our flight tomorrow night."

"Can we come along?" asked Max, bouncing a perfectly placed orange peel off of Aarons head again.

"Of course," said Roger. He listened to Aaron finish his rant at Max for hitting him in the head again. "He's on his way now so we should start walking to the park entrance."

Their timing was perfect, they arrived at the entrance just in time to see Roger's dad arriving.

"Hey Mr. D," said Aaron. "We want to come along too. Is that OK?"

"Hello guys. Sure you can come," replied Calvin. They all got in and drove away headed to Grandmas house.

"I need a few items for the flight tomorrow that are hidden in a place I've wanted to show you."

"What place?" asked Roger. "I have been through every inch of that huge house playing games with Jenny and I never noticed any secret place there."

"That's why it's called a *secret*," laughed his father.

"OK, sounds good dad," said Roger, "But it must be a really good hiding place."

Roger turned on the radio to listen to some music as they all drove across town.

They pulled up to Grandmas house to see Chester barking at them through the large front room window. He was sounding the alarm that someone was there. Grandma came to the door as they walked up the front steps and greeted them happily.

"So what are you all doing here?" asked Grandma Enid.

"I've come to show them the lab," replied Calvin.

Grandma had a startled look in her expression. She was not aware that Calvin had shared this valuable information with them.

"It's ok mom, these three pretty much know everything about Randy and his secret work."

"Calvin Dexter!" she scolded him, "Why would you involve these three young children in this dangerous work."

"Hey G-ma, we're not young children," replied Max, "I'm going to be sixteen next week." Max was the only one who called her

G-ma. It was a little nickname she had given her about eight years earlier.

Grandma stood there a few moments looking at them, "Fine, fine," fussed Enid. "If my son thinks you are old enough to know about it, then fine."

She led them toward the back of her large home. They followed her out the back steps and over to grandpas workshop. Grandpa Kevin's workshop was behind the house in a large garage. Calvin had gotten his tinkering habit from his dad. They both loved to work on old classic cars and fix broken things.

As they all entered grandpas shop, they could see an old classic car partially covered in the corner. The shop was similar to the one at Roger's house as far as the setup. The old shop had tools and car parts scattered about, a work bench and stools on one side. Grandma liked to be in the shop because it reminded her of Grandpa Kevin.

Aaron noticed the similarities of this shop and the one at Roger's house and asked, "Mr. D, does this shop have a special addition down below, like your shop?" He was hinting at the secret lab.

"No Aaron, it does not have the lab, but it does have this." He kicked the rug on the floor causing it to roll up a little revealing a large door hidden in the floor.

They all watched as Grandma pulled the rug up and moved it to the side of the hidden trap door. She lifted a small latch and pressed a secret code in the small lock under a latch and pulled on a handle that had popped out after she pressed the code. The large door in the floor opened revealing a huge compartment. Chester leaned over the edge and peered down into the large hatch along with the others.

"Is that what I think it is dad?" asked Roger.

"It is son, Cruiser 4.0," replied Calvin. "This is where I hid it shortly after Randy was killed along with some other parts."

In the secret space was a large device. It was the size of a large bicycle, without wheels and had two seats in a tandem position. It was the Ducati motorcycle styled cruiser, the one Calvin had told Roger about the other day. Next to it were a few small boxes with some strange looking parts.

"Just a few people knew about this hiding place," said Enid looking at Roger.

"I didn't know that you were involved in Randy's projects Grandma," said Roger.

"Oh yes, he would take small trips over here when he was first building the cruisers. He would dock right over there," she replied and pointed out the back door at something in the distance.

She was pointing at an older power pylon on the back of her property that was holding high power lines. There were other pylons that were all chained together running past her house. They were not as tall as the newer ones and went right through her back yard as well. There was also a small platform with a ladder built on it a short distance up from the ground.

"Randy would come here to get cookies and milk late at night when he was working in the lab. He knew I had trouble sleeping after Grandpa died and would pop over to see me for visits," she said smiling. "I sure miss those visits. They made me happy and would always cheer me up."

They all stood and smiled at Grandma Enid as she told them the stories of Randy's visits and how he would share his latest discoveries with her. Roger thought how fun that would have been to zip across town for one of her delicious cookies or even a fresh brownie with cold milk and then return back home to work in the cool lab in a matter of minutes.

"This is what I need," said Calvin. He pulled a small silver handled case from the hatch, closed the door and stood up. He kicked the rug with his feet again causing it to unroll and cover the hidden hatch in the floor.

He placed the case on the workbench and opened it up. There were a few USB drives and some more manuals inside. He looked through the entire contents of the case and then closed the lid and locked it. Just as he finished closing the case a man appeared in the door way of the shop.

"Hello there." They all looked up to see Carl standing in the doorway. He had just returned home from work.

"Hey Carl," said Aaron and he gave him a high five as he walked in to greet the rest of them.

"I was just coming to take out the trash cans and I saw the shop door opened back here, so I thought I would stop by to say hello," said Carl.

He gave Max and Roger each high fives glancing around the room to see what was going on. "So what are you all working on in the shop?" asked Carl.

"I was just looking to borrow a tool," replied Calvin and he moved and stood in front of the case that was on the workbench, blocking it from Carl's view.

Calvin saw that Carl had caught a glimpse of the case but Carl acted like he didn't see it and took a step back. As he moved he tripped over Chester, causing a startled yelp from the small dog. Chester was unhurt but he caused Carl to stumble and fall. As he was starting to fall and reach out to catch himself, a small handheld radio tumbled out of his jacket and onto the floor, skidding away from him. Carl caught himself on one knee and both hands on the floor and quickly jumped back up.

"Are you ok little buddy?" he asked the unhurt dog Chester.

He began to quickly scan the ground for the radio that had fallen out. The radio had skidded to a stop at Aaron's feet, who reached down, picked it up and went to hand it to Carl. But something caught Aaron's attention and his eyes widened momentarily. On the back of the radio was a small insignia. It was the familiar eagle with two lightning bolts coming up from behind it. He remembered seeing it on the platform and on the computer screens in the lab when the systems booted up.

"Thanks, that's my friend's radio. I was fixing it for him," said Carl as Aaron handed it back to him.

He put it in his pocket quickly then looked at the old partially covered Chevy car in the back of the shop. There was an odd sense coming over all of them that this random visit from Carl was indeed strange. He usually kept to himself and wasn't around that much. Aaron was trying to keep his cool about seeing the eagle insignia on Carl's radio. They had just recently come across it and were unaware of where it really came from. Every time they had seen it, it was connected to Randy and now a stranger had it. Roger remembered seeing Carl use the radio the other day when they were there. He saw him from the upstairs window using it the night of his Grandmas birthday party. He hadn't paid attention to it that night, but now he saw it again and he thought it was very curious. He looked at Aaron and could tell by his face that something had spooked him about Carl.

"Well, I need to be going," said Carl and he walked toward the door to leave.

"See you later," said Roger and Max.

"Thanks for taking out the trash cans Carl," replied Grandma.

"Sure," said Carl and he nodded and left the shop.

As soon as he was gone and they heard his apartment door close Aaron spoke up instantly.

"Did you see the eagle insignia on the radio he dropped?" he blurted out.

They all looked at him and listened as he explained to them what he had seen when he picked up the radio and gave it back to Carl.

"Something is definitely up with that guy," said Calvin. "He was acting very strange, especially when he saw the case on the counter. I saw him catch a glimpse but he pretended he hadn't seen it."

They all listened to Calvin as he spoke, "I have seen that eagle insignia in a few places now. There is one on the launch platform and on the monitors when Tory powers up. I think I will go and ask Jeffrey tomorrow at work. His office was moved a few months ago to the dam facility. I might go over first thing in the morning to talk with him. He might know more about it," said Calvin.

They closed up the hatch, locked the shop and headed back into the house. They were eager to get inside and eat some of Grandmas famous cookies she'd been baking all morning.

"These are the best cookies ever Grandma," said Roger and he patted his belly, now full of cookies. "My favorites are the sugar ones," said Aaron, "I love the sugar too," replied Max.

"Thanks for the snack mom. I wish we could stay longer but it's a school night. I've got to get these hooligans home," said Calvin as he leaned over kissing her on the cheek.

During the drive home Max kept punching Aaron because he kept letting out cookie burps, grossing her out. Calvin dropped off Max and Aaron at their homes and returned home. When they arrived home his dad parked the truck and took the silver case he brought from Grandmas inside with Roger for the night. As they walked into the kitchen they saw Alicia sitting at the table with a cup of warm tea. She looked frazzled and appeared a little tense.

"Are you ok dear?" Calvin asked his wife.

She took a sip of tea in a bit of a trance and then looked up at both of them. "I can't take it anymore, they are driving me crazy!" she said.

Confused, Roger and his father looked at each other and then at Alicia.

"What are you talking about mom?" asked Roger.

At that moment they heard a crash and the sound of something breaking in the living room. Alicia jumped and continued to stare at Roger and his dad.

"THOSE TWO!" she said pointing to the living room as two little robots came speeding into the kitchen, Servo in the lead followed by Sparky. "They are out of control and won't stay put for a second," she cried.

Roger smiled to see the robots zip around the kitchen in a game of tag. Sparky caught Servo then turned quickly and immediately left the kitchen at high speed, heading upstairs with Servo close behind. As they left the kitchen they were so close to Alicia's face that it made her hair blow from the speed of the breeze they caused as they passed by her.

"HEY, watch it!" yelled Jenny as she came into the kitchen as the two robots were quickly leaving, nearly taking her out. "What is with those two?" she asked with a smile, pointing over her shoulder.

"That is so cool," said Roger, "who else is lucky enough to have two pet robots flying around their house?"

"We'll lock them up Alicia," said Calvin, "so they don't stress you out."

He looked over at Roger, "Isn't that right son?"

Roger caught on quickly, "Yes dad, I'm taking care of it right now mom."

He looked at his sister, "Come on Jenny." They quickly left the kitchen to calm the two robots down and put them away for the night.

Calvin took a mug from the counter and sat down to have some tea with his wife and to help her unwind from the stressful day of babysitting two young energetic robots.

Chapter 30

Flight and Deception

Friday had finally arrived thought Roger as he climbed out of bed. The day of our flight is here. His mind raced because he was so excited to get into the cruiser tonight. He was very familiar with how it worked because of all the study he had done during the week in his flight manual. Roger walked into the kitchen to get some toast before heading to school. Jenny was watching cartoons at the counter, on the TV. Sparky was buzzing right next to her shoulder watching with her. They were both glued to the show. Roger laughed when he saw that it was the cartoon show *The Jetsons*. It was a cartoon about spaceships and robots. He smiled seeing sparky the robot watching a cartoon showing a bunch of robots.

Calvin was on the cell phone and Roger could hear the conversation he was having.

"Jeffrey, I've seen it etched on the launch platform and on the computer screens in the lab when Tory comes online."

Calvin had mentioned he wanted to ask Jeffrey about the eagle insignia's that they had come across.

"I have no idea where it is from, I was hoping you might know something about it," said Calvin into his cell phone.

Roger was putting bread in the toaster while he was eavesdropping on his father's phone conversation with Jeffrey. He opened the fridge and took out the milk pretending not to listen, but his father saw him and they both made eye contact. Calvin winked at Roger indicating it was okay for him to listen to his conversation.

"OK Jeffrey, I'll talk with you later today," said Calvin and ended the call.

"So, did you hear all of that?" Calvin asked.

"Well, part of it. What did he say about the symbol?" asked Roger.

"Jeffrey said he has seen it before but really didn't know what it was. He said Randy might have made it up but he couldn't talk because he was very busy this morning and had to go. I'll meet him for lunch today and discuss it further," said Calvin.

He looked down at his watch and saw that it was time to leave for work. "Don't forget, tonight at 6:00, meet here to go take a cruiser flight," Calvin whispered to Roger as he left the house.

"*Duh dad, like I would forget that,*" replied Roger, as he smiled at his dad.

The school day seemed to crawl. Roger was walking to his last class when he quickly came to a stop. He saw down the hall that Gary was coming his way with his posse next to him. They were being obnoxious pushing kids and giving wedgies to smaller kids as they moved through the halls. Roger turned and went down a different hallway to avoid them but it was too late. They had spotted him alone and made a direct path to him. He was walking fast towards the gymnasium when he heard them calling him from behind.

"Where is your little girly bodyguard Dexter?" they called and started running to catch up to him.

He heard their footsteps turn into running steps so he took off running. The bell rang for students to be in their class, but his next class was on the other side of the school. He didn't care about being in class at this moment. He just wanted to avoid these bullies. He rounded another corner as he was sprinting away. The hallways were now vacant as he ran. The others students were all in their classes, except for the ones on his tail. He ran down a flight of stairs to the first floor and could hear them jeering at him as he fled.

He rounded another corner and down another set of stairs he had never been on before. He was now in the basement and running down a short hallway. At the end, there was a door with old rusty pipes and wires overhead. He hit the door with his body hoping it would fling open, but instead came to a full stop. The momentum he had as he hit the door popped the lock and it opened a crack. He pushed on it again and it flung open. He then quickly went into the boiler room behind the door. He had just slammed the door shut and could hear Gary calling him as he approached the closed door.

"Roger. Where are you Roger?" taunted Gary.

Roger quickly scanned the area near the door. It was very dim and lit by a small yellowish light bulb in the distance. Roger found a piece of pipe in a small pile of debris that was just long enough to be used as a wedge and he quickly jammed it in the frame just in time to secure the closed door. He immediately heard Gary slam into the door with his full momentum and saw it give a little, but it held tight and was blocked securely to keep the boys out. They called him names in frustration from the other side of the door as they pounded and pushed on it trying to get it to open, but it held, keeping them out.

"We will wait out here all day you wimp," yelled Gary as they pounded on the blocked metal door.

"Oh yeah, just leave me alone you jerks!" Roger replied back through the closed door.

He turned to scan the room he was in looking to see where he had just trapped himself. The boiler room was very hot and not well lit. The old room had a damp smell of mildew and old rags. Loud noises hummed in the background from the machines and giant fans that supplied heat and air conditioning to the school. Large electric panels lined the wall on one side of the room. The ceiling was lower in places as he walked toward the back of the large room. Pipes and large conduits full of cables sprawled everywhere on the ceiling. A small amount of dust covered the basement floor, showing the absence of people coming down here.

A loud noise suddenly came from behind him. He jumped and quickly turned. One of the boilers had turned on and he could see the small flicker of flame inside the metal case. He looked to his side toward the ceiling and his eyes followed a group of pipes that went across the room. The pipes disappeared into a dark narrow crawl space. He looked and saw another group of pipes heading the opposite direction leading to a crawl space that went to a different section of the school he was below. He decided to follow the first set of pipes to see if they would lead to some kind of an exit from this spooky basement. As he got farther down the small corridor he came to a solid concrete wall and the pipes went through it with no room for anything else to follow. It was very dark so he pulled out his cell phone to use the flashlight app. He saw that there was a giant vent on his right where the pipes disappeared. The vent had a large metal grate cover. He was turning to go back to where he started when something caught his eye. On the wall next to the vent was a small emblem carved into the wall. It was an eagle with two lightning bolts.

"No freaking way," he said out loud, *"you gotta be kidding me. There is no way I'm going in there,"* he thought to himself. He backed out of the small crawl space and went back into the loud boiler room.

He paused and thought of his brother Randy and wondered how this eagle insignia he had seen before was possibly tied to him.

"Did Randy work down here for some reason?" he thought to himself, then paused for a few minutes deep in thought.

He had to go back and see if he could open the vent cover. He had to see what was in there. He took his cell phone and with the light from it led the way back into the crawlspace to the vent. He looked and found two latches on the giant vent and twisted them to open it. As it fell open, he saw that it was wide enough for him to duck and enter. He held up his phone and looked forward and backward to decide which way he should follow. He found another eagle insignia on the side of the vent followed by two more a short distance away. He pulled the vent door closed to hide his tracks in case Gary got past the jammed door and tried to follow him. He walked bent as he followed the eagle insignias to see where they led him. They were spaced pretty far apart and hard to see but he found more as he walked forward.

"I can't believe I am in here doing this," he said to himself, "this is so crazy," he thought as he continued down the dark endless tunnel. He continued further and suddenly he knew where he was. He was under the main offices of the school. The vents branched off in different directions to the offices above. He knew this because he saw a little bit of light up ahead and as he was slowly approaching the opening, he could hear Mr. Tolman talking with someone in his office. He slowed down and started to crawl to the vent opening so he could hear what was going on inside of the room. The vent he was in, rose slightly in the wall of the room just above the floor. It sounded like there were two people in the office talking to Mr. Tolman. Roger heard a woman's voice with a thick Russian accent. He closed his cell phone to hide the light and looked through the small vent opening that he was hiding inside of. The vent cover was on the wall of the principal's office, it was barely big enough for him to squeeze through if he needed to. He could see the University Gymnastics coach Natalia standing there. She was very pretty. She approached Mr. Tolman as he was speaking to her. He appeared to be agitated as he spoke to her.

"I told you I want double the money this time," said Mr. Tolman, as he leaned back in his office chair.

Natalia was standing across from him as he sat behind his desk.

"We had an arrangement and now you want to change it at the last minute," she said, her voice rising in anger.

"We already talked about this Natalia. Look, you now want me to do more than we originally agreed to. I agreed to help you get the Dexter boy. Now you want me to help you get his friends and family as well. That's more work and deserves more money." He then got up and stood to face her, more agitated now. "If you don't like it, you can find someone else."

Natalia turned and looked at someone. Roger could not see who it was from the vent and pressed closer to try to see. He caught a glimpse of her partner and saw Nikolay nod his head back at her.

Natalia turned to face Mr. Tolman, glaring at him.

Rogers mind and heart were both racing. He knew they were talking about him, his friends and family. He wanted to run out to warn them all, but he had to stay to see if he could hear more about what they were planning.

"We can come to some sort of arrangement", she said now in a softer voice. She approached him like a snake, sneaking up on its prey.

She gently pushed him back down into his chair and walked slowly behind him as he sat. She slowly dragged her hands across his shoulders calming him. She was reaching into her coat to get something when a cell phone ring tone could be heard across the room.

Roger jumped and knew that it was Max's ring tone coming in on his cell phone. He tried to cover it and stop the ringing as fast as he could, but it was too late. Natalia turned in the room and was facing the vent in the wall where Roger was hiding. Nikolay also heard the noise and quickly had gotten up and was walking cautiously over to check where the sound had come from.

"Where could he be?" asked Max, waiting for Roger to answer his phone. School was over and she and Aaron were tired of waiting outside the building for him. They had missed their bus and were going to walk home with him.

"It went to voice mail," she said, as she hung up her cell phone. "Try it again," said Aaron. She took out her phone and dialed again.

Roger was being as still and quiet as he possibly could. He held the phone tightly in his hands and pressed it against his chest as he knelt just inside of the vent. He was trying to keep his breathing as soft as he could while his heart felt like it was going to leap from his chest.

"What was that noise?" questioned Nikolay.

"I don't know, it came from over there in the wall," said Natalia, as she pointed to the vent.

Mr. Tolman was sitting in his office chair and had spun it slightly so he too was facing the wall staring intently at where the sound had come from.

Max's ring tone once again started playing on Roger's cell phone causing Nicolay's eyes to widen. He instantly began to make quick large strides across the office toward the vent in the wall.

Roger jumped, being startled by the phone again and was trying to turn around in the vent to crawl back the way he had come. But Nikolay had reached the vent and was peering inside with Natalia now standing next to him.

"Someone is in there," said Nikolay.

He scanned the vent looking at all of the corners for a latch to open it. Not finding one, he took the vent with both hands, his fingers wrapped in the small vent openings with a tight grip and jerked hard. The vent cover broke off the wall with pieces of drywall falling into the room as he tossed it to one side. He was kneeling down as he reached his head in the vent opening and could see a boy trying to crawl away.

He reached in to grab Roger and caught him on the foot as he attempted to flee,

"Gotcha," said Nikolay.

Roger tried to kick and pull his leg free of the man's tight grip on him, but was not successful. Nikolay, a large and strong man pulled him back toward the vent opening. He continued to struggle as the large man pulled him like a prize from the vent and into the principal's office.

"Well, well," said Natalia, "look what the school has living in its walls."

Nikolay's grip holding Roger was very tight and held him securely so he could not wiggle free.

"What are you doing in my wall!" shouted Mr. Tolman.

He was now standing in front of Roger with an angry stare. Roger was very scared as he stood there in the room confronted by the three adults.

"I was trying to get away. Some guys were chasing me," explained Roger. "You know Gary Crawford and his posse, they were after me."

Natalia and Mr. Tolman stood there looking at him.

"I don't think so," replied Natalia breaking the silent stares.

"Honest," cried Roger as he started to try to explain what had happened.

Natalia cut him off and instructed Nikolay to release his tight grip on him. Roger rubbed his folded arms as he stood there. They were sore from his tight grasp.

Mr. Tolman approached him starting to speak in anger, but Natalia held up her hand to silence him as she kindly seated Roger in his chair.

Roger was looking at Natalia's pretty face and big brown eyes.

"We have been meaning to talk with you, Roger."

"How did you know my name?" he said angrily and turned to Mr. Tolman, "how much are you getting paid to give up me and my friends?"

He tried to stand up but was pushed back down into the chair gently by Natalia.

"What is going on here?" demanded Roger.

In a soft motherly voice Natalia answered, "Settle down Roger, it is ok." She was now standing behind him as he sat in the chair.

"We need to ask you a few questions Roger, but not here at the school."

She was holding a small device about the size of a cell phone that she had taken from her coat pocket. She put it next to Rogers head and it instantly sent a small beam of what looked like a lightning bolt right into his neck. She had stunned him and he went limp in the chair, unconscious.

"Nikolay, pick the boy up and carry him to the car."

"What did you do, where are you taking him?" asked Mr. Tolman.

"He will be fine. We are taking him with us. It is of no concern to you" she replied.

Nikolay picked up Roger and flung him over his shoulder like a bag of flour. The school was nearly empty as most of the teachers and students were now gone for the day. Nikolay and Natalia exited the back door the of the school offices toward their car. Roger was unconscious and hanging over Nikolay's large broad shoulder as they walked toward their SUV a short distance away.

Max and Aaron had given up on Roger and were starting to walk home. They had just passed the back of the school near the faculty parking lot when they saw the back door of the offices fling open and a large man exit with a young boy draped over one of his shoulders. A dark haired woman in a bouncy pony tail was following him as they approached a parked SUV.

"Hey, look. The university coaches," said Max when she noticed Natalia.

"Who is he is carrying over his shoulder?" questioned Aaron.

They both watched as the man flopped the unconscious boy into the back seat of the car. The man had shut the door and was walking around to get in the driver's seat when another girl quickly approached him at a full run. She slammed into the man with her shoulder down like a football player, knocking him to the ground. Natalia was reaching into her coat pocket when the girl who had just taken out Nikolay did a spinning kick, knocking her right in the side of the head. Natalia fell to the ground unconscious.

"Did you see that?" exclaimed Max. "Hey that's Laura!" as she took off running toward Laura.

"Wait, you can't-" said Aaron as he took off after her.

Nikolay got to his feet and was face to face with Laura. He threw a punch at her, but she dodged it and landed her fist right in his face. He staggered and stepped back as she did another spinning roundhouse kick aiming for his head. He caught her leg with his large hand stopping her momentum on the spot. She staggered as he held her calf sneering at her.

"Is that the best you've got sweetheart?" asked Nikolay, trying to provoke her as she stood there on one leg.

Instantly, Laura hopped and quickly spun her body using her free leg to kick him in the face causing him to drop her leg he was holding. This caused her to fall to the ground, but with grace she quickly caught herself and spun back to her feet facing the stunned Nikolay.

Nikolay threw a strong punch but failed to connect with Laura as she dodged it. She stepped closer to him and hit him in the face with her elbow, then quickly kicked his feet out from under him and he fell hard on his back. She punched him in the face as he lay stunned on his back. She hit him again with two fast rabbit-like jabs that knocked him out cold.

"Laura, what are you doing?" Max screamed as she arrived on the scene. "Those are the university gymnastics coaches."

Laura turned quickly, startled that someone was there.

"Hey Max," she said smiling at her after she recognized her.

"*Laura!*" gasped Aaron as he arrived. "What are you doing?"

She was quickly searching through Nikolay's pockets for the keys to the SUV. She found them along with a hand gun. She quickly took them both and hurried over to the car.

Max and Aaron both gasped. They had just spotted Roger in the back seat of the SUV.

"Listen, I don't have time to explain. Get in the car now," she ordered them as she opened the driver's side door and climbed in.

"NOW-, we have to go NOW!" she barked.

Max and Aaron looked at each other with confused expressions then quickly got in the car. Laura slammed the SUV into gear and quickly sped away escaping from the two obviously fake university coaches lying unconscious on the ground in the back parking lot of their school.

Chapter 31

Blown Cover

The SUV turned a corner at high speed, the wheels screeched with Laura at the wheel. "Hang on, we are going to be taking a lot more corners at this speed," said Laura, as the SUV swerved again around a city corner.

Max was in the back seat next to Roger while he lay unconscious, trying to hold him steady as Laura drove the SUV erratically. Aaron was riding shotgun by Laura holding on tight to the grab handle.

"How does Roger look, Max?" Laura asked.

Max leaned over to check on Roger. "He looks ok, I guess. He's breathing just fine. He looks like they knocked him out or something," replied Max

"OK," replied Laura. She was busy looking at the traffic she was speeding through as she maneuvered the SUV in and out of lanes.

"What is going on Laura?" asked Aaron. "Why did you kick the gymnastics coach in the head and beat up her assistant?"

"Listen you guys, there is so much to tell you but we don't have time right now. We need to get to Rogers house and into the lab right away. They'll be coming for us."

"Who'll be coming for us?" replied Max and Aaron, "And how did you know about the lab at Roger's house?"

Laura looked over at Aaron, "Because I dated Randy. I had a bug in the shop so I could listen and keep tabs on everyone, but Calvin destroyed it the other day."

Roger moaned and was starting to gain consciousness. He was slowly trying to sit up looking very groggy.

Max reached over to comfort Roger and help him sit up. "Hey bud, it's ok. We are here," she said looking at his face as she held it with one of her hands.

"*Where am I?*" asked Roger in a soft voice. He was becoming more alert now and quickly sat up in the back seat and looked up at Laura driving the SUV. A car horn sounded as Laura swerved the SUV hard to get around the car and they all jerked from the sudden movement.

"*Hey, what the- Laura*, Is that you?" Roger asked.

Laura turned briefly as she sped through traffic and looked back smiling at him.

"Yeah it's me, how are you feeling?"

Roger was now more coherent "I'm doing ok, but how did I get here?" he asked. "I was in the principal's office talking to-" he immediately sat up more alert. "*Guys-, the coach is bad and so is Mr. Tolman.*"

He quickly explained to them how he found the vents under the school when he was running from Gary. He told them how he went inside after finding the eagle insignia and following it right up to Mr. Tolman's vent in his office. He went on to describe how he had gotten caught in the vent. He explained how they dragged him out of the vent and into the office, how they questioned him and then, he was tazered unconscious by Natalia.

"She got pay back for that," said Aaron.

"What do you mean?" said Roger.

"*Laura kicked her in the face.* I saw it. *She was Awesome,*" he said as he looked over with dreamy eyes at Laura as she drove.

Max told Roger about the fight Laura had in the school parking lot with the two coaches and how Laura had rescued him.

"Look, it is a long story, but I was assigned to protect your brother Randy," explained Laura. "I met him in college. I was undercover and was meeting with his dorky roommate Jeffrey. I pretended I needed my grade changed so I could get introduced to Randy and meet him. I was assigned to protect him while he was working on projects for the company."

"What do you mean *projects for the company*," replied Roger.

"I was working for a very wealthy, powerful man at the time. I later found out that he was a very bad man and using his company for funding university's science departments to develop special weapons projects for him. He paid off certain professors who came to him with talented students. He would take the inventions the students were creating and use them to build and run his empire. The longer I worked for him the more I learned about how evil the guy was and the things he was doing. This man actually recruited Randy to work for him and his company secretly at the university. Randy was working on some big project, a weapon of some kind that he needed for his company. It was a huge project and he was planning something very big. I don't know what it was, but I know he invested some other countries money in it."

The three in the back seat were stunned as they listened to Laura.

"What do you mean Randy used to work for the evil guy?" asked Max.

"His name is Volkov, he hired me to get close to Randy and protect him, in case other interested countries or businesses wanted to steal him away. I worked undercover as a bodyguard for Randy at first, but things changed and I," she paused a moment and then swerved the SUV around another vehicle sounding its horn as she drove.

"I actually fell in love with Randy, we hit it off so well and spent so much time together. I loved him dearly. I quit working for Volkov after Randy was killed in the explosion at the lab. I stayed out of contact with Volkov, changed my hair and disguised myself. I tried to keep informed as best I could with my resources. I wanted to find out what he was up to the past year so I stayed undercover working at the diner.

She looked at Roger, "I was tailing Natalia today when I saw that she and Nikolay had you, I had to save you. I found out about their fake plan tomorrow to take you to the University for a tour. I was going to tail them after they had you to see where they were really going to take you, but I was scared when I saw you being hauled out of the school unconscious. So I chose to save you now."

"They were pretending to be coaches?" asked Max.

"Yes Max, they would have kidnapped all of you and then taken you to their secret location. But that is blown now, they will he coming for all of you very soon."

This comment scared the three of them. They looked at each other and then back to Laura.

"We need to get to the lab at your house Roger, get the cruiser and head out of town before they get there," said Laura.

"Let me call my dad," said Roger as he took out his cell phone.

He looked down and saw that he had two missed calls from Max when he was hiding in the vent. Just then his phone started to ring again, this time it was his dad.

"Dad," answered Roger hurriedly.

"Hey son, I just wanted to call to see when you were going to be home?" he said.

"I'm on my way home now." He quickly said, "Laura is driving me, Max and Aaron to our house. Someone is after us dad!"

"Who is after you?" Is it that bully Gary again?" asked his father, "I am going to call his parents and-

"Dad!" Roger cut him off, "it's not Gary. It's the coaches from the University, the ones who wanted us to come and visit tomorrow."

He went on to tell his father what had happened at the school, nearly being abducted by them and how Laura saved him.

"How soon until you will be here," asked his father.

"About five minutes," replied Roger.

"OK, I have Jeffrey here with me so he can help get the stuff from the lab ready. Your mom is not here right now, she is at Grandmas house with Jenny. I will call her and tell her to leave and get somewhere safe."

"OK dad, see you soon," then he ended the call.

Aaron looked a little worried, he was an only child and his parents were both gone. His father had a business trip and his mother had joined him because it was their anniversary during his father's trip and it was a good excuse to get away together.

"Mrs. Jenkins is staying at my house with me this week while my parents are gone," said Aaron. "So my family is safe." He asked, "Do you think Mrs. Jenkins will be safe?"

"She should be fine," said Laura. "She has no knowledge of any of this."

"My mom is gone for two weeks on business as usual so I don't have to worry about her," said Max.

"OK, we need to get somewhere safe after we get the cruiser," said Laura, "I know just the place."

Laura drove the speeding SUV into Roger's driveway and pulled to a sudden skidding stop by the shop. Calvin was standing guard with a shotgun as they arrived. He quickly hurried over to meet them as they all were quickly getting out of the car.

"Laura, it's good to see you," said Calvin as he gave her a quick hug. "Thanks for saving the kids."

"No problem Cal, but we need to hurry and get to the lab. Volkov is probably well informed about what happened by now and will be sending reinforcements."

"Volkov?" he asked. Then his face sunk as he remembered that name. He had heard it years before during his time in the Army.

"He's the one after your family," she said as they closed the car doors and all hurried towards the shop. She explained a little more trying to get Calvin up to speed as they went to the shop as quickly as they could.

Roger looked up to his open bedroom window and whistled with two fingers. Instantly, two little flying robots came zooming out of the window and down to him. He turned and entered the shop followed by Servo and Sparky.

He shut the door and followed the others to the secret closet that was the entrance to the lab.

"Jeffrey is already down there waiting for us," said Calvin as he pulled the secret lever in the cabinet opening the door to the lab.

Laura stood there looking at Sparky hovering, in amazement.

"Who made this little one?" she asked, "I have met Servo many times before but not this little cutie."

"Servo created her the other day with parts I had in my room," said Roger.

"She what?" replied Laura.

"She created her from Jenny's toy helicopter and spare iPod parts I had in my bedroom," said Roger.

Laura was momentarily speechless about little Sparky and her eyes were glued to her as the little helicopter buzzed around the shop and went into the closet entrance following Servo down into the lab.

They all entered and closed the secret door and went down in to the lab. They greeted Jeffrey who was already busy at work on his laptops, working with Tory setting up the systems for launch.

They saw Jeffrey hard at work on the computers. He didn't look up but waved a hand saying, "Hi guys."

As they all stood in the lab Laura began to quickly update them on Volkov and the last year she had spent undercover. They all listened intently to Laura as she quickly told them all about the surveillance she had been doing on Volkov and his employees. She had also been watching Roger and his family as well to see how close Volkov's men were to them. She was pleased to see that they had taken the cruiser out and had a good understanding of how it worked. "I saw your maiden voyage the other day with cruiser 5.0 and you seemed to handle it pretty well Cal," she said.

"You sneaky little girl," said Calvin smiling at her. "Thanks for watching out for my family, it means a lot to me Laura."

"You're welcome Cal," replied Laura, "But we all need to go right away. We need to get the *cruisers* and hurry to the tower and launch."

"*Cruisers?*" replied Calvin, "there's more than one in here?"

"Of course there are," replied Laura. "Remember I almost married your son, he showed me everything about this lab."

She took Calvin's hand and paused a moment, looking at him.

"I want you to know that I really did love your son. I fell in love with him the first week I was supposed to be protecting him."

He smiled back at her. "I know Laura. I could see the way you looked at him. I knew you really cared for him."

"I'm sorry you had to find out this way, I wanted to tell you but I needed to see what Volkov's intentions were with you. So I had to stay back and observe," said Laura.

"I am just glad to know you have been watching out for us, they would have gotten Roger today if you hadn't been there."

"So where are these other cruisers?" asked Roger curiously.

"Tory," said Laura as she faced the wall of monitors to talk with her.

"It is so good to see you again my dear, how have you been?"

"I am doing well Tory. Thanks for asking."

"We have unfriendly people inbound after us, we need to leave now in the pods." said Laura.

"What is the passcode for evacuation?" asked Tory.

"0311" replied Laura, as she whispered over to Calvin standing next to her, "it is the date I was supposed to marry Randy."

"PASSCODE CONFIRMED," sounded Tory.

They all turned as they heard the loud sounds of gears turning and the loud bang as locks and latches disengaged as the whole back wall to the lab slowly rolled backward and swung open like a giant gate, revealing a very large room. The lights quickly flickered on and they all headed into the room. As they passed the water cooler that held the cruiser 5.0 model, Laura took it under her arm like a football as she passed by.

The room they entered was a little larger than the lab. It was full of objects and devices that were strange and they had no clue about what they were. On one side was a large control panel. There were three work benches that all had a football object sitting on them.

"What is this place?" Jeffrey asked. "I never knew this was here."

"No one did, except for Volkov, Randy and me," said Laura. "He had it secretly built by contractors from Russia at the request of Randy. But there is one good piece of news. Volkov never actually oversaw the construction and he thought the secret lab was being built under the lab at the college. Randy somehow had tricked the contractors into building it here, managing to keep the secret that it was built at your house Calvin. Volkov thought it was destroyed in the explosion at the college. He thought he lost everything Randy had been working on. So that is why he wants you Roger."

"Me," said Roger, "Why does he want me?"

Laura was quickly moving through the new lab gathering items and pressing buttons at one of the control consoles on a far wall, apparently powering up some kind of systems as she spoke to them.

"He wants what is in your head Roger," said Laura

"What are you talking about Laura," queried Roger.

"We don't have a lot of time, we need to get out of here with all four of these cruisers," said Laura, as she motioned to the tables holding the football shaped cruisers.

She opened the door of a large cabinet and took out three white duffel bags and tossed them to Aaron, Max and Roger.

"Put a football cruiser in each bag." said Laura as she turned to Calvin and told him to get the last one and keep it close. "We will use the one I have and the one you have Calvin to escape with on the platform," she turned to face Roger.

"Roger, there is something Randy did to you one night while you were sleeping," she said.

This had Roger's attention along with the rest of them. She flipped on some more lights and switches then they heard a deep hum coming from some odd looking devices on the side wall.

"Randy scanned your eyes one night while you slept. He was creating your passcode and ID for his entire systems, giving only you full access to everything that he had created. He not only gave you access to everything, he also implanted his entire program of all of his inventions into your brain by the scan. The code is hidden and embedded throughout the electrical energy in your brain. As long as you are alive, the code and all of his work can be downloaded from you."

"You're kidding me, right?" said Roger, as he looked at the shock on his father's face.

"Servo is the key to getting it from your brain. She has been programmed to be your bodyguard for your safety as well as protecting the data in your head."

Roger immediately got a splitting headache trying to process all the information she had just dropped on him.

"They are here!" announced Jeffrey.

They all looked at the computer panels that Laura had turned on. There were security cameras around the perimeter of the house up above. This room had the only access to these cameras they were seeing. There were some cameras located on the tower and the platform. They were looking at one camera angle that showed a large black SUV. It had pulled into the driveway of the house, the man Cooper was behind the wheel. Two more black SUV's were right behind that one. They could see the car doors open, Natalia and Nikolay got out with Cooper. Natalia held an ice pack on the side of her head and looked very angry. Cooper flicked a burnt cigarette to the ground and crushed it with his foot as he looked around the back area of the house, his gun drawn. The other SUV's doors opened and men with small machine guns quickly setup a defensive area around the stolen SUV they had arrived with. The men approached it with guns drawn and took cautious steps toward it to see if anyone was inside.

"Everyone in here now," said Laura as Jeffrey ran over to join her. "Tory close the door and protect yourself," she ordered.

The large lab wall that had opened earlier slowly closed and they heard huge locks bolt into place securing them in the new lab.

"We need to leave ASAP," she said.

"How are we going to get out of here and to the tower?" asked Calvin.

"*Didn't you all read the manuals?*" she said sarcastically. "Seriously."

"We need power cables to connect with, Laura," said Calvin.

"Chapter 36 in the manual shows you how the cruiser transforms the molecules in your body and alters it so that you can go underground while in a transformed cruiser, remember?" said Laura. "I learned this on cruiser 5.0 with Randy and I also helped write the manuals," she added.

"*I know that,*" replied Jeffrey. "But we still need a power source."

Laura had just typed something in a computer terminal and a wall section of the lab slid open, revealing giant overhead power cables that were fastened and terminated right above them near the platform.

"*Is this what you are looking for?*" she asked sarcastically.

It looked like a mini train station where the end of the rail tracks stop, only this was where the power lines came to stop. They were constructed right on the launch platform and were used to tap into the power grid and connecting cruisers to the power.

They all quickly dressed into their flight suits and helmets. There were three power gloves with them. One of them was the one that they used on their first flight. The other two were sitting by the football cruisers on the tables. Calvin took the one he had used for himself and tossed one over to Roger who caught it then slid it on. Laura took the last one and put it on. She turned to Calvin, "I'll take Roger and Max with me. You take Jeffrey and Aaron."

Calvin placed the sphere on the new mini platform below the power lines. Aaron and Jeffrey took their places on the mini platform standing above the football sphere. It was just like they had experienced on their first flight. Servo and Sparky were zooming around pressing buttons on terminals and preparing for launch. The sphere they were standing over immediately grew around them as they were instantly sitting in the fully charged cruiser ready to leave. Servo pressed some controls that made the sphere rise on the platform and make contact with the power cables and they were ready to launch. Sparky came over, docked with the sphere at the top and everything looked ready to go.

"Calvin, head to Chicago, we will be right behind you," said Laura on the helmet radios.

"OK, hurry and get out of here, see you on the lines," replied Calvin.

He pushed the throttle slowly forward. The cruiser formed an elongated sphere of energy as they appeared to dissolve into the lines and speed off underground following the path of the power cables leading them underground and away from the lab. They emerged a few miles down from the house as the power lines transitioned out of the ground and up into the air toward the tall towers ahead. They were now out in the open and connected back to the power lines high up with the towers.

"OK," said Laura. "You two, bring the bags with those two cruisers over here and let's launch."

Laura set the cruiser she had brought with her from the front lab down on the platform. They all took their places standing next to the sphere on the platform resting quietly below them. Instantly the oval sphere grew around them and they were now sitting ready for departure. Laura quickly pressed some buttons on the console and the lift rose up to the power cables and made contact. Servo sped around the new lab briefly and then docked into the top of the sphere ready for departure.

"Are you all ready?" asked Laura.

"Punch it," said Roger. "Hit it," replied Max.

Laura was in the left seat and she slowly moved the throttle forward. The sphere did just as the one before it and dissolved into the lines as they rocketed off, speeding briefly underground as they headed towards Chicago following Laura's directions.

Chapter 32

The Getaway

"ALL CLEAR," said Nikolay as he stepped back from the SUV lowering his gun. He had just finished searching it and found no one in it. They had arrived at the Dexter's house and were looking for Laura or Roger. They proceeded into the house and made a full sweep through all of the rooms searching for anyone. When the search turned up empty, they proceeded toward the shop in back. They entered with their weapons drawn and searched the entire shop for any person or some sort of clue where they might be. Cooper was standing by the small fridge in the shop. He opened it and helped himself to a cold bottle of root beer soda.

"Where can they be?" asked Natalia.

"The SUV is here and so is the fathers work truck. They must be hiding somewhere."

Nikolay took out a small computer tablet and turned it on. On the screen a large map of the city appeared. On the map a small blue dot was moving quickly across the map.

"Jeffrey was supposed to put the trackers on the boy and his father tonight. But since he appears to have fled with them, it looks like he has activated them for us to follow."

He turned the tablet to show Cooper and Natalia the map and the blue dot that appeared to be the location of Jeffrey.

"Very good work Nikolay," said Natalia.

She then turned to face Cooper. He just finished a long gulp on his soda bottle. "Radio Carl, get a status update from the Grandmas house," ordered Natalia.

Cooper took out his radio and contacted Carl for an update. A few moments passed and he reported. "Natalia, the boy's mother and younger sister are also there. He is apprehending all of them now, then he plans to take them back to the base at Canyon Dam."

"Good, good," said Natalia. "Now radio the base and dispatch the helicopters to intercept the rest of the group that just escaped. Give them the coordinates and tell them to meet us back at headquarters when they have them."

"OK," said Cooper, as he made the radio call.

"We need to return back to the base, I want to be there when Carl brings the others," said Natalia.

They all turned, leaving the shop, heading back to their SUV's.

Alicia was trying to hurry Grandma Enid into getting a few items so they could leave.

"We need to hurry Enid," exclaimed Alicia. "Calvin said that they would be coming after us very soon."

"Chester, where is Chester?" said Grandma Enid. "I can't leave without him."

"Jenny, quickly go and see if you can find him, he might be out back."

"OK, mom," she said as she hurried out back, looking for the dog.

As Jenny came out of the house, she heard Chester's playful barking in the back yard. She saw that he was playing with Carl. They were on the ground frolicking and appeared to be having a good time.

"There you are Chester, mom sent me to get you, boy." She fell to her knees patting them, signaling for him to come over to her. He saw her and bounded over, jumping into her lap and began to lick her face.

"Chester, stop," she said laughing, "we gotta get going."

Carl quickly got to his feet, "Oh, are you going somewhere?" he asked curiously.

"Yes, my mom is in a hurry to leave," she answered.

"Where are you off to?" asked Carl suspiciously.

Jenny didn't like the tone he was using and his questions, it was making her feel uneasy. She had heard the urgency in her mom's voice that someone was coming for them and that they had to leave.

"Uh, I'm not sure Carl, she just told me to get Chester," said Jenny as she turned to walk quickly toward the house.

Her heart was beginning to race a little because Carl was acting very strange and it made her nervous. She was at the back steps holding Chester close and started to walk up the steps quickly and was beginning to open the back screen door, when suddenly Carl's hand appeared over her shoulder and slammed the screen door shut. He quickly covered her mouth from behind and began to drag her backwards off the stairs. His grasp on her was secure and she couldn't fight or struggle as he dragged her backwards, muffling her screams of panic and fear. Jenny had dropped Chester when she was grabbed, he was barking and very upset. Carl reached into his pocket and took out a small device that he placed on her neck. It was the same kind of device that Natalia had used on Roger in the principal's office earlier that day. The device shocked Jenny and she jerked quickly, then fell unconscious. He then turned, used it on Chester, causing a small yelp from the dog and then no movement. They were now both unconscious, he placed Jenny into his van and then scooped up the still body of Chester and placed him next to Jenny.

"What was that noise, was that Chester?" asked Enid.

She and Alicia had heard the noise in the back yard but did not know what it was exactly. They decided to investigate walking to the back of the house. They opened the back door and saw Carl standing in the back yard using his radio to talk with someone.

"Hello Carl, what are you doing home from work so early?" asked Enid.

"I was just talking with Jenny. She and Chester went up the driveway toward the front of the house playing," he said as he pointed to the driveway.

Alicia and Enid could not see the driveway from the back porch, so they went down the steps over to where Carl was pointing.

"She's right over there," Carl pointed. Alicia and Enid walked next to him and began to peer around the corner looking for Jenny and Chester. He reached over and shocked Alicia on the neck, she fell instantly to the ground. Enid heard her go down and looked back to see Carl standing over Alicia's unconscious body, holding his Taser. Enid was startled to see him, then she grew angry as she realized what had just happened. She jumped at him, trying to punch him in the face. He easily deflected her blows and pulled her to him, holding her arms tight. He smirked saying, "Take it easy old lady." With an arrogant smile he stepped back and then zapped her on the side. She too fell to the ground unconscious. He dragged each of their unconscious bodies to the van and loaded them in the back next to Jenny and Chester.

Chapter 33

The 2 Cruisers

"Keep in close formation," said Calvin over the intercom radio, "I don't want to get separated."

He was speaking to Laura as she followed him in the second cruiser down the lines. They were picking up speed and really moving fast. She had maneuvered the cruiser close to him on the second set of power wires on the tower. She was pulling up beside him as they raced toward Chicago.

"I'm at your 9:00 o'clock Cal," said Laura, as she pulled up next to him and gave a wave.

The sight was amazing. They were all in two spheres racing away attached to power lines headed towards Chicago. The spheres looked like little orbs attached to the cables as they flew side by side. Roger was riding shotgun with Laura and gave a friendly wave to Calvin and Aaron, but they didn't see Jeff looking back at them.

"Hey Jeff, can you see me?" asked Roger.

There was no answer and then the sound of Aaron laughing. *"He passed out."*

They all chuckled. They saw that the sun was setting in the distance and Roger started to comment on it, "Look at that-" and then his head fell forward and his eyes closed. He looked like he just passed out.

"Roger, are you ok?" asked Laura as she reached over and shook his arm.

"I'm just a little groggy. I haven't felt right ever since I got tazed at school." groaned Roger, "My head has been killing me and I-I just can't explain what I keep seeing. Weird objects and diagrams keep coming in and out of sight in my vision. I keep hearing a bunch of sounds and ringing in my ears followed by what sounds like Randy talking in my head."

"Oh no," said Laura, then she paused to catch herself. "You'll be fine," she said quickly trying to cover up what she just slipped.

"What is wrong with me Laura?" asked Roger, "Do you know?"

"I think I do Roger," she answered, "I think Natalia may have activated you."

"Activated me, what are you talking about?"

Laura was busy at the flight controls and flying the cruiser, but she looked at him and then continued, "When she hit you with that stun gun, it must have reacted to the implanted information Randy put in you. Somehow it appears to have activated one of the modes of his hidden systems that he implanted inside of your body. The one that he attached to your cells."

"What the HECK are you talking about?" questioned Roger.

"Roger, everyone's body has its own electrical signals that make it function. When your brain tells your hands to move, it sends an electrical signal that travels through the cells in your body to its destination. The signal is carried through your body in the form of electricity. When you became implanted by Randy, he uploaded his program into you and attached it to your cells and muscles. When Natalia shocked you, I think it made something happen to the program he put inside of you. It seems like somehow they may have been loaded into your brain."

Roger looked at her, "I think I understand what you are talking about Laura. For some strange reason I am beginning to understand Randy's programs and I actually know how this whole sphere works now. Watch this." He reached up to the control keyboard and his fingers sped as he typed on the keyboard.

"Randy had done a lot more programming on these spheres. The manuals that we had been studying were way outdated. They had a lot of basic information in them, but now my mind is racing with new information, it is so cool," offered Roger as his fingers continued to fly across the keyboard typing and entering commands.

The front display now showed a computer system at a bank.

"I know how to use the network insertion module he made. As long as we have Servo attached to this sphere I can tap into any system in the country that is drawing on power."

They watched the computer display and saw him looking at financial records and bank account information at the bank he pulled up. Then he changed screens and pulled up a computer system at the airport. It was a reservation ticketing system of a major airline at the international airport at Chicago O'Hare.

"Do you want me to book and pay for you a free flight anywhere?" he said, as Laura and Max were watching him type. He was now showing them a screen with flights to other countries around the world.

"Let's go to Paris tomorrow," he said. Then he put them all in first class for a flight the next day at 6:00PM in first class.

"We don't have tickets for that," said Max.

"Yes we do Max," She saw him type in some information and it now showed that all three had paid flights and confirmed boarding passes to Paris.

"This is not right," said Max. "I can't believe you can do that."

Roger looked at her and told her, "We don't have to go. I am just messing around getting familiar with Randy's systems. But this network insertion module is a very powerful thing to have."

"That's right guys," said Laura. "And Volkov is prepared to KILL you, or anyone else for it. This module is what Volkov was planning to use for something big. We really need to keep it from him."

"Son," said Calvin. "That is enough. We need to focus on getting to Chicago for now. Then we can meet and discuss how this new piece of information will help us to find out more."

Roger had been sharing his main screen with the main screen in Calvin's cruiser. They all were watching his demonstration between the two cruisers as they fled.

"OK dad," Roger said as he logged out of the systems.

A few minutes later a sound came over the radio intercom systems. The voice was unrecognizable and there was a crackle like someone saying something.

"Pull over and stop the cruisers," sounded a man's voice in a thick Russian accent.

They were spooked by the voice and no one said anything as the voice repeated the announcement, adding a statement that freaked them out, "or we will shoot you down."

Roger and Aaron looked around and spotted two fast moving black military styled helicopters on their tail. They had never seen helicopters like these before. They did however recognize the eagle symbol with two bolts of lightning painted on the front of the helicopters. It was just below the windshield on the nose. The helicopters were shining spotlights on the two fleeing cruisers.

"They're right behind us!" shouted Roger to everyone on the intercom.

"You have ten seconds to comply or we will shoot one of you down," said the pilot from one of the helicopters.

"What do you want to do Calvin?" asked Laura.

"I think they are bluffing, they don't want to kill us. They only want to capture us."

After Calvin said this one of the helicopters fired a weapon of some sort right over Roger's cruiser. The weapon fired a large bolt of energy like a stream of lightning right by them. It was not like any military device any of them had seen on TV or in the movies. It was a giant version of the electrical stun gun that Roger had seen Natalia use before.

"That's it," said Roger. "Sparky, get over here to my cruiser right away."

"What are you doing?" asked Laura.

Sparky immediately came zooming over and docked on top of their cruiser. The cruiser she just abandoned continued working and stayed on path as Calvin piloted it.

"Sparky is more than you think. Servo created her and uploaded the Weapons module, Randy designed, into her computer CPU and memory."

"What does that mean?" asked Laura.

"I have no idea, but I know about every project Randy was working on and how to use it. My headache is gone, but new things are popping up all over in here," replied Roger as he pointed to his head. "Watch this, give me the flight controls Laura."

He took his set of controls and pressed a few keystrokes on the keyboard. Instantly the cruiser disconnected from the power lines they were attached to and began to fall like a rock. Their stomachs fell as they started to plummet toward the ground. They were falling and about twenty feet from hitting the ground when suddenly the cruiser had two engines pop out of the top and come bursting alive. The cruiser stopped falling immediately, then shot back up like a jet airplane. They were propelled inside the floating cruiser back up to the sky, rising higher and higher above the power lines they were once connected to. The sphere was flying like an airplane as it soared away from the power lines.

Roger maneuvered the sphere around as one of the helicopters following them tried to move in close on their tail behind them. It was trying to stay on their rear but Roger was flying the sphere like an acrobatic airplane and had pulled into a steep climb, gaining altitude fast in an attempt to try to lose him.

"So much for being attached to the power cables," he said to Laura.

"How is this possible?" said Laura as Roger piloted them into a full loop with high G-forces, pulling on their stomachs and rear ends pressing them hard into their seats.

"Randy was so smart, he designed this thing to draw on the static electricity that is in the air. It uses very little power because it stores enough of it to run in the cruisers power systems. It immediately charges itself and stores enough extra energy from being connected to the power cables. The static electricity in the air well that is everywhere, keeps this thing on a constant charge."

Roger pulled a tight turn trying to lose the helicopter that was on his tail. It was gaining on them when it fired another electrical burst, missing them on their left side.

"Where did you go?" asked Calvin on the radio.

"We are taking care of business dad, just keep on your current heading and we will catch up," said Roger.

Roger pulled another full loop and had positioned himself on the rear of the helicopter that a moment earlier was on his tail. He pulled a trigger on the flight control and the same type of electrical energy that was once shot at him now burst from the front of their sphere aimed directly at the helicopter that was in front of him. It hit the helicopter and knocked it violently to the side, frying its electrical systems, causing the engine to cut out. The pilot had no control of the helicopter as it began to fall to the ground. It hit with a hard blow and dust and metal pieces of wreckage flew in different directions as the spinning blades broke apart when they hit the ground. Roger pulled a circle and flew in close to observe the wreckage and look for signs of life. He knew everything was fine with the downed pilot as he slowly approached the crashed aircraft. He saw the pilot unbuckling his seatbelts and he looked up at Roger giving him the bird.

"Did he just flip us off?" asked Max.

Roger laughed, "Yes I believe he did."

Roger turned the cruiser and sped off into the air to go after his father and the other helicopter that was tailing them.

"Dad, where are you?" Roger said on the radio.

There was no reply as Roger continued to try a few more times. He was very worried that there was no response and he pushed the throttle full blast rocketing toward where his dad should be on the cables.

"Calvin, Aaron, Jeffery, can you hear us, come in," said Laura on the radio, panic in her voice.

They saw some flashes like lightning bursts in the distance as they approached a large open canyon. The bright flashes of light were from the weapons that the helicopter was firing at his father's cruiser. They were easier to see because it was now dusk and the sun had nearly set.

"I think I see them," said Laura, pausing, "Oh no!"

As they approached the scene they were high in the darkening sky. They saw that the other helicopter had landed next to a smoking cruiser on the ground. The cruiser looked like it had been shot down by the helicopter and had crashed to the ground. Numerous black painted hummer military trucks had surrounded the grounded cruiser. Roger saw a small army of soldiers all loading Calvin, Jeffery and Aaron into one of the Hummers. Their hands were bound as they pushed them in the back of a vehicle. They saw a couple of the soldier's motion and point up at them hovering in their cruiser. It was a very stealthy cruiser but the lights on it gave away their position. Flashes of energy bolts went whizzing by them on both sides as the soldiers fired numerous times at them. Roger hit a few keys on the keyboard and turned on some sort of energy shield. It was a good thing because the next two bolts hit them directly and knocked them back quite a few feet. They were undamaged but violently shaken as they were jolted backward after the strikes.

"We need to get out of here Roger," said Laura. "This cruiser can't take another hit like that."

"I can't leave them, we have to save them," cried Roger.

"They won't kill them Roger, they want you and what is in your head. We have to leave so they don't get you. NOW, Roger," she yelled.

She took over the controls when Roger didn't respond or retreat. She had been observing him fly and closely watched him and how he had maneuvered the cruiser. She had a good feel for it as she piloted them away and climbed upward speeding out of reach of the weapons firing at them.

Roger was in shock seeing his father and best friend being taken by Volkov's men.

"Roger!" snapped Max, getting him out of his gaze. "We will get them back. We just need a plan, we need to be smart and patient about it."

"We have to, we have to!" cried Roger, as tears rolled down his cheeks.

"My mom and Jenny, where are they?" Roger said startled, as he reached for his cell phone.

He dialed his mother's cell phone and it went to voice mail.

"Mom, please answer your dang cell phone," he said as he dialed her number again.

This time someone answered the phone. Only it was not his mother or Jenny. It was woman's voice, a familiar voice.

"Roger," said Natalia in her thick Russian accent, "so good of you to call."

"*Who is this?*" yelled Roger, "WHERE IS MY MOM!" he demanded.

"*She is fine Roger,*" replied Natalia in an evil tone. "She is sleeping, along with your little sister and grandmother."

Roger was stunned to hear that she had captured some of his family members. "If you hurt them, I will-"

"You will what Roger?" she cut him off.

Laura was leaning over to Roger and could hear both sides of the cell phone conversation and whispered to Roger, "That's Natalia, she is Volkov's main accomplice."

Then Natalia spoke, "Remember I now also have your little friend *and* your father." She sneered back at him.

"You will do what we say Roger." He could hear a little whimper in the background. It was Chester, his Grandmas dog.

"If you do not do what I say, then your family will end up like this annoying little animal. What is his name, *Chester?*" asked Natalia.

"Don't hurt Chester, please don't hurt-

"BANG," the loud sound of a gunshot from the phone rang in his ear and the whimper was gone.

The gunshot on the cell phone was so loud that Laura and Max heard it and flinched. They were now listening in on the radio intercom because his mic and earpiece in the helmet were close to the phone.

"No, no, you didn't," cried Roger.

"YES! I did Roger, he is gone and so will your family be unless you give yourself up Roger. Come to the Dam first thing in the morning or you will lose another dear family member. Do you understand boy?"

"You are a witch, you monster. Who kills a defenseless little dog?" screamed Roger as angry tears filled his eyes.

"The same kind of person who killed your brother, Roger."

Chapter 34

Hiding Place

Roger was in shock as Laura piloted the cruiser away from the city and toward the mountains. She took Rogers cell phone from him and turned it off then asked Max for her phone.

"These phones can be used to track us, I need to destroy them!" said Laura.

She opened a small latch and a tiny window on her side and tossed the phones out over a rocky canyon that they were flying over. The phones smashed on the rocks below, destroying them and eliminating the possibility of them being used to track their movements as they fled.

Roger sat motionless, his ears were ringing as he tried to process what he had just heard Natalia confess.

"Roger, Roger," said Laura loudly. "Max, snap him out of it!" said Laura.

Max shook Roger a few times to get his attention.

"*She, she, killed Randy and Chester!*" stuttered Roger as Max shook him by the shoulders.

Laura's face was furious as tears rolled down her face. "I had a feeling she was involved with Randy's death, but I wasn't sure," said Laura.

"We need to go to the police!" said Roger.

"Right," said Max, "and get thrown into jail or turned over to the CIA or something."

"No way," said Laura, "we need to go somewhere to make a plan and hide."

Laura typed in some coordinates on the flight computer and then turned the cruiser toward the mountains.

"Where are we going?" asked Max.

"We are going to my old cabin back in the mountains. My parents left it to me after they died years ago," Laura told them. "Randy and I used to take cruiser rides up there while we dated. He did a lot of testing on the power lines that ran through the mountains up there. It's secluded and very few people know about it. I think it will be a great place to hide out."

"I think I saw that place. Is it by a lake?" asked Roger.

"Yes it is," replied Laura. "How did you know about it?"

"I remember seeing it in one of the video segments Randy made while he was testing his early cruiser model. He went flying into that lake testing a high speed turn." Roger laughed a little from the memory of Randy skipping across the lake as his dad stood by watching and also laughing.

"Oh, I remember seeing that test video. We laughed so much about that," said Laura.

"Max, do you still have the other cruiser back there with you in the bag?" asked Laura.

"Yes, just the one," replied Max.

"Dang," said Laura, "that means they have the other one now. It was in Calvin's cruiser when they caught him."

"Oh well, they don't know how to operate it," replied Roger.

"Hopefully they don't get the information from your dad or Jeffrey," said Laura.

"I wonder if Jeffrey ever woke up from passing out before they caught them," laughed Max.

They all laughed a bit which broke the tension in the sphere as they glided quietly through the sky into the mountains toward the cabin.

"We'll need to stop and get some food and supplies before we get there. I haven't been to the cabin for a long time," said Laura.

They were following an old country road up in the mountains when Laura pointed out a small general store that hunters and local people used for goods and food.

"We can get some supplies over there at the general store. I know the old guy who runs the place. I used to always stop there for milk and cereal when I would drive up to the cabin in the town of Snow Ridge on the weekends," said Laura. "Let's set down over there in the trees, out of sight."

"Roger, I need your help landing this thing," stated Laura.

Laura gave the controls over to Roger to land. She had never landed a free flying cruiser before and he obviously had the skills to do it. Especially now that his brain programming had been activated.

Roger took over the cruiser and brought them to a hover in the trees, landed and powered it down. Sparky and Servo undocked from the cruiser and flew around as security guards protecting Max and Roger while Laura went to the store to get some groceries and other items they might need while hiding out.

Laura entered the store and the owner Bernie was seated behind the counter watching Wheel of Fortune on a small black and white TV. There was no one else in the store and he looked startled to see Laura.

"Well, well, I haven't seen you in a while Laura," said Bernie smiling, "what a nice surprise!"

"It has been a long time Bernie," replied Laura, as she approached the counter and leaned over to give Bernie a hug.

"I didn't see your car pull up," said Bernie.

"I parked around back by the bathrooms Bernie. It's always a long drive up here and I really had to go."

"So were you at a costume party before you left?" asked Bernie, pointing to the white flight suit she was wearing.

She laughed, "No Bernie, my friends and I were goofing around and made some suits for us to go parachuting in. They turned out to be really comfy for lounging and driving. Who would have guessed?"

Bernie laughed and came out to help Laura get some items from the shelves.

"Well you sure look cute young lady." They talked a little more and she answered some questions he asked her about Randy's death. She paid for the items and said goodbye to Bernie. She headed back to where Max and Roger were waiting with the cruiser.

After she got back in the cruiser, Roger lifted off and headed towards the cabin following the coordinates Laura had entered in the flight computer. They were about fifteen minutes away from the cabin by air. The night was beautiful and the full moon was bright with clear skies.

 The minutes passed when Laura spotted the cabin. It rested on a small hill surrounded by trees.

"That is not right," said Laura. She had a startled look on her face as she looked down at the approaching cabin.

It had the lights on and looked like someone was in it. The garage located on the side was closed and there was a jeep parked in the front of the cabin.

"No one knows about this place," she said, "only Randy and your dad. It's on private property, fenced off all the way back in the woods. Set us down over there and stay away from the cabin so whoever is in there doesn't see us land," said Laura.

Roger landed the cruiser perfectly and quietly a few hundred yards away completely out of view from the cabin. They quickly powered down the cruiser and caught themselves as the seats disappeared beneath them as the sphere dissolved back into the football shape. They removed their flight suits and the power gloves then stashed them along with the cruisers in some bushes. They hid the supplies next to the suits and slowly began to cautiously approach the cabin. Laura took out the gun she had taken from Nikolay during the attack in the school parking lot. Servo and Sparky were hovering quietly next Roger as they drew nearer to the cabin.

"Who do you think is in the cabin?" asked Max.

"I have no idea, maybe some poachers or squatters," replied Laura.

They all slowly crept up to the side and then to the front window of the cabin and peered in the windows. A fresh dinner sat on the kitchen table, accompanied by a steaming cup of fresh coffee. The cabin looked very well kept and clean. Someone had been living in it. This struck Laura as very strange because it was so clean. They saw a very long haired man in a sweatshirt, his back facing them. He was sitting at a computer terminal typing very fast on the keyboard. They couldn't see the man's face from the angle they were at from windows, the curtains were drawn and it was hard to see the man in the room.

"Follow me," said Laura as she crept to the front door. She took out a hidden key that was under a fake rock next to the porch and quietly put it in the lock and slowly turned it, unlocking the door. She turned the handle so that the door barely opened a crack and then kicked the door open loudly, startling the man at the computer. She quickly went in with the gun drawn and pointed at the man at the computer. The stranger instantly jumped grabbing his gun quickly from the desktop and spun around aiming the gun at Laura and her group rushing in. Servo and Sparky sped in hovering quickly taking positions on each side of the man with their little arms out ready to shoot energy bolts at him.

They all stood in silence facing the startled man who was now calm with a huge grin growing across his face and lowering his gun to his side.

"Roger," said the long haired man. "You have grown so much this past year."

Roger's eyes filled with tears as he ran across the room and into the outstretched arms of his big brother Randy, burying his tear filled face lovingly into his brother's chest.

The End of Book 1…

Acknowledgments

I want to express my thanks to my editor and co-writer Tami White for all of her time, enthusiasm, and passion and numerous lunch meeting edit sessions. Those times were special and fun. Thanks James Ellis for the great looking cover and design.

My children Talya, Tory, Brayden, Jayce, Aymee, and Irelynne. They kept the enthusiasm alive to write and gave me quiet time. For your patience you deserve a long awaited trip to the beach on each coast.

Thanks so much to those who inspired the characters and helped out with my book. Samantha, Bray, Tate, Tanner, Breanna, Claire, Sonora, Manzee, Aubree, Hunter, Toby, Aaron, Chris, Jeff, Gary, Kevin, Grandma, David, Darin, Colee, Kevin (the other one), Ben, Grandpa, Jason, Todd, Kevin (yes another one), Peter, Mike, Alex, Ben, Sasha, Michelle, and my kids.

Getting this book to its finished format would not have been successful without my precious wife Gaylene, for running our household so well, making it possible to allow me the time to write. My heartfelt love and gratitude to you.